DEAD VESSEL

THE LIFE AFTER SERIES

DEAD VESSEL

AMANDA FASCIANO

4 Horsemen
Publications, Inc.

4 Horsemen
Publications, Inc.

4 Horsemen Publications, Inc.
1497 Main St. Suite 169
Dunedin, FL 34698
4horsemenpublications.com
info@4horsemenpublications.com

Cover by S. Wilder
Typeset by Niki Tantillo
Editor Kristine Cotter

Library of Congress Control Number: 2022947621

Print ISBN: 979-8-8232-0120-9
Hardcover ISBN: 978-1-64450-874-9
Audio ISBN: 979-8-8232-0118-6
E-Book ISBN: 979-8-8232-0119-3

This Book Is Dedicated To

As always, the Life After series is dedicated to my family.

Without their constant support, I couldn't do this.
To Marc B. Lee, whose cheerleading I couldn't
do without.

To Wil Wheaton, he knows why.

Last, but absolutely not least, to my many friends who
support, cheerlead for me, and generally are wonderful.

Table of Contents

CHAPTER 1

Batter Up!

Cadence Riley skipped back a step to dodge the baseball bat that whizzed by her head, missing her by a mere inch.

"Get out!" yelled the ghost of the elderly woman swinging the bat. She advanced past the king-sized bed in the main bedroom, forcing Cadence away from the walk-in closet in which she had found the old lady. She kept swinging and Cadence kept ducking as she walked backward through the dim room, closer to the door to the hallway.

Even though the bat was made solely of spirit energy, instead of wood or aluminum, it would have hurt Cadence as if it had been the real deal since she, too, was a ghost. Irene Woods swung the bat again, and again, Cadence danced back out of the swing's arc. Irene grew frustrated as her bat did not connect, and the old woman gave a grunt of frustration.

"Get out of my house!" the old woman yelled in anger.

"It's not your house anymore," Cadence said, trying to stay as calm as she could under the circumstances.

"The hell it isn't!" Irene shook her head in denial. "It's mine, and no squatters are going to make me give it up! My husband and I built this house from the bottom up. I've been here fifty years. It's mine!" She stomped her foot in frustration and vanished from the room. Cade rolled her eyes at the woman's temper tantrum and left the main bedroom of the house to find her partner, Snow. He had tasked himself with watching over the paranormal team that was there, at the behest of the current owners, to investigate. It didn't take Cadence long to find him, as he was just down the hall in another bedroom.

Derrick was the youngest of the paranormal team and was still in college. He was busy setting up a camera in the bedroom that the twin boys of the family shared while Lauren, the team's psychic, was sitting on the bottom mattress of their bunk beds. The young man angled the camera toward the bed, then flipped the viewfinder screen closed once he was satisfied. His hazel eyes glanced over toward Lauren in concern, and he ran a hand through his short, curly, light brown hair as he tried to think of something to break the silence. "So, … how old did you say this place was again?"

"Do you even listen to the briefings?" Lauren said, irritation plain in her voice; it was obvious her annoyance was directed at Derrick and not the stuffed animals she was moving toward the end of the bed so as to make more room for herself. "It's sixty years old. It was built by Howard and Irene Woods when they had just gotten married. He died twenty years ago; she died ten years ago. And if you ask why we are here, I will throw something at you."

Derrick grinned at her and shook his head. "Nah, that I know; reports of curtains opening and closing, TV going on and off, things being tossed around, and the kids being yelled at by someone who isn't there." Derrick moved toward the door but paused in the door frame, then looked back to Lauren. "Do you think they're here tonight?" he asked.

The pleasantly plump woman, who was in her late thirties, looked up at the unexpected question, as this was something they had gone over in their briefing before coming to the home. "The family? No, they went to stay with boys' grandparents," she replied, distracted as she readied herself to attempt communication with whatever was here. She pushed a few stray strands of her long, wavy, black hair from her face so they would stop tickling her nose.

"No, not them. The ghosts from Lexington that we helped, the ones that talked to you. This is the first investigation we've done since then."

Lauren stiffened; an involuntary shiver went through her as she recalled that night at Lexington Asylum. It had been the first time she had channeled a spirit, or let one channel through her, since she had been a teen. The event at Lexington was when she learned her ex-husband Dan had died. She had then watched, unable to help, as he was consumed entirely by a shadow creature. The images still haunted her, and she still had nightmares about it. It had taken her almost six months to deal with Dan's death and trust herself to go back into a situation like this. She honestly still wasn't sure she wanted to continue investigating, but between Aiden's cajoling and the desperate pleas of the family for help, she had reluctantly agreed.

"I don't know. Ask Aiden; he's the one they talk to," she replied tersely. Aiden was the team's tech guy. He was also the one that Cadence and her partner, Osmund Snow, spoke to the most.

"I see Lauren is still pissed," Cadence said, her voice quiet as she watched the interaction between the two living investigators.

"Well, her last experience didn't exactly go well, now did it?" Snow's English accent was crisp and elegant as he spoke. "The poor woman went through quite a shock, what with everything that went on that night. To be in the position of confronting a non-human creature, then to see through your eyes as her ex-husband was ripped apart in spirit form mere seconds after she found out he had died."

"Yeah, I know. I don't begrudge her anger. I just wish I didn't feel like it was directed at me. I'm not the one who summoned that creature. Her ex-husband was."

"She'll get over it in time, Cadence. That's all anyone needs; time. And it is wonderful to see that despite all that happened, she hasn't given up on helping people."

"True," Cade said with a sigh.

Derrick had caught Lauren's tone and frowned, looking over at her. "Lauren, you know—" he began.

"I'm fine," she said, interrupting him. The speed of her answer and her readiness to cut him off indicating she was anything but. "You have the camera all set?" she asked. She wanted to switch the topic before the conversation progressed too far down a road she wasn't ready to go down yet.

"Hmm? Oh, yeah," he replied, nodding as he let the topic drop.

"You should probably go see what you can get from the living room since that's where they first noticed things happening with the television and the curtains. Get another camera from Aiden and see what kind of evidence you can get."

"You sure?" He did not feel right leaving her alone.

"Yeah," she said, trying to give him a convincing smile. "I'm sure. It will be easier for me to do my thing without you in here messing with my senses."

Derrick sighed and turned away, heading out the door. Cadence dodged backward out of his way. She was an athletic, thirty-year-old woman, or had been when she was alive. Her dark blonde hair was pulled back into a ponytail and bounced a bit as she moved back. The chuckle of her partner drew her attention.

"He can pass through you, you know," Osmond Snow said as he gave her a wry grin. Salt and pepper hair framed a face that made it impossible to tell his actual age. Cadence had initially guessed he was somewhere between 30 and 50. Though she had never asked him specifically, she pegged him in his mid-forties since he had once spoken of having children when he died.

"Yeah, yeah," she muttered in return. "Whether the breathers can or not, it's still creepy as hell. It feels weird, too."

"Is Mrs. Woods still in the master bedroom?" Snow asked, looking down the hall toward the room in question.

"No," Cadence replied. "After trying to attack me with a bat, she vanished."

Snow sighed and shook his head. "I think we should locate Mrs. Woods before the poor old lady does something horrible, and we have to ask Aiden to bury evidence again."

"Why didn't she go through processing when she died?" Cadence and Osmund left the children's bedroom and looked up and down the hall.

"Apparently, her attachment to the house was so strong that she never bothered leaving. She had been a housewife since she and her husband had built the house. With nowhere else she needed to go, aside from the usual jaunts to the store, she just chose to stay. The poor woman fell asleep one night and died in her sleep. In her mind, she woke up the next day and simply continued on," Snow explained.

"Which, I guess, explains why we didn't know about this place?" Cadence asked. She and Snow had been in their office when one of the spirits who worked in the observation bay had come in and advised them of the situation. The ghosts who worked in the observation bay kept an eye on all kinds of things in the territory that Snow and Cadence were responsible for covering. This wasn't the first time one of them had come in with an urgent or surprise case.

"Yes." Snow nodded. "It's a good thing they caught what was going on with our paranormal group. If they hadn't noticed Aiden and the others gearing up to go out, we wouldn't have known to be here."

"True. Still, it would have been nice if we'd had a little downtime between getting back from the Eberly house and coming here."

"I'm sorry, Cadence. Are you annoyed because they interrupted time with your brother, or time with your boyfriend?" Snow's tone implied he was teasing, as they made their way down the stairs.

Cade promptly rolled her eyes and sighed. "Oh, for the love of God, Ramon is not my boyfriend. We're friends. And look at you, getting more sarcastic as time goes on. Face it, Ozzie, I'm rubbing off on you." Ramon was an orderly at Lexington Hills who had been murdered by a patient when he was a young man. He had taken a liking to Cadence, but she had been doing her best to keep him at a distance. Her brother was also a ghost, having been murdered in a massacre at his college dorm house.

Snow made a derisive noise at her comment and led Cadence past where Derrick was setting himself up in the living room and out to the garage, where Aiden had set up his so-called central command. Shelves lined either side of the garage, filled with various boxes and plastic tote tubs. There were black stains on the concrete where the cars usually parked, though neither was there, and the faint smell of gasoline and motor oil lingered in the air. In the open area vacated by the family's automobiles was a large folding table that held a bank of computer screens. At the table sat Aiden in an uncomfortable-looking folding chair.

He was a tall, lanky man with shaggy hair that he was apparently letting grow out, as it almost reached his shoulders now. Warm brown eyes kept watching the screens as one hand rested on the computer mouse. Two splashes of color beside the mouse caught Cadence's attention, and she smiled. Ever since he had started working with Snow and Cadence, he had begun keeping two felt pieces by him when he was by his computers or doing anything vaguely associated with the paranormal. They had agreed that if they were around, they would let him know. So, he had a white felt snowflake marked "Snow" for Officer Snow to knock off the table and a green felt clover marked "Riley" for Cadence to knock off.

Cade laughed and looked over at Snow. "I thought he would just keep those at home. I didn't think he would bring them here."

Snow chuckled. "I suppose we should let the old chap know we're about, eh?" The two ghosts made their way to the table. Cadence pulled the felt clover off while Snow brushed the snowflake to the floor. Aiden jumped at the unexpected motion.

He arched a brow and bent down, picking them back up. "No cameras in here, no recorders," he murmured. "Guys, if that's you, do it again, so I know it wasn't just the air conditioning or something."

He put them down, and as soon as his hands left the felt pieces, the two spirits smacked them off the table once more. Aiden grinned.

"Sweet."

"What's sweet?" Derrick asked, coming into the garage.

"Oh, nothing, I was just talking to myself," he said. He knew if he told Derrick the spirits were here, the kid would blab it to Lauren. It had taken a lot of convincing for Lauren to come, and he didn't want to upset her now. "How is all of the setup going?" Aiden switched the topic as he picked the felt pieces up again and pocketed them this time.

"We're about done. I have the DVR cameras set up in the upstairs hall, the kid's room, living room, basement, and kitchen. Got an extra EMF for me? Lauren thought we should split up, so she has the other one upstairs in the kids' room."

"Yeah," Aiden said as he rose from his chair. He went to a plastic case and opened it, pulling out a Mel Meter. "There you go; temperature and EMF all in one. Hey," he paused and gestured to the ceiling. "How's she doing?"

"Well, she's here," Derrick said with a shrug. "That's progress, right?"

"Yeah," he said with a nod. "I just want to make sure this isn't too much for her. You and I could have done this on our own if push came to shove. I think helping the kids out is what convinced her to do it, though. I just hope we're doing the right thing, making her get back on the horse."

"I hope so, too, but ... she seems the same, you know?" Derrick shrugged. "Angry, shaken, not talking unless she has to."

Snow and Cadence left the two men in the garage. "I'll check out the basement; you go back upstairs to the master bedroom. See if she is hiding up there once more," he said.

Cadence nodded and made her way back to the stairs. She peeked back in on Lauren, who was sitting on the bunk bed still, her eyes closed, slowly opening herself up. Lauren picked up her head suddenly, and without opening her eyes, looked straight at Cadence.

"Hello?" she asked quietly.

Cadence didn't reply, not wanting to engage with the skittish psychic. She turned and continued down the hall, looking for Irene. It didn't take long to find her. She was in the main bedroom, quietly seething.

"Now who is here?" she muttered to herself as she sat, rocking back and forth on the foot of the bed, staring straight ahead. "More people, more people are here now. Scaring them away by bothering their brats was supposed to work, but no. They bring in more people to muddy up my house. Guess I'll have to deal with this the old-fashioned way."

She got up from the bed and went to the large walk-in closet. The light in the closet went on and Cadence frowned; it would be likely someone would notice that.

"Mrs. Woods," Cadence called. The old woman's head popped out of the closet.

"Who's there?" the old woman called crankily, her eyes narrowed in suspicion.

"You don't need to scare them. They're just a nice family," Cadence suggested.

The old woman frowned and disappeared back into the closet. "Where's my baseball bat?" she asked herself. "These infernal people keep moving my things."

"Mrs. Woods, come on now, there's no need for that." Cadence had no intention of letting the woman bring the bat into the situation again.

"No need?" the woman said, incredulity tinging her voice as she exited the closet. In her hands, she now carried the same ghostly baseball bat that she had tried using on Cadence before. "Of course, there's need. I tried to be nice and let that family stay, even though they don't have my permission to be living in my house. But now they've taken to tearing down walls and trying to change things. This is my house! My house! I still live here! They can't do this kind of thing without my permission!"

Snow made his way into the main bedroom. "They've seen the light," he warned Cadence under his breath. Sure enough, she heard footsteps coming.

Lauren was the first one in since she had been just down the hall. She was followed quickly by Derrick. Lauren closed her eyes for a moment, audio recorder in her hand, while Derrick panned the camera around the room. The psychic took a sharp breath.

"You okay?" Derrick asked, as he looked at her with worry.

"Spirits," she replied. "More than one spirit, but one of them is furious." She frowned.

She moved forward and put the recorder on the bed. "We would like to communicate with you," Lauren said calmly.

"Oh, I'll communicate with you, missy!" Irene said as she hefted the bat above one shoulder.

"Woah, woah, woah," Cadence said, her voice quiet, but firm, as she put a restraining arm on the woman. "You are not going to hurt her."

"I WANT THEM OUT OF MY HOUSE!" Irene yelled at Cadence. She then turned to look at Lauren. "GET OUT!" she shouted.

Snow and Cadence frowned at each other, knowing that this would be a nice little Class A EVP for Aiden to have fun with. Nothing they had to worry about yet unless the woman's anger made her appear on film.

"Who are you? What is your name?" Lauren asked. She was completely unaware the dead octogenarian was ready to try to knock her block off with the spiritual energy equivalent of a Louisville Slugger.

"I am the owner of this house, missy!" Mrs. Woods stated. "That's who I am!"

"What do you want? Why are you scaring the children?" Lauren continued after a moment.

"What I want is for you all to LEAVE!" she yelled again.

"Mrs. Woods, come now," Snow ventured, being careful to keep his voice pitched to a calm, quiet level. "Put the baseball bat down." He managed to get the spirit-made bat away from the woman, and he set it back in the closet.

Derrick walked too close to where Cadence and Mrs. Woods stood, and the Mel Meter spiked, giving out a squealing alarm.

"Got a spike!" he called out needlessly. "It went from a zero to a point eight. The temperature is dropping, too! Down to 62 ... 60 ... EMF is up to a 1.2." He focused his camera on the piece of equipment he was holding to get a visual recording of his readings.

Cadence frowned, annoyed with the old lady now, but not worried like she would have been when she was brand new. She moved the old lady back, away from Derrick. For his part, the young man was annoyingly persistent in following the cold spot as it moved across the room. Snow saw Derrick following Cadence and shook his head at the boy's determination. He flicked off the closet light. He was rewarded when Derrick ran to the closet to see if he could get evidence there, but by the time he got there, Snow had moved.

"Almost feel bad about that," Snow murmured to Cadence. "It's like pretending to throw a stick for your dog to chase and watching him run off while you hide the stick behind your back." Cadence chuckled quietly.

"Are you aware you are dead?" Lauren asked, trying to ignore Derrick, grateful when he moved to the closet and the squealing alarm of the Mel Meter stopped.

"I'M NOT DEAD!" Irene screamed in fury.

"I'm afraid you are," Snow replied quietly to her.

She looked at Snow, anger burning in her eyes. "No, I am not!"

"Really? When was the last time you saw your kids or grandkids?" It was Cadence who asked this.

Irene frowned, thinking about it.

"Or the last time you had to go to the grocery store or talked to a friend on the phone?" Cadence asked, adding to the things Mrs. Woods had to ponder.

"Kids are busy," she frowned. "They don't have time to bring the grandkids over."

"Or call you?" Snow ventured.

Irene frowned. "I'm not dead," she said, sounding less sure.

"Seems to have died down," Derrick said.

"You go back to the living room. See if you can get anything," Lauren instructed him. "The kids' room is covered; I left a recorder in there, along with the DVR camera. I'd like to stay here. See if I can get anything else."

"I know a place that will be safe," Cadence said. She grabbed Irene's and Snow's arms and teleported them to the attic of the house. There were no cameras set up in here, no investigators to try to follow cold spots or EMF spikes. The smell of warm dust was heavy up here as they stood among forgotten boxes and furnishings. The attic was mostly untouched by the new family and contained a lot of things that had belonged to Mrs. Woods. To one side was a large portrait of her, her husband, and their three children done in oil paints. The children were little and the couple was young. The happiness of the family in the painting was unmistakable and genuine.

"Good thought," Snow said with a nod of approval. They could talk and try to reason with the woman without interruption or distraction.

Irene looked in between the two of them and frowned once more. "I am not dead."

"I'm sorry, ma'am, but yes, you are," Cadence said.

"I am not dead," Irene persisted, but her tone was petulant and far less confident than it had been before. It seemed more a statement borne out of stubborn determination than true conviction. Her eyes moved to the portrait of her young family, and she frowned.

Cadence looked at Snow and arched an eyebrow. "I'm going to check on the others. Maybe you can get somewhere with her." Snow nodded, and Cadence left the attic.

Cadence passed by Derrick in the living room. He had returned there as instructed and was taking advantage of the comfy green couch as he tried to conduct his own EVP session. There was a green glass bowl on the end table next to him filled with potpourri, which made the room smell like flowers. Cadence resisted the urge to tousle Derrick's curly hair just to mess with him. While funny, however, it would not be worth the energy it would take.

She made her way to the garage where Aiden sat and she watched the monitors over his shoulder. Lauren had gone back to the kids' room since the activity in the main bedroom. It seemed that Snow was succeeding in keeping Irene distracted, as she hadn't reappeared. Finally, Derrick got up from the couch and made his way back upstairs to Lauren.

"You get anything else up here?" Derrick leaned against the doorway to the boys' room as he talked to Lauren.

"No," she said with a sigh, rising from the bed she had been sitting on. Lauren stretched, then looked back over to the young man. "What about you? You have any luck downstairs?"

"Not a bit," he said with a shrug. He nudged a toy car that was on the floor with his foot. "Maybe the bedroom thing was all it was going to do tonight."

"Maybe," Lauren said and grabbed the recorder off of the dresser. "Let's go see what Aiden wants to do."

Cadence popped back up to the attic. Snow made his way over to her, leaving Irene looking at an old, framed wedding portrait of her and her husband.

"They're going to talk to Aiden. They haven't gotten anything since the bedroom, so they may pack it up," she told her partner.

"Follow them," Snow said. "I'll stay with her for a few more minutes."

"Any progress?" She glanced back over to Irene as she asked Snow.

"Hard to tell yet, but I think perhaps," he said in reply.

"Could we get her classified as a haunting spirit? She seems attached enough to the house to qualify, I would think," Cadence said.

"Possibly," Snow admitted after a moment of thought. "But with her reaction to the family currently living here, she might be deemed more of a dangerous, haunting spirit. That comes with a whole other set of problems, and to be frank, I am more of the opinion that she should be allowed to move on and be with her husband."

Cadence nodded and teleported back into the garage. Aiden had set out his little felt pieces again, Cadence noticed. She moved to the table, knocking the green felt clover off the table just as Lauren and Derrick entered the room.

Aiden picked the clover up off the concrete floor as he turned to regard his friends coming in. "What was up with the bedroom light?" He had seen the light go on in the stationary camera they had set up in the hall.

"Something was in there. I was getting mad readings!" Derrick said, his voice portraying his excitement at that.

Lauren just shrugged and handed Aiden her audio recorder. "I was getting spirits in there. One was very angry. But after the light went out, there was nothing else."

Aiden nodded. "Let's pack it in, then. It's almost three in the morning. Derrick, want to go get the stuff from upstairs?"

"Sure," the college student said as he nodded, handing over the Mel Meter and his camera to be packed up.

Aiden looked expectantly at Lauren as Derrick left the garage. "So?"

"What?" she asked as she began to busy herself with unplugging things and coiling up cords.

"Are you okay?"

"And that makes like the hundredth time one of you two has asked me that tonight," she said with a grumble of displeasure.

"Well, we're worried about you," he said, shutting down his computer and unhooking things from his setup.

"Thanks. I'm okay."

"You seem mildly pissed," Aiden said.

"I'm not pissed!" she snapped in anger. Aiden gave her a pointed look at the tone of her reply, and it made her stop. "It's just … I don't know," she said with a weary sigh.

"Yes, you do. You're still mad at Cadence and Snow for letting Dan die."

Lauren looked over at him sharply as Cadence held her breath, waiting to see where this would go. Lauren sighed. "Look, I know technically they didn't let him die. He had a heart attack. But I saw his ghost, his spirit. I saw that woman reach out with some kind of glowing knife and cut him. Then that shadowy creature went after him like a shark after a bloodied swimmer."

"Just so we're clear, you do know he helped call that shadow creature, right? He brought it into being. The heart attack he had was caused by that thing."

"Yeah, I know," she said, a tear slipping from her eye before she wiped it away in an angry, jerky gesture. She then returned to coiling up the cords. "It just still hurts."

"I know," he said gently. He walked over to Lauren and put a hand on her shoulder. She stopped coiling the cords and stood still for a moment as she tried to get ahold of her emotions. "But I also remember you guys helping out a grieving young man that was pissed off to no end that the woman he loved had been murdered. I'm here for you, Lauren. Just like you guys were for me. You know I won't bullshit you, but trust me, while it may never stop hurting, it does ease up so you can breathe again. I promise." He paused and then decided to add the one thing he knew she needed to hear, but wouldn't want to acknowledge. "And you need to forgive yourself."

She put down the coiled cord harder than she meant to. "Excuse me?"

"You need to forgive yourself," he said again, turning to close a case that was packed up. "See, my anger? It came from me blaming myself for what happened to Bethany. Maybe if I had gotten to her work earlier and not been late, she wouldn't have been taken. If I had driven around more looking for her, maybe I could have found her, have saved her." He shrugged to Lauren.

"See, I figure you're blaming yourself for not having taken him more seriously when he said something was following him. For not checking on him sooner because we all kind of just thought he was hiding from us for being a coward that night he ran out of the asylum. I also figure maybe you're mad at yourself for not stopping Cadence from lashing out at him with the knife.

"Thing is, we'll never know. And it's very probable, especially in Dan's case, that nothing would have changed. He still would have died, and the spirits still would have had to find a way to deal with that shadow thing before it went out and killed other people. At least with the way it did go down, he was able to atone for what he did. It sucks, but he ended up doing the right thing."

Lauren frowned as a couple of silent tears slid down her cheeks. Snow rejoined Cadence unseen, following Derrick back in. "I guess," Lauren said, looking down to the floor and admitting to herself that Aiden was probably right.

Derrick stopped, looking between them. "Is everything okay?" His voice betrayed uncertainty.

"Yeah," Aiden said as he took the equipment from him. "We're good."

"What did I miss?" Snow asked as he approached Cadence.

"Aiden, helping Lauren to accept the fact that she's not to blame for Dan," Cade said.

"Good," Snow said with a nod. "She needed to hear that."

"How is Mrs. Woods?"

"Confused, I think. The poor woman is quite stubborn in her opposition to accepting the fact that she has died. We may do well to bring Miss Saxon in on this."

"Bethany?" Cadence could not keep the surprise from her voice. "You think it's a good idea to bring her in on a case Aiden is investigating?"

"I don't see the harm. Miss Saxon can help Mrs. Woods accept things, and she is very good at what she does. I think she and Aiden have both moved on from the worst of their heartbreak over each other."

Cade shrugged as the group began lugging their equipment out to the van. "I guess," she said as they turned to follow them, getting into the back of Aiden's van with the equipment.

"Well, this should go smoothly at least," Snow offered, climbing into the van after her.

"What do you mean?"

"What evidence do they have? A video of a light turning on and off? Some temperature and EMF fluctuation? Some probable EVP voices? I doubt they have anything damning. Nothing we'll have to ask him to cover up."

"Oh good, so we can go home, then," she said with a grin.

"We still have to be able to say we've done this part of it for the paperwork," he chided. "Work before play, Cadence."

"You are no fun, Ozzie," she said as she pretended to pout.

"Ah, good; you must not be rubbing off on me as much as you thought."

The Dreaming Path

Aiden had moved since they had last visited him six months ago. He had left the one-bedroom walk-up apartment he had occupied for so long and moved into a two-bedroom apartment in a different building. In the old apartment, all of his equipment had been strewn throughout the living and dining rooms. In this apartment, however, all of the paranormal group's equipment occupied the second bedroom. His computer desk was set up on one wall of the bedroom, while heavy-duty storage shelves lined the opposite wall to neatly store the ghost hunting paraphernalia.

"Nice place," Cadence said as they roamed the apartment while its occupant put equipment away.

"Indeed, a bit nicer than the last one," Snow said with a nod of agreement.

"Seems incredibly familiar to me, though," she said with a frown, looking around.

"Perhaps you have been here before?"

"Who knows?" she said with a sigh. "I went to a lot of places as a cop." She kept looking around, the familiarity of the place bothering her. It took a few minutes for her to realize that she had, in fact, been there before. There had been a murder investigation here a few years ago. She had been a beat cop at the time, not a detective, so her role had been to secure the scene and keep curious onlookers out. "So now we just amuse ourselves until he reviews the evidence," Cadence said, looking back over to Snow and he nodded. She watched Aiden put the felt clover and snowflake on his desk and look around the room.

"You guys here?" he asked.

"Should I?" Cade looked at Snow as she spoke.

Snow shrugged. "We might as well give the fellow a heads up. That was our agreement, after all."

Cadence nodded and knocked the felt objects off of the desk. Aiden grinned and picked them up. "This is so cool." He chuckled to himself. "I'll check the stuff over in the morning, but right now, I need to get some sleep. Feel free to turn on the TV if you want to watch it." He left the room, heading to his bedroom.

"Nice of him to offer," Snow said. "That should help alleviate your usual boredom."

Cadence shot Snow a look and shook her head. "Sure, sure, make fun of the new girl. Besides, it's not like I can turn the damned thing on. You're the one who is good with the electronics."

"Actually, I was thinking that if you could set aside your electronic whims for a time, I might teach you something."

"And what would you be teaching me tonight, oh Jedi Master?" Cadence said with a wry grin.

"I'm no Jedi Master," Snow said with a shake of his head. "I could never pull off the brown robes, or the green skin, for that matter."

"Obi-Wan didn't have green skin, and I kind of figured that reference would go over your head."

"Everyone knows Star Wars, Cadence, even the dead."

"If everyone knows Star Wars, then how come you didn't know about Obi-Wan?"

"Oh, I know about him. I just always thought of myself as more of a Yoda type."

"You consider yourself to be more like an 800-year-old Jedi Master?" Far too many mildly insulting comments sprang immediately to her mind and she couldn't decide on which to reply with so, she simply chuckled and smirked. "Far too many snarky comments and way too little time. So, what did you want to teach me?"

"I think you're ready to dream-walk on your own," he replied, ignoring her sarcasm.

"Really?" She couldn't mask the surprise in her voice. Every time she had broached the subject of learning to do it on her own before, he had always demurred. He seemed to prefer to shove the topic off for another time.

Snow nodded with a smile. "Indeed. Once he falls asleep, I'll tell you how to go about it."

"Is it difficult?"

"I don't think so, but then I've had a few decades of practice. You should be able to pick it up in one night. You're a bright student," he said with a shrug. They left the computer room together and made their way to the main bedroom.

"He's not asleep yet," Cadence said as they entered. Aiden was just settling down into bed.

"It's very late. I'm sure it won't take long," Snow said to reassure her. "In the meantime, it's important that you get your mind in the right frame."

"And how do I do that?"

"When we usually do this, you entrust your mind to me, correct?"

"Yeah," she said.

"Well, to do this, you will be moving your consciousness yourself rather than entrusting me to do it for you. You will place yourself in Aiden's mind rather than me doing so. You'll take his hand as you usually do, to form the connection, and then move your mind into him."

"Why do I get the feeling that it's going to be trickier than I had imagined?"

"Isn't everything?" he said in reply.

"Touché."

"To begin with, you'll need to move your consciousness into him, but the hard part is leaving a piece of your mind behind, like a kind of tether to yourself. You have always followed my touch, so to speak, to return to yourself; you followed my mind, my consciousness. Without me as a go-between, you have to rely solely upon yourself."

"What happens if I don't find a way back to myself?" She was concerned about how badly this could foul up.

"Well, for now, I am here. If I think you are taking too long, or if I sense there is trouble, I can come to get you, in a manner of speaking."

Cadence took a deep breath. "Alright. Well, I guess there's no time like the present." She frowned, though, suddenly not so sure that she needed to learn this just yet.

"If you would rather wait, we can," he offered.

"No, no, it's fine. I'm not sure why I thought it would be easier, but I did," she shrugged. "But hey, what's the worst that could happen, right?"

"Without me here as a safety net? Without knowing what you are doing? You could lose yourself permanently in his subconscious. Become a ghost of his dreams."

She gave him a disheartened look. "It was a rhetorical question," she said with a slight whine in her voice.

"Ah, right." He looked down to the floor and cleared his throat before lifting his ice-blue eyes to her again and giving her a somewhat sheepish smile. "Sorry."

Cadence sat down on the bed with a sigh. Aiden had fallen asleep; his breathing was deep and even. Cade frowned slightly and took his hand.

"Relax," Snow urged. "I'm here. Nothing will go wrong."

Cadence nodded, reassured a bit, but still not thrilled at the prospects of all that could go wrong.

"Close your eyes and just relax for a moment. You're too tense about this now to get anywhere." She took a deep breath and forced herself to try to relax. There was nothing to get worked up about, she told herself. Snow was here; he wouldn't let anything go wrong. Once Snow could see her relax a bit, he continued.

"You have contact with him, so it should be easy for you to search out his mind. Picture him in your mind and once you feel you have a solid hold on the image, follow it. You should find yourself in his dream."

Cadence sat there, eyes closed, holding Aiden's hand. Yet she couldn't find his mind. She could picture him in her mind, but she wasn't sure what Snow was talking about when he said to get a hold of Aiden's mind in hers, and she couldn't feel any connection. She tried for over an hour, only succeeding in growing more and more frustrated. At length, she opened her eyes.

"It's not working." She sighed.

"Hmmm." He frowned.

"Sorry."

"No need to be. You don't have to be perfect at everything right off the bat, Cadence." She frowned at him for that comment.

"Give me a few and I'll try again."

"Would you like to take him up on his offer of television?" Snow offered, thinking that perhaps a change would benefit her.

"No, there usually isn't anything worth watching on at this time anyway, unless you like infomercials."

"Info … Mercials?"

She chuckled at the perplexed look on his face. "How is it you know about Star Wars but have no idea what an infomercial is? They're basically commercials for products, but instead of 30 seconds, they last 30 to 60 minutes."

"Why in God's name would anyone willingly watch something like that?" he asked, flabbergasted.

"I have no idea. Maybe they're masochists." They continued chatting for a while until the light of sunrise began to color the blinds in a pale glow.

"Shall we try again?" Snow suggested.

"I'm not sure what you mean, to feel his mind. I think that was my problem; I'm not sure how to go about feeling for someone's mind."

"Take my hand; let me see if I can show you." Cade reached out and took Snow's hand, as well as Aiden's. She closed her eyes. "Now focus on me. I should be easier for you to find since we're on the same plane of existence," Snow coached.

It was like a match lit in her mind. She focused on Snow and it seemed like he was instantly there, this bright flame in her mind. She reached for it and he pulled her into his mind.

"You see?" She heard him speak in her mind. "It will be like that, only not so strong, not so bright, because he is still flesh. Watch." He held her mind in his as he went searching for Aiden. Cadence watched and saw a glow appear, though it was dimmer and smaller than the brilliant fire she had gotten from Snow. He released Cadence, and they both returned to the present, sitting on Aiden's bed.

"Think you can do it now?" Snow asked.

"Yeah," she nodded. "I think so." She closed her eyes and concentrated on Aiden. There was a small spark of recognition in her mind, and then she saw the dim flame. She reached out and threw herself into it.

He was walking down the hallway of his old apartment building, but the building looked run down and abandoned. He had a camcorder and an EMF detector and he seemed to be actively hunting instead of watching from the monitors like he did most of the time. Wispy white curtains hung in front of the windows, tattered and worn with age. With each step, his foot brought up plumes of dust. Cadence hung back, just watching as the tall man moved through dusty rooms that seemed bathed in silvery twilight. They didn't need anything from him, so there was no need to disturb him. She watched as he turned a corner and went out of sight before turning to follow her path back out.

Opening her eyes, she saw Snow smiling. "Very good!" he declared.

"Yeah?"

"I honestly thought you would need my assistance getting back out. But you had no trouble at all, did you?"

"No, just retraced my steps." She shrugged. "Hardest part was getting in."

"Wonderful! Did you talk to him?"

"No. I didn't see a need to bother him." She shook her head.

Snow nodded. "Very good. You did very well indeed." He looked pleased with the progress his protégé was making.

A few more hours were spent whiling away the time with Cadence practicing dream walking before Aiden woke. The man was completely unaware that his subconscious had played host to an audience. When he got out of bed, Snow and Cadence made their way to the computer room to wait for him while he showered and dressed. He entered the computer room with a cup of coffee and smelling like Irish Spring.

"Okay," Aiden said with a sigh as he sat down at the computer with his coffee. "If you guys are still here, I'm about to look at what we got last night." He flipped on his computer and looked around the room, unable to see Snow or Cadence. "And if you aren't here, I'm just talking to myself like a crazy person. But that's okay."

Aiden hooked up a camera to the computer and video of the hallway came into view on the screen. He marked down a couple of times on the tape where orbs could be seen, likely Snow or Cadence moving down the halls. He also marked down the times that the light in the main bedroom went on and off.

The camera from the twins' bedroom had nothing, despite Lauren's many attempts at communication. The living room camera also had nothing other than Derrick pacing around or sitting on the couch as he did his EVP sessions. Aiden unplugged the camera and put it away.

"You guys did a hell of a job keeping the visuals to a minimum last night," he said, commending his unseen guests. "Let's listen to the audio." He grabbed the case of audio recorders and plugged the one marked as Lauren's in. Despite her multiple attempts at contact, the only time anything was ever picked up was in the main bedroom.

The squealing of the Mel Meter Derrick was holding and his excited chatter couldn't mask the old woman's voice as she shouted for them to get out of her house. Aiden diligently wrote down the times as placemarks and what was going on in the recordings. He then did the same for Derrick's recorder, which gave the exact same evidence.

"Well," Aiden said as he leaned back in his chair and laced his fingers behind his head, "you guys did great at keeping the evidence to a minimum. Although, I'm not entirely sure that helped us out too much. That is, unless you convinced the woman that the house isn't hers anymore." He looked around the otherwise unoccupied room and sighed. "Not that you can tell me anyhow."

Snow had been right. Other than the EMF readings, the light going on and then off, and a few faint EVPs of Irene yelling at people to get out of her house, there hadn't been anything of note. There was nothing that Cadence and Snow had to worry about.

"Well, you know what that means," Snow said as he indicated to Cadence that it was time to go.

"Paperwork?" Cadence asked with a face like she had smelled something awful.

"Paperwork," Snow said with a grim nod.

CHAPTER 3

Sam's Call

Snow and Cadence sat at their old-style metal desks, which were pushed together so that they faced each other, both dutifully bent over their paperwork. A large map was hung on the wall beside the desks with different colored pushpins in various areas. A couple of seats occupied the far corner of the office, but otherwise, the room was sparsely furnished and decorated.

When the cellphone in her jacket pocket rang, Cadence was glad for the interruption and she set down her pen. Her paperwork was almost done, but any interruption was always a welcome one. She pulled out her phone and answered it.

"Riley," she said by way of greeting.

"Hey, Cade," the familiar male voice at the other end greeted her.

She couldn't help the smile that came to her face. "Sam! How are you?" Her smile faded, however, as she noted the tone of her brother's voice.

"I'm good," came her brother's tentative reply. "But I would appreciate it if you and Snow could come by. There are some disturbances going on here that are upsetting the balance."

"On our way," she said as she rose and hung up her phone.

Snow arched an eyebrow as he saw her rising. He hadn't expected that since most calls from her brother were just chats. "Is there a problem?"

"He said he wants us to come over. That there's some kind of disturbance upsetting the balance?"

"Construction," Snow said with a sigh, setting down his pen as he rose. "Usually, construction of some kind is what can upend the balance in a place. The ones who don't believe they are dead, like Mrs. Woods, when their surroundings are being changed, their realities are challenged, and it's quite upsetting to them. It's one of the reasons we're calling Miss Saxon in on Mrs. Woods's case. We may need to ask her for help with this one, too, if there is a problem."

They left their office and made their way to what Cadence called their hall of doors. It was a long hallway that had doorways that acted as portals to the most commonly visited haunted sites in their region. They opened and passed through the one marked with the address of the large three-story tall Victorian home that had served as a college dorm. In its prime, it had been pale yellow with white trim. Now, however, it was a sadly abandoned building with cracked, peeling, and faded paint, a stark reminder of the bloodshed that had happened there a decade prior. It was almost midday, and the sun shone down on the building, as well as on the construction workers going in and out of it.

Cadence and Snow wove in between the living people and their machines and made their way inside. Sam was waiting in the hallway, looking a little agitated.

"Hey," he greeted his sister, hugging her. There was a definite familial resemblance between the two, although Sam seemed like a brighter version of Cadence. His hair was a light golden blonde as opposed to her darker honey-colored blonde. His eyes were a bright green, as opposed to her muted jade-colored eyes. He also possessed a cheerier disposition, in contrast to his sister's sometimes dour and always sarcastic demeanor. Although he was the younger of the siblings, he was the taller of the two and would often rest his chin on top of her head when they hugged. Their differences and similarities never failed to make Snow smile.

"Hey, what's up?" she asked. "Are they finally tearing this place down?"

"No," he replied somberly, brushing a bit of his shaggy blonde hair out of his eyes. "They're opening it back up."

"You've got to be joking! Since when does the college open a murder scene back up to the public?"

"I guess now. Look, Cade, I'm the only one here who knows we died. This construction, it's starting to make some of the others question things." A construction worker carrying a ladder passed by them as he headed upstairs, closely followed by another carrying painting supplies.

"Maybe it would be best to let them move on?" Snow suggested.

"I'd be all for it, but for the fact that some of the ones questioning things are making trouble. I'm not sure they'll want to move on."

"You think they could become violent?" Snow asked, concerned. Sam's emerald-green eyes conveyed his worry as he nodded in response.

Snow frowned. "And if they become violent, that could bode very ill for this place being reopened for students."

"Personally, I don't care if it is open or not," Sam shrugged. "It's the construction and the problem it's creating that has me worried. One of the girls keeps trying to leave."

"I didn't think a haunting spirit could leave the site of their haunting," Cadence said, looking at Snow.

"They can't," her partner said quietly.

"And if they try?" she asked, not liking the look that was on his face.

"If they try, it could possibly end in their non-existence," he replied.

"Well, shit." Cadence sighed. "We have to find a way to stop them from leaving, stop them from finding out they are dead, and stop whoever is behind this from reopening the dorm."

"Cadence, I doubt you can stop the dormitory from reopening," Snow chided.

"I don't see how any self-respecting parent would sign up to let their child live at the site of a massacre," she countered.

"The college might not advertise that fact." Sam shrugged. "Why are you so buggy about this?"

"Sorry, I just have a problem with people idly taking showers in the exact spot my brother and his girlfriend were killed," she replied heatedly.

"Calm yourself, Cadence," Snow warned. "They can remove you from the area if they think your personal feelings are interfering with your work."

Sam stood there, looking at the two of them, his sister and her partner. "Cade, if I'm okay with it, you have no right not to be," he said at length. "This is my tomb we're talking about."

Cade didn't like it, but clenched her teeth together and eventually nodded. "Fine, fine. So, what do you want us to do?"

"Well, firstly, I just wanted you guys to be aware of the situation. That something was going on here. If Sandra catches on, I don't know what she'll do."

"Sandra is the one you're worried will become violent?" Snow asked.

"Yeah," Sam replied. "Ever since this started earlier this week, she's become a little bit unstable."

"Shocking, Sandra is the problem," Cade said under her breath, her tone highly sarcastic. Both Sam and Snow gave her a look and she spread her hands in a defensive gesture. "Alright, no more commentary from the peanut gallery," Cade said. "What else?"

"Well, honestly, I would like to know what their plans for the building are. Is it going to be an administrative office, or if they are going to continue using it as a dorm? I also would like to know why it's being reopened. I don't mind the building being used; it's just that that timing seems a little weird to me. We're just past the ten-year anniversary."

"Suspicion must be a genetic trait in your family," Snow remarked, to which both siblings grinned.

"Maybe if they are reopening the dorm, it means they found something out about the case," Cadence said. "Maybe they solved it."

"It was unsolved?" Snow asked, surprised.

"Yeah," Cadence sighed. "It was the middle of the day, which meant people coming and going was normal, as the students had all kinds of schedules. There were no witnesses and everyone who was here and not in class was killed."

"And you don't recall?" he asked Sam, who shook his head.

"No. It was a guy; I can tell you that. But whoever it was, he was wearing a Halloween mask and wielded a machete. Even if I was alive, that doesn't make for a solid lead. I think it's probably even less of a lead since I'm a ghost. Last I checked, we aren't exactly reliable witnesses."

"You really were watching me, weren't you?" Cade chuckled softly.

"Yeah, well, it's not like I could watch CSI anymore. You had to be my cop show." He grinned.

"I can go to Andy, see if he knows anything about your case, or can find it out. Maybe he can look into why the college is opening the place up now, too."

Snow regarded Cadence with a bit of trepidation. "Do you think that's the wisest course of action? You two have only had a few months to heal from your demise."

"It'll be fine, Snow. It's been over six months. He seems to be doing okay when I check in on him."

"Look, I've got to get back," Sam said, gesturing to the back of the house that comprised the communal living room and kitchen.

"Of course," Snow said. "If you have trouble with this Sandra that you can't handle, give us a call."

"And I'll be in touch when I can get any more answers about this," Cade added. The siblings hugged each other goodbye.

CHAPTER 4

A Memorized Massacre

"**W**e've never discussed the details of your brother's murder," Snow said once they sat back down at their desks. "Would you mind if we did so now?"

"You think we'll be able to solve it?" she asked with a skeptical look.

"No, that was not exactly what I had in mind. I was thinking more along the lines that knowing what happened may help us in handling some of the more troublesome spirits there."

Cade thought about that for a moment and nodded. "I can tell you what I know from the police file. I studied it so often, looking for any clue, I practically have the thing memorized. I was in class when it happened, and Sam and I haven't spoken of it either."

"That's quite understandable. None of us prefer to discuss the details of our death. It's an uncomfortable topic. I'm sure more so in your brother's case."

Cadence nodded once more. "I will say that Sam's little tidbit about the guy wearing a mask was new to me, but it makes sense as to how the person could have remained unknown and unseen. The murders happened a couple of days before Halloween in 2012, and you know college kids. Half of them were going to class wearing masks and crap."

She closed her eyes, able to recall the file and its information in perfect detail—so perfect, in fact, that it appeared on her desk. The manila-colored folder was showing age, with its corners worn and crinkles and small tears on the tab bearing the case number. Snow didn't move; as much as he was curious about what was in the file, he didn't want to break her concentration and wanted to see if the visuals would change as she told the story.

"Near as the cops could make out, the person came in by the sliding glass door in the living room located in the back of the house. They think Sandra was the first one killed, that the killer slit her throat from behind. The back of the couch she was sitting on faced the sliding glass door. Then he climbed over her to kill the other two girls that were watching TV in the room. The same machete-style weapon was used for all of the kills. One of the girls in the living room apparently tried to run; she was found on the floor almost to the door of the living room, lying face down, stabbed in the back seven times."

As Cadence spoke, the file remained unopened; however, pictures from the crime scene began to appear around the file, one by one, as she talked about each kill. He could see the young blonde woman slumped over on the couch, the cushions and rug around her stained with blood. Another picture appeared of a young black-haired woman with tanned skin, her throat also sliced open. The third picture to materialize showed a pale, freckled woman with curly red hair. She was face down, her clothing soaked with blood, the multiple stab wounds evident.

"A male student was in the kitchen at the dining table, his back to the living room. He was killed from behind; another throat slice. He still had his earbuds in and music playing when the cops found him." The picture appeared and showed a young brown-haired man face down on a textbook that was too blood-soaked to even tell what subject it might have been. The brown linoleum floor also had a good-sized pool of blood on it, and in the blood rested a dropped pen.

"Another body was found in the laundry room, stabbed multiple times and then stuffed in the dryer, which the killer then turned on." Snow winced at the picture as it appeared. The dryer front was covered in blood, as was the button that turned the machine on. The dryer door was open, and the legs of an officer were visible against the door. The inside of the door was also covered in blood. An arm protruded grotesquely from the open dryer, bent at an unnatural angle. Cadence continued on, unaware that she was manifesting the pictures as she described the scenes. "From there, the perp went upstairs." She paused, a grimace on her face as she braced herself for the part of this that would lead to her brother's death.

"One girl was found in the corner of her bedroom. They think she had been begging for her life or had tried to fight him off, due to the defensive wounds on her body, before he managed to kill her. Another guy had been taking a nap, they figured. He was stabbed multiple times, lying on his bed. We're not sure which of the two bodies upstairs was first, since their rooms were right across from each other." The two pictures materialized. The first showed the young man, who could possibly have been big enough and powerful enough to fight off the attacker had he been awake. Whatever clothes and bedding he had were completely covered in blood, and the stab wounds shredded the shirt to tatters. The young woman's body was slumped against a wall in the corner of her room. It looked like she had perhaps been kneeling, and there were clean tracks through the blood on her face. The killer had taken the time to terrorize her. Her arms and hands had been cut multiple times, but it was the stab wounds to the chest that had killed her.

"They all agreed that my brother and his girlfriend Eri were the last," Cadence continued. Although her voice was monotone, a tear slipped from her closed eye. "They were found in the bathroom together as if they had been hiding up there. The bathroom door had been broken down forcefully. Sam had defensive wounds on his hands and arms and was stabbed in the gut a couple of times before the guy managed to nearly decapitate him."

Snow turned his head and closed his eyes. He had gotten to know the younger Riley well over the past few months. He had no desire to see the young man the way

Cadence had described the scene. "Eri was the last and the worst. The guy disemboweled her. My brother's body was covered in his girlfriend's entrails." Cadence shuddered a bit and stopped talking. The file and gruesome pictures disappeared from the desk as she pulled herself out of her memories and opened her eyes. Snow would have had to have been blind to miss the haunted look in them.

"About half an hour later, one of the other kids who lived in the house came back from class. He found the student who had been killed at the kitchen table and then the girls in the living room. He high-tailed it out of the house and called 911.

"They pulled me out of class a couple of hours later. My Psych professor looked annoyed at the interruption, but when the news broke, all of my professors were understanding." Cadence had wrapped her arms around herself as she sat there recounting the tale, reliving the memories. She could see the classroom in full detail as the officers stepped in and called her name. She could even remember the stubble on the officer's cheeks and the smell of his cologne as they escorted her out of the classroom to sit her down in an office and tell her. She remembered the icy feeling of dread that shot through her. Of course, she had been more afraid for her father, who had been serving in the armed forces in the Middle East. The fact that something could have happened to her brother hadn't even crossed her mind.

"I'm so sorry," Snow said at length. "I shouldn't have asked you."

"No, it's okay," she said, wiping away the errant tear. "You are right. There might be some detail or fact in all of that mess that will help us deal with what is going on there now. I should ask Sam about it, too. Who knows? Maybe he can tell me something that would make all the difference in the case. I could pass the info on to Andy, and he could finally get the son of a bitch who did it."

"Cadence, you know we can't get involved in things like that. We can't go around solving the breathers' crimes."

"I know," she said with a frustrated sigh. "I just would give anything to be able to solve this one."

"I know," Snow nodded. "I do understand. When I died, I thought I would finally get all of the answers, be able to somehow put everything right. All the crimes that had crossed my desk and remained unsolved, or those that happened to people I knew." He paused, as if weighing his words or choosing what to say next.

A knock sounded on their door and Bethany Saxon stepped into the office after Snow called out an invitation to enter. Bethany was a petite blonde with delicate features whom they had met while working on one of Cadence's first cases after shuffling off her mortal coil. She had always struck Cadence as looking like a cross between an angel and a porcelain doll.

"Am I interrupting?" Bethany asked. "I got your message."

"No, not at all," Snow said, letting the conversation drop as he waved Bethany into the office.

"How can I help you?" she asked, closing the door behind her.

"We have need of your expertise at guiding those who have died to their life after mortality," Snow explained.

"Oh? They usually come through my office," Bethany said uncertainly.

"True, my dear, but this poor woman doesn't truly realize she is dead. She is holding onto her home rather stubbornly and has gotten quite active with the breathers now in her home to scare them away."

"We were kind of hoping you could come with us and do your guidance thing to get her to move on and stop scaring the kids," Cadence translated.

"Oh, sure, I guess. Um … Am I allowed to do that?" she asked. Bethany had only been dead and working on this side of life for about a year longer than Cadence and seemed to keep mostly to her home or office.

"I don't see why not." Snow shrugged. "It is in the line of duty, after all."

"Oh. Okay then," Bethany said with a smile.

Cadence looked pointedly at Snow. "You're seriously not going to tell her?"

"Tell me what?" Bethany asked.

Cadence sighed as Snow remained quiet. "Aiden will likely be there," she answered.

Bethany smiled a bit at that. "It will be good to see him in person again."

"You're not going to have an issue with him being there?" Snow asked.

"No." She shook her head. "I'm fine with it."

"Well, good, I'm glad to hear it," Snow said, relieved. "So now it just remains to be seen which house we go to first; Mrs. Woods's home or Mr. Halleran's apartment?"

"Mr. Halleran?" Bethany asked.

"Don't worry about Andy." Cadence shook her head to Bethany. "I'll be dealing with him, no one else. And I doubt he's available yet," she said, swinging her gaze around to Snow. "So why don't we finish off this paperwork from last night and then go on to Mrs. Woods's house and see what we can do about her?"

Snow nodded, agreeing, bending once more to his file of papers. "We shouldn't be too much longer, Miss Saxon, if you wouldn't mind waiting?"

"Oh, no, I don't mind," she said with a smile.

CHAPTER 5

Anger & Denial

The house that Irene Woods haunted was empty of the living. The family was away for a second night so that Aiden's group could attempt to contact the angry spirit in the house and get it to move on. When Cadence, Snow, and Bethany entered the second-floor hallway of the home through their hall of doors, the house was dark. Aiden and his compatriots were just pulling into the driveway, the lights from Aiden's van visible through the beveled window on the front door. The house may have been quiet, but silent unease was widespread through the atmosphere, which made it clear that all was not well.

Cadence ducked into the main bedroom to see if Mrs. Woods was in there, since that had been where they had found her the night before, and stopped just inside the door, her jaw dropping. What Cadence found this time was completely different from an angry ghost with a baseball bat. Snow and Bethany followed her to the doorway of the room and stopped, just as shocked at what they saw. The drawers of the dresser and night-stands had been opened wide, and it looked like they had all been emptied. Clothing and other items were strewn all over the room; the bed itself was unmade to the point that the bedspread was hanging over the dresser mirror across the room. The closet had also been cleaned out. Shoes, hangers, clothes, and boxes had been tossed out of the closet and into the room.

"This does not bode well," Snow said solemnly.

"Was she like this the last time you were here?" Bethany asked, a bit wide-eyed.

"Not this bad," Cadence answered. "She was angry, but not full-on temper tantrum angry."

A glance into the boys' room showed the same kind of disarray. Toys and clothes had been tossed all over. It looked like a tornado had hit. In what was either a macabre moment or a lucky throw, a teddy bear hung from the ceiling fan by the bow around its neck. A crash from downstairs broke their awed reverie and alerted them that Mrs. Woods was not done with her temper tantrum yet. Bethany took a deep breath, preparing her-self for the hard work that seemed to lie ahead of her.

The rest of the house had been dark, but now the lights in the kitchen were on. That was where they found Irene Woods. She was standing on the dark brown gran-ite-topped kitchen counter island and was pulling down the family's stainless-steel cookware. From the ceiling hung a wrought iron pot rack, and she was throwing each piece as hard as she could to the floor. All of the dark wood kitchen cabinets and drawers were open, but it seemed as if she had not gotten around to throwing things from those yet.

"Mrs. Woods," Snow greeted her, his mellow voice breaking the momentary stillness in the house as the last of the pans clattered to the floor.

She turned sharply, startled at being addressed, her grey dress with the purple flowers flaring out as she did. She narrowed her eyes, recognizing Snow and Cadence from the previous night. "You all get out!" she shouted, climbing down from the kitchen island as if she were alive. "Get out! I've got knives right over there, and I am not above using them."

Through the window, Cadence caught sight of the trio of ghost hunters walking up the sidewalk. She was hoping to have this done by now. With the way Irene was behaving, she didn't want to have to worry about their safety.

"Mrs. Woods, let me introduce you to Miss Saxon," Snow continued.

Irene Woods, for her part, looked suspiciously at Bethany. "What do you want? You here to tell me lies again?" she asked, returning her gaze to Snow and Cadence.

"We weren't lying last night, Mrs. Woods," Cadence said, trying to rein in her irritation at the old woman's antics. "You are dead." Cadence heard the front door open and the three breathers walk in. It was only a matter of time before they found the damage Irene had done.

"More lies!" the woman yelled, sweeping a glass off of the nearby counter and sending it to the floor, where it shattered on impact.

"Mrs. Woods," Bethany began, trying to interrupt the woman before she caused more damage. "I'm very pleased to meet you. I was hoping we could talk some."

"I don't want to hear any more of your lies!" the old woman shouted and picked up a knife, throwing it at Snow. It passed right through him and lodged itself into the door frame right as Derrick rounded the corner with his camera in hand. His eyes were as wide as saucers as he watched the hilt of the lodged blade wag back and forth from the force of the impact. He turned the camera toward the knife and filmed it as it slowed to stillness.

"I just came around the corner into the kitchen," he said, his voice shaking a little as he documented what he had seen for the videotape, "and this knife barely missed hitting me. Look how close to the edge of the door frame it is. And look how deeply embedded it is in the wood."

This shocked Irene into silence for a moment, but then she frowned. "More people in my house," she muttered.

"Mrs. Woods, would you like to go somewhere where people won't be barging into your home all the time?" Bethany asked.

"I'm not going anywhere," the woman said, stomping a foot. "This is my home!"

Lauren and Aiden followed Derrick into the kitchen, both pausing when they saw the state of the room and the knife in the door frame. Aiden held a camera in his hand, as well as an EMF detector. Derrick's free hand held an audio recorder. Lauren held an audio recorder, but nothing else.

"And it's a charming home," Bethany said calmly, making Cadence envy the other woman's sweet and even disposition. Sometimes Cade could talk sense into people; other times, she just got fed up with their bullshit. This was one of those short-temper nights, it seemed.

"Well, I'm glad you feel that way because I'm not leaving it!" Mrs. Woods declared, swiping another glass off the counter and sending it shattering to the floor.

"We're here to speak to the spirit of Mrs. Irene Woods," Lauren said as the glass went sailing off the counter and smashed on the tile floor. "We mean you no harm; we just want to communicate with you." The three investigators exchanged wary looks. They had known the ghost was angry, but this was getting downright violent.

"Like we said last night, Mrs. Woods," Cadence said, "when was the last time you went grocery shopping, talked to a friend or family member on the phone?" She felt a great sense of urgency to get Irene away from the breathers, as she didn't want any of them getting hurt.

"She's here," Lauren said as she opened herself up to sense the spirits. "There's more than one spirit here, but she is here. I can feel her anger." The two men nodded but didn't say anything, not wanting to disrupt her concentration. "Mrs. Woods, you need to move on, let your spirit rest, and leave this family in peace," the psychic urged.

"This is my house!" the ghost of Mrs. Woods said, but she sounded slightly less sure of herself. She looked around at the different décor, the furniture that was not hers, the three investigators, and then the three other ghosts. She frowned again. "My house," she repeated, but it sounded less angry and more plaintive.

"Mrs. Woods, I can see how much this house means to you. How much the family you raised here means to you," Bethany said quietly. "But wouldn't you rather be somewhere where you can watch over your own family and make sure they are okay? Wouldn't that be better than staying by yourself in this house while you watch other people making their own memories here? Doesn't this new family deserve the same chance to raise their family in happiness that you had?"

"Mrs. Woods," Lauren said, "your family loves you very much, and they want you to move on, to rest in peace. I spoke with your son, Zachary, today. He wanted us to tell you that although they miss you, they are fine. He wanted me to tell you that it was okay for you to go on."

"I…" The old woman paused at Lauren's words, looking a little lost and defeated. "I'm dead?" she asked finally.

"Yes," Bethany said with a gentle nod. "You are. Would you like to come with me? We can talk about things and get you where you need to be to rest in peace."

Mrs. Woods took one last look around the kitchen, almost desperately, hoping something would jump out for her to once more latch onto to prove that she wasn't dead. But they were right. She couldn't recall the last time she had gone to the grocery store or talked to her kids or grandchildren. Without another word, she turned back to Bethany and nodded.

"Wonderful," Snow said softly. "Miss Saxon, do you have things in hand, or shall we accompany you?"

"I can take her back. We're fine," Bethany said with a smile and held out a hand for the old woman.

Mrs. Woods took Bethany's hand, and they turned, walking a few steps before Bethany teleported herself and Mrs. Woods away.

"She's gone," Lauren murmured. "The angry presence is gone. There was a wave of deep sadness, and then she was gone. I think she's accepted that she died and has moved on."

Cadence looked to Snow. "Should I talk to her?"

"Let them believe they were the ones that got her to move on for now. Let them have the victory. Give Lauren a bit more time before you try to communicate with her again. Let's go. That way, she's not picking up on us either."

"You want to go back to the office? I'll go for Andy."

"I'm not letting you do that alone, Cadence. You only just learned how to dream-walk on your own. I'll stay out of it if you wish. But I want to be there, just in case."

Cade frowned, but nodded. Part of her was actually glad he was going. Knowing she had an audience there might help her keep it together. She was also tired. It had been a couple of days since she had slept and given what could go wrong with dream-walking, she didn't want to try her first solo one right now, especially with the emotions involved with Andy being the subject.

Snow and Cadence clasped hands and teleported into the living room of Andrew Halleran's apartment. As was usual for Andy, the place was a mess. Dishes filled the sink and the trash needed to be taken out. Magazines and mail covered the coffee table. Darwin, Cadence's old cat, was lying placidly on the brown leather couch, but turned his head when they appeared. He meowed a greeting to them.

Cade couldn't help but grin. "Hey, Darwin," she greeted him and went over to the cat. "Where's Andy?" she asked, not seeing her old partner in the apartment. Darwin meowed again and jumped down off of the couch, padding his way into the bedroom. Cade cast a glance back to Snow, who had lingered back from her, and he nodded to her.

"Let's go," he said, gesturing for her to lead the way.

Cadence entered the bedroom with Snow a few steps behind. She paused as she saw Andy's form on the bed in the dark room. The emotional pain took her by surprise, but she frowned and did her best to wall it off. She looked in on him via her television at home, but seeing him in person was different. It brought back all the memories of the last time she had been here, to say goodbye to him. She shook her head and stuffed those feelings away. She would do as she usually did. Deal with it later. She moved to the bed and sat down beside him, slipping her hand into his.

"Do you want my help?" Snow's voice was quiet, as he was trying to be as unobtrusive as possible, knowing this wasn't as easy on her as she was trying to make it seem.

"Let me see if I can do it myself," she said.

"Of course," he nodded, moving to a far corner of the bedroom to give the former partners their space.

Cadence took a deep breath and closed her eyes. She found the dim flame of his mind and followed it into his dream.

She found herself in a graveyard, and it was raining. The sky overhead was a dark gray and rain was pattering down in a gentle but steady rhythm. The weather and light combined to make the greens seem brighter and more vibrant, while the browns seemed darker and earthier. The color of the slate headstone that Andy was kneeling by seemed to almost match the color of the sky.

"I'm so sorry, Cade," Andy said, his voice a harsh whisper.

"I told you to stop blaming yourself," she said. She was proud of the fact that she managed to keep her voice even and calm, reflecting none of the turmoil inside her. This was the first time since saying goodbye that she had spoken to Andy. It was also the first time she had ever seen her name on a headstone. While she had accepted and adjusted to her new life, this stark reminder of her death still managed to unnerve her.

The sound of her voice startled him so badly that he tried to rise and spin around to face her too quickly, which basically just landed him on his behind in the wet grass. Cade chuckled a bit, then reached out and offered him a hand up. He stayed on the ground for a moment, looking up at her with his eyes wide.

"Cade?" he gasped at length.

"Last I checked," she said with a nod, her hand still extended toward him to help him up.

"What ... How ...?" He was stammering in shock.

"You expect me to give away all of my secrets?" she asked with a grin, using Snow's line. She wiggled her hand in front of him. "Come on, get up."

He took her hand and rose, moving in to hug her in one fell swoop. "I miss you," he said, and she could feel his breath move her hair. She could feel the strength of his arms wrapped around her and she closed her eyes tight, unwilling to let herself fall to pieces.

"I miss you, too, but please tell me you aren't still blaming yourself," she said, doing her damnedest to ignore the stinging in her nose that usually indicated she wanted to cry.

"No … I'm not. Still, wish I'd been faster or done something differently. But I know it wasn't my fault. His trial is set to start in a couple more months."

"Sage's?" she asked, and he nodded. "Good luck with it," she said. "I hope you guys put the bastard away for good."

"Thanks. I am sorry."

"Why?"

"I … I thought that's why you were here?" he said, backing up a step to examine her face.

"What part of the conversation did I miss? Why do you think I'm here?"

"Ashley." He looked at her, confused. "I thought … Because I feel terrible …"

"Who's Ashley?" She felt lost in this conversation for a moment, and then a light began to dawn on her.

"A neighbor … she and I … we …"

"Are dating?" Cadence said, prompting as she saw where he was going.

"Yeah," he said, looking down.

"Great!" she exclaimed as she ignored the pain that once more shot through her, doing her best not to register it at all. He, meanwhile, looked shocked.

"Great?"

"Yes! Andy, I told you to move on. I mean, I'm dead. No matter what we feel or felt for each other, there's nothing that's going to happen now. I want you to move on, to be happy, live, love, laugh, and all the rest of the crap they put on greeting cards." She smiled at him. "Andy, I'm truly happy for you. Now be happy for yourself, dammit, or I'll kick your ass. Ghost or no ghost, you know I can do it."

He allowed himself a chuckle and wiped his face. "God, I don't know why I'm seeing you. I thought it was guilt."

Cadence took the opportunity to change his dreamscape slightly and put another headstone next to hers. She pointed to the headstone, which was marked with her brother's name. "That's why I'm here, Andy. I need your help."

"With Sam's case?" he asked, utterly confused about this change.

"Yes. Have there been any new developments?"

"Cade, nothing's changed on that case in a decade."

"Are you sure?" She couldn't keep the disappointment from her voice.

"Yes," he said. "Why would you think something had changed?"

"They're reopening the dorm where the massacre took place."

"The college is?" He was surprised at this news.

"Yeah, and I can't understand how they would think that it's a good thing to do. Andy, can you do something for me? Look into it. Find out why they are reopening it, if they are going to use it as a dorm again, and who is behind this push to get it done. The timing is just too weird. This is coming right on the heels of the ten-year anniversary of the murders, and it just seems off."

Andy thought about it, and she could see the wheels turning in his head. "The timing is suspicious," he said after a moment. "But even if I look into it, it's not like I can tell you anything."

"Yes, you can," she said. "I can come back, like now, and talk to you again. It'll almost be like we're working together again."

"Cade," he said as he looked down, his voice dropping to a soft tone. "I … don't know if I can do that. Seeing you … it still hurts. If I'm going to move on like you say you want me to … Seeing you again isn't going to help."

"Like picking the scabs off a wound," she said, closing her eyes against the hurt as she realized what he was saying. "I get it."

"I'm sorry."

"No, don't be," she said. "I should have thought of it myself. I'm actually a bit embarrassed that I didn't. Look, if I ask someone else to visit your dreams and talk to you about it, could you look into it for me? Please? It would help both me and Sam."

"Yeah, sure," he said, his voice gruff. "I am sorry, Cade."

"Oh, good grief, would you get a new line, please? Don't be an idiot. You have nothing to be sorry for, Andy. I'm happy for you. I truly am." She smiled at him, then disappeared from his dream.

Cade sat on the edge of the bed, her mind back in her own body, so to speak. She kept her eyes closed for a minute as she fought to control herself. The urge to cry was too strong, and Snow had seen her in tears too many times for her comfort.

"I know you're back," he said quietly from a corner of the room behind her. "I can tell by the way you're sitting. Do you want to go or sit for a minute?"

She held up a finger, indicating a moment. She needed to get a hold of herself, but her throat felt too tight to speak. She opened her eyes and blinked back the tears, willing herself not to cry. It had hurt a little when Andy confessed he had moved on. However, his asking Cadence not to come back had just about killed her again. She would have to tell Snow to go in to get information from Andy next time. But she wasn't able to do that just yet.

To Snow's credit, he just stayed where he was, in a dark corner of the room by the dresser. He knew she wasn't comfortable with people seeing her when she thought she was vulnerable, and he didn't want to trespass on her emotions. He knew it had to have been hard to go in and talk to her former partner. They had been close friends who had a great love and trust for each other, despite not acting on that love to take it further.

Finally, Cadence rose. She couldn't talk yet, and tears had moistened her cheeks in spite of her trying to force them away. She wouldn't keep her current partner waiting. She would just go home once they got back and do her paperwork in the morning. Once she was on her feet, Snow made his way to her but stopped when he saw the tears, and a sign of something that alarmed him even more than her open vulnerability, which he knew she hated.

"Do you need more time?" he asked gently, worry creasing his brow.

Cadence shook her head, then did something he hadn't expected at all. She turned and threw her arms around him and wept. When she had cried before, right after her death, she had done so on her own, preferring to keep him at arm's length. He held her and let her cry, rubbing her back gently as she did so. Darwin watched them steadily, tucked in against Andy's body.

"Come on," Snow said after her tears had begun to abate a little. "Let's get you out of here."

Cadence felt the familiar shifting as they teleported and she finally released hold of him. She knew it should have surprised her when she found herself not back in their office or in the hallway that separated their apartments, but at Lexington Hills, however, the pain she was feeling was mixed with almost a cold numbness, and she wasn't fazed much by the different destination, even knowing that their arrival would trigger Ramon to come to them. Despite her hatred of people seeing her in a weakened state, she just couldn't muster the desire to care.

The hospital had closed its doors in 1979 and had played host to a few paranormal groups and even cultists since then. It also housed one remedy to Cadence's current state, or at least Snow hoped so—Ramon. The orderly had worked at the hospital until he had been murdered back in the 1940s by one of the patients there. Ramon had made no secret of his admiration for Cadence to Snow. Snow was hoping that maybe Ramon held the key to keeping Cadence from spiraling down into desolation. Desolation was a state that could kill a spirit. He didn't know what had happened with Andy, but he could see the signs. The creeping of a blueish-gray in her color and the lack of facial expression. Thankfully, they never had long to wait for Ramon to appear, since he was charged with keeping track of everyone in the hospital.

"Hi!" Ramon said, surprised to see them. Then he frowned as he saw Cadence and the state she was in.

"Good evening, Ramon," Snow greeted, as he noticed Cadence didn't even flinch a bit from being seen like this. "I hope we're not intruding?"

"We shouldn't be here, Snow," she muttered under her breath. Her voice was monotone. Snow, for his part, ignored her protest.

"Not at all," Ramon said, coming forward to them, concerned. "What's wrong? Are you hurt?" Ramon looked to Snow, having seen the same concerning signs on Cadence's face.

"Cadence here has just had a very painful conversation with someone. No physical wounds for you to tend to, but I believe there are plenty of emotional ones. I thought that together you and I could help cheer her up."

"Of course," Ramon said. "Come on; I don't think I've ever had a chance to show you the common room." He led them over to a room off of the lobby. He didn't want to take them up to the patient rooms. He knew as well as Snow that Cade wasn't comfortable with people seeing her like this. The dining hall and kitchen areas didn't have the best of memories either, not since the shadow creature six months ago.

He sent out a pulse of will as they entered the common room so that they would see it as he had seen it back in the hospital's heyday. The parquet linoleum was intact, not torn up or moldy. The sofas and tables were there and showed no sign of wear and tear. The soft glow of lamps illuminated the room. Cadence sat down on the nearest sofa almost as if she was on automatic pilot, and the two men sat on a couch that was beside the one she occupied.

"Is that what I think it is?" Ramon's voice was hushed as he gestured to the blueish-gray splotches coloring Cadence's face like some strange rash.

"I believe so," Snow said just a quietly. "We have to pull her out of this or she could lose herself." He then turned and focused on Cadence, who was staring straight ahead, not registering much of anything. He cleared his throat to get her attention. "What happened?" Snow asked her.

"Nothing," Cadence said. She hoped to deflect their attention but knew she wouldn't be able to. It was annoying, but because they cared about her, they were doggedly persistent in their desire to take care of her.

"That wasn't a nothing, Cadence," Snow said, his voice gentle. "What happened?"

"Um ... Well, he will look up the information about the dorm, but you'll have to go talk to him to find out what he got. He, uh ... He doesn't want me coming around anymore." That declaration even stunned Snow. He had seen pictures of Andy with some other woman on his dresser when he had been over in the corner of the bedroom. He had thought that was what had Cadence so upset. He had never thought Andy would tell her not to come back. He saw where Andy was coming from, but he hated that it was hurting Cadence so much.

"I'm sorry," he said, knowing that his words wouldn't cover what she was feeling. "I will, of course, talk to him about it. And we do have others we can go to for help in the physical world. Aiden …"

"Aiden's not a cop," Cadence said with a sigh. "I'm sorry. It's stupid of me to be reacting this way." She shook her head, feeling foolish as the numbness began to wear off just a little.

"Not at all." Ramon shook his head. "It takes longer for us to heal because we have far fewer distractions, fewer options open to us to work toward healing. He's had work, friends—"

"Dates," Cadence threw in and was proud that she managed to keep the venom from her voice.

"Exactly," Ramon said with a nod. "Whereas you have had only work, and let's be honest, even those you speak with through work are far fewer. He has a whole police station of people. You have Officer Snow, me, maybe a handful of other spirits who are aware like we are."

"You have your brother," Snow said, hoping to remind her of one definite bright spot she had in her new life. His plan was beginning to work. He could see the splotches of blue and grey fading from her face and light returning to her eyes.

"I know. I know. I'm thankful I have him, and both of you. It's just … Andy was my partner and best friend a long time. I said goodbye to him when I died, and then tonight. That's the only time I've interacted with him in the last seven months. I … I guess I expected too much from him and from myself both. He was …"

"He was the last tether you had to your old life, and he cut you off," Ramon said. "So, you feel lost, adrift, like one of those floating balloons at fairs that kids let go of.

But you aren't adrift, Cadence. You are here, where you belong, making a difference and helping people."

"Everyone moves on differently, Cadence," Snow said. "Maybe he can handle moving on just fine until he sees you, and then seeing you brings back all of the pain of losing you." He paused as his phone rang and he frowned, pulling it out of his pocket. "Excuse me," he said, rising and moving away from them to answer it.

Ramon switched to the couch that she was sitting on and reached out to take Cade's hand in his. "I'm sorry. I know how hard this has to be for you, and I know what he meant to you."

Cade shook her head. The cold numbness she had felt in the wake of the emotional pain was receding and now she just felt foolish and embarrassed. "No, I'm just feeling stupid and emotional." Much as Cade might not have wanted to admit it to herself, maybe Snow had been right to bring her here. She had just been going to fall to pieces at home in private. But in bringing her here, Snow and Ramon had reminded Cadence that she did have friends who cared for her, that she wasn't as alone as she had felt in that moment. Cade also realized that she was trying to move on, too. She knew that Andy hanging on to the idea of her was unhealthy. Maybe hanging on to the idea of him was just as toxic for her.

"No, not stupid and emotional, normal," Ramon said comfortingly. "It's completely normal for you to react like that to what happened. He was important to you, I get it. You don't think the rest of us grieved for what we lost?"

"No, I know you did. I just thought I was done with it, you know?"

Ramon nodded and smiled gently at her. "It's funny how a thing can sneak up on you at the strangest time and remind you very pointedly of what you lost. Things still get to me at times."

"Still?" she asked, knowing he died over eighty years ago.

"Still." He nodded.

"I'm sorry to interrupt," Snow said, returning. "But it would seem Miss Saxon needs some help with the reports regarding Mrs. Woods."

"Oh?" Cadence asked, rising from the couch. "Is she giving Bethany trouble?"

"No, not at all. She is just having a hard time making heads or tails of the paperwork since this is a unique situation. I'm going to go give her a hand. I'll see you tomorrow, Cadence."

"I can come," she said, and Ramon rose as she did.

"No, it's fine. You stay here for a while, then get home and get some sleep. I'll see you tomorrow."

She arched an eyebrow at him, wondering if he had brought her here when she was upset as a way of contriving more time for her with Ramon. Her partner did seem dead set on setting the two of them up at times. Snow merely smiled and teleported out.

"He's worse than a mother hen," she said with a sigh as she sat back down.

Ramon laughed, sitting back down as well. "He cares about you. You should have seen him after the shadow creature had a hold of you. While I was patching you up, he couldn't sit still, kept pacing around the room. It's sweet."

Cade nodded, relenting. "Yeah, I'm lucky. I have two guys willing to deal with me and my stupidity. Three, if you count my brother."

Ramon laughed again at her grin. "I think siblings are contractually obligated to be there for you. Besides, I keep telling you it's not stupidity. It's just life."

"Newsflash, Ramon, we're dead."

"And yet we still continue to live. Just not in the most conventional of ways," he said with a shrug.

She chuckled and shook her head. "How is it you always have the best way of looking at things?"

"Oh, I didn't always. I spent probably my first five years dead hating everyone and everything."

"I can imagine being murdered would tend to have that effect on people, especially if they have to stay where they were killed. But I have to be honest; from what I know of you, I cannot see you as being some kind of angry, sullen spirit."

Ramon shrugged without elaborating further on his past. "I'm just trying to say that we all deal with this in our own ways and our own times. You will get through it, though. You didn't let that shadow creature get you. I'd imagine you're strong enough to not let this get you, either." He was relieved to see the gray gone from her. He had seen spirits succumb to desolation, descending into nothingness slowly because of too much pain from the loss. He didn't want to see her go through something like that.

She smiled and leaned over, kissing Ramon on the cheek. "Thank you. Though honestly, I would rather take on another shadow creature than have to deal with this emotional crap. I've never been good at it."

He smiled at her and returned the kiss to her cheek. "You're very welcome, Cadence," he said softly. "I'm glad you felt safe enough to come here."

"About that … As much as I don't want to hurt your feelings, Snow made the decision to come here, not me. I was just going to go home and cry myself into a stupor. But I'm glad he brought me here. This is better," she said with a smile as she gave Ramon's hand a gentle squeeze. Ramon smiled and squeezed her hand back.

New Ghost on Campus

Cadence walked into her office the next day; the smile on her face told Snow she was feeling much better. The thought that Andy didn't want to see her still hurt. However, between Snow and Ramon, she had realized that maybe it wasn't all that bad. She offered Snow a playful salute as she closed the door behind her.

"I must say, I am a bit surprised to see you looking so chipper today," he said.

"I am surprised, too. It's weird, but I'm in a great mood."

"I'm glad," he said, his sincerity obvious in his voice and face. "I was worried about you last night."

"Yeah," she said with a wince of embarrassment. She slipped into her seat at her desk. "Sorry for the waterworks."

"Not at all," he said, waving her apology away as unneeded. "I was expecting something to crop up soon, anyway."

"You were?" she asked, surprised.

He nodded. "We're coming up to the holidays. Usually, a person's first holiday season on this side is hard for them."

"The holidays were never exactly a great time for me the last few years I was alive, anyway. I hadn't even registered it was that time of year. Besides, I did a lot of thinking last night, and I realized I'm happier here. Most people probably aren't."

That admission took Snow by surprise. "You're happier?"

"Yeah," she said with a nod. "It's weird, right? I did a lot of thinking last night after I came home, and as strange as it is, I am. I have more here than I did there."

"Are you being serious or trying to throw me off?" he asked, wondering if he had somehow pulled off a masterstroke of brilliance by taking her to Ramon last night.

"Yeah, I'm serious," she said and laughed a little at his question. "You're a terrific partner; we have a great relationship. My brother is here and I get to hang out with him every so often. The work is honestly more interesting and less grim than earthly police work. Aiden's cool to work with, and then there's Ramon."

"What about Ramon?" Snow asked in a teasing tone and with a devilish grin.

Cadence gave him a look. "I know what you were trying to do last night. You've been playing matchmaker between him and me practically since the beginning."

"Not entirely since the beginning," Snow said, hedging a little. "Besides, he likes you and you like him, so what's the problem?" Snow asked.

"That's the thing, Ozzie," she said as she shrugged. "There isn't one anymore. If there ever was one to begin with. I realized last night that for all my talk to Andy about him moving on, I was the one hanging on to some stupid romantic notion of what never was and could never be. His telling me not to come back was probably the best thing he could have ever done for me. So, whatever can happen between Ramon and me, I think I may be ready to explore those options. I might take things slow. I was never very good at the relationship thing when I was alive; I doubt death will have suddenly improved that skill. I think I'm ready to try, though. It's weird. I'm braver in death, at least in my personal life, than I ever was when I lived."

Snow smiled, genuinely happy for her. "I'm glad things worked out so well last night, Cadence. I truly am."

"Thanks. How did your paperwork go with Bethany?"

"Oh," he said with a dismissive wave. "She had called to ask a question. She didn't need my help. I made the excuse to leave you two alone."

"You are such a brat!" She laughed and tossed a pen across the desk at him. He easily ducked it and it clattered to the floor about a foot behind him.

A knock at the door drew their attention to it as it opened. Alistair Croft, the tall, imposing, dark-skinned man who had been Osmond's mentor when he died, entered. He closed the door behind him and gave them an amused smile from behind his beard.

"Things are going well, I take it?" His deep voice resonated in the room when he spoke. He stooped over and picked up the pen, tossing it lightly back onto Snow's desk. The light reflected off of his bald pate as he moved.

"Yes," Snow said with a smile and nod. "Very well, thank you. What can we help you with, Alistair?"

"I was hoping we could clear a few things up. I am aware of your taking Miss Saxon from Guidance out into the field last night."

"Irene Woods never went through processing when she died, so we thought it might help her move on if we brought the processing to her," Cadence said. She hoped the explanation would keep Snow out of trouble if she was the one that gave it. Cade didn't give a rat's ass if Croft was upset with her. She knew, however, that it deeply troubled Snow when he thought he had disappointed Croft in some way.

He kept his smile, but narrowed his eyes at both of them. "I'm in something of a conundrum here. You see, no one can argue with your results. You two have done some remarkable things since being partnered together. However, your methods of execution are sometimes more outside the box than some are apparently comfortable with."

"Are we in trouble?" It was Snow who voiced the question that both he and Cadence were thinking.

"Since so far, I'm the only one who knows about your adventures last night, no. As I said, your results are terrific. However, I would warn you to be careful. Working with Guidance is fine, even if it is a bit unorthodox to take them out into the field. However, your sojourns to communicate with that paranormal group a few months ago got a few people up in arms, so to speak. Knowing you were doing so again, bringing Guidance out into the field, or visiting your former partner, for that matter," he said with a pointed look to Cadence, "those things would not be looked on kindly by others."

"Well, it's not like we've let evidence slip out," Cadence said, trying to defend their actions. Croft made a defensive gesture with his hands.

"Don't get upset. I'm not here to yell. I just wanted to warn you to be careful. If what I'm hoping gets approved does, then it won't matter much, anyway. But for now, you do need to be careful. Taking Miss Saxon out on a regular basis may raise eyebrows."

"Who is getting bent out of shape about how we do things, anyway? I thought we answered to you," Cadence questioned.

Croft let out a deep laugh that sounded almost musical in tone. "Child, I am not the highest authority around here. Nor am I the only one to read your reports."

Cadence bristled a bit at being called a child, but let it pass without comment.

"What exactly are you waiting on approval for?" Snow asked.

"The specifics aren't important right now. I'll let you know if or when anything changes." He nodded to them and then turned, leaving them and closing the door behind him.

Cadence looked to Snow, confused. "So, he came in here to warn us to be careful, but that we might not have to be careful if something that he won't tell us about happens?"

"Apparently," Snow replied, looking just as perplexed by his former mentor as Cadence was.

"Ozzie, I know you like the guy, but he's weird."

"I seem to have a fondness for strange people," he quipped as he tossed her a file of paperwork to be filled out.

She grinned as her phone rang. "Ooh, saved by the bell."

"The paperwork will still be there after your call, you know," he retorted.

"Riley," she answered her phone, pretending to ignore Snow. "Oh! Hey Sam," she greeted him. Her smile at hearing her brother's voice faded and turned into a frown at whatever he was saying. "Okay. Be right there."

"What's wrong?" Snow was on his feet as she was hanging up the phone. He knew from the change in her face and tone of voice that something had happened.

Cadence rose as well. "Sam says there's suddenly a new ghost there."

"What? That makes no sense," he said as they made their way to their hall of doors. "Or did one of the construction workers die?"

"He said he didn't want to go into detail. He just wants us there," she said as she opened the door that let them out at the corner of the street the large Victorian stood on. It was late afternoon; they made their way through the yard and into the open door of the house, unseen by the men replacing the windows. Sam was waiting for them in the hall.

"Hey, thanks for coming," he said nervously, running a hand through his shaggy blonde hair.

"No problem," she replied. "What's got you so wigged?"

"Mike Caulfield showed up today," he said, eyeing his sister.

"Who? Wait … Mike Caulfield? Like, football linebacker Mike Caulfield?"

"Yeah." Sam nodded, glad his sister remembered the guy.

"Who is Mike Caulfield?" Snow interjected.

"Mike Caulfield lived here," Sam explained. "He was a senior when I was here as a freshman, and he generally liked to make my life a living hell. He had the room next to mine."

"He was also the kid who called in the murders," Cadence explained. "He wasn't killed here. He lived. He graduated. What the hell would he be doing here?"

"He doesn't remember," Sam said. "Freakiest thing is, he looks like he did ten years ago. He doesn't look like he aged at all."

Snow frowned deeply. "It could be he has died and returned to a point of profound trauma for him. Let's go talk to him, shall we?"

Sam nodded and led them back toward the main living area, and Cade adjusted her view of the dorm to be from when the co-eds remembered it. There they found four other spirits: three young women and a young man. The young man, whose hair was close-cropped and dark, was tall and had the muscled bulk of a weightlifter, wrestler, or football player. The young man was sitting there, just staring straight down at the floor, rocking back and forth. The young blonde woman was diminutive compared to the man she sat next to. Her hair was up in a side ponytail and she was pretty, if sharp-featured. She held one of his hands in both of hers, and his other hand remained limp at his side. The other two women were on the opposite couch; one was obviously of Latin American descent, and the other was a pale redhead. They were engrossed in some TV show that only they could see. The blonde woman moved her concerned gaze from the man she sat beside to the door at the arrival of Sam and the other two.

"Holy shit, Cadence?" the blonde woman asked.

"Hi Sandra, how are you?" Cade replied. She had never liked Sandra, or Mike, for that matter, since they both liked to pick on her brother. They had been one of the "it" couples on campus and it made sense to Cadence that they would be together since they were both jerks.

"Haven't seen you come by to protect your little brother in ages," the woman said. She then checked her watch. "Shit, I have class. Mike, are you gonna be okay?"

"Yeah," he mumbled, giving the first signs of life Cadence had seen, as he had seemed unaware of anything when she and Snow had walked into the room.

Sandra seemed reluctant to leave, but rose and began making her way out of the room. She paused by Cadence, looking her up and down. "Jesus, get laid or something, girl. You look thirty!" She then turned and headed out, having made what she thought was a great parting insult.

Snow rolled his eyes but kept quiet, letting Cade take the lead for now.

Cade moved forward and knelt in front of Mike, who was sitting on the couch, just looking down at the floor. "Mike, do you remember me?"

"Cade Riley," he said, his voice sounding hollow and emotionless. "Sam's sister."

Cade turned, casting a worried glance at Snow and Sam, then turned back to Mike. "Mike, what's wrong?"

"I don't know ... But something is. Things don't feel right."

"What do you remember, Mr. Caulfield?" Snow asked, his English accent catching the attention of the two girls remaining in the room, who immediately started whispering among themselves as they watched the conversation.

"I went to the basement. I was looking for something. I ... I don't remember. I came upstairs, and everything is strange."

"Mike, why don't we get you up to your room? You can lie down, okay?" Cadence suggested. She knew that the other spirits weren't aware of the fact they were dead. And she didn't want to start having a conversation that might reveal this fact in front of Julie and Nelia.

"Since when do you care?" he asked, even as he rose to his feet and began to shuffle his way out of the living room toward the stairs in the front hall.

"Since you're not yourself," she responded.

"See?" he said, pointing in the hallway and stopping. "Look, the bike rack is gone from the porch. The curtains are gone too, and the plants. What the hell is going on?" he asked, wide-eyed, afraid.

"It's okay, Mike," she soothed. "Let's get you upstairs and we can talk, okay?"

"Is this a joke, Riley?" he asked, looking over Cade's shoulder to Sam. "Some joke to get back at me?"

"No, Mike," Sam replied, shaking his head. "No joke. Let's get upstairs, okay?"

The big man was still upset, but he nodded and climbed the stairs, heading down the hall to his room. He stopped dead in his tracks when he opened the door. "Where's all my stuff?!" he yelled.

Cadence, Sam, and Snow hurried in, shutting the door behind them. "Dude," Sam said. "Chill out. Do me a favor, okay? Close your eyes. Remember your room. What it looked like, where everything was."

He looked at Sam uncertainly, but did as he was asked, closing his eyes. The room rippled and shimmered until a messy dorm room came into view. Clothes were strewn on the floor, the unmade bed, and the back of the desk chair. Textbooks and papers shared space with a computer on the desk. In one corner of the room, a stereo stood, and a pile of CD cases littered the floor around it. The walls were plastered with posters of bands or partially clothed women.

"Okay, good, open your eyes," Sam said.

Mike did so and freaked as he saw his room was back in order. "What the fuck is going on?" he demanded.

"Sit down, Mike," Cadence said as gently as she could. He was beginning to wear on her nerves a little bit.

He went to his bed and sat down on the bunched-up sheet and blanket, his pictures of scantily clad women looking down on him from their places on the wall. "What the hell is going on?" he asked, frustrated with not knowing as he looked between the three of them. "Why do you look so much older? And who is that guy?" He gestured to Snow, the only one in the room he did not know.

The three of them shared an uncomfortable, uncertain silence as they looked at each other. Snow gestured for Cadence to take the lead, and she sighed. "Mike, the guy is Officer Snow. As for what happened, we're trying to figure that out. What is the date today?"

"October 28th, 2012. Why?"

Cade looked at Sam and Snow again. That date was one day before the massacre. She wasn't sure if telling Mike he was dead was going to make him more hysterical or calmer. She wanted to choose whatever answer would make him more inclined to answer their questions, but she was unsure which way to go. Sam and Snow shrugged in unison, neither one of them having a clue which way was best, either. Finally, she decided to go with the truth.

"Mike, over ten years have passed since that date."

"What? Now I know you guys are pulling a sick prank. That's impossible."

"Which is why I look like I'm thirty," she said, trying to prompt him to think it through.

"Then how come Sam doesn't look any older? Or Sandra, Julie, Nelia, Chase, any of them. Nice try. You did your makeup weird or something, and you and your brother cooked this up to get back at me."

"Then why can't you remember how long you were in the basement for?" she retorted.

He furrowed his brow, thinking. "I went down there looking for Halloween crap for the party. I remember now, don't know why I couldn't before. I was digging through the storage area down there. My foot hit something…" He struggled to remember, but shook his head after a few minutes.

"I woke up down there what … about an hour or two ago?" he asked, looking to Sam, who nodded. "You're telling me I've been missing for ten years?"

"Not…exactly, Mike," Cadence said with a frown. "And this is where things get kind of crazy. See…we're dead."

"Huh?"

"Someone came in here on the afternoon of the 29th. He killed every one of us that was home," Sam said. "That's why my sister looks so much older, but I don't. Me, Sandra, Chase, Julie, Nelia, Eri, a few others. We all were killed by some masked asshole with a machete."

"The thing is, Mike, you weren't among those killed," Cadence said as she crossed her arms over her chest. "I have no idea why you are trapped here in the spirit world at the age I last saw you, because you were the one who found the bodies, Mike. After the massacre, you called the cops."

He looked between them all, confused and scared. "That's impossible. I don't remember that. You would think I would remember coming home and finding a bloodbath."

Cadence turned to Snow. "We've got to figure out what the hell is going on here because the last I knew, he was still alive."

"Sam," Snow said, looking at Cadence's brother, "did anyone go into the basement today? Perhaps a construction worker or someone who could have disturbed something?"

"Yeah," Sam said with a nod. "They've been going up and down for a couple of days, working on the wiring."

"It's possible, I suppose, that there could be a psychic impression left by Mr. Caulfield. The trauma of finding everyone dead could possibly create that. Perhaps the workers tromping through brought it up."

"But would that psychic trauma impression act as a ghost? I thought those things were more like recordings, residual hauntings," Cadence said.

"I'm right here," Mike said, grumbling his discontent at being talked about.

"Sorry, Mike. We're just trying to figure out what is going on," Cade said.

"How come if we're dead, Sandra was going to class? And how come she's here at age thirty?" he asked, pointing to Cadence as he asked the last question.

"Sandra and the others don't know we're dead, Mike," Sam explained. "They go through every day as if it was just a normal day. She says she is going to class, but she doesn't go anywhere. She just thinks she does. I'm the only one here who is aware we're dead. I'm kind of the caretaker for everyone else. Cade is dead, too, but she died a little less than a year ago."

"How'd you die?" he asked curiously.

Snow and Sam exchanged a look, but Cadence ignored what amounted to the rudeness of the question. She knew he didn't realize it was rude. She also realized that even if he had known, he wouldn't have cared. "I became a cop after what happened to Sam and the others here. I died in the line of duty."

"Mr. Caulfield," Snow interrupted "we're going to have to investigate exactly why you are here, why now, and figure out what to do with you."

Mike blinked. "What to do with me? What do you mean?"

"Mike, no one here but me knows we're dead," Sam said, repeating himself as he took a seat in Mike's desk chair after tossing a few pieces of clothing to the floor. "It could be a catastrophe for some of them if they found out."

"How bad?"

"Depending on the person? They could end up somewhere they don't want to be."

"You mean like Hell?"

"If that's what they believe in, yes," Snow said, not seeing the point in mincing words.

"Sandra, especially, is volatile," Sam said, continuing. "You know how she is when she gets mad. She may not always be my favorite person, but I don't want that for her. If you stay here while they investigate what is going on with you, you can't tell her what you know."

"If you would rather come with us, we can set you up with a place to stay while we do our investigation and you go through processing, if it is necessary."

"Processing?"

"Guidance counselors for the dead," Cadence said with a shrug. "We know a nice one who is good at her job."

"Yeah, but Sandra's seen him," Sam said, frowning. "She'll come back looking for him and get downright pissed if he isn't here."

"Where is she, anyway?" Cadence asked. "I thought she couldn't leave."

"She didn't," Sam shrugged. "In her mind she did, and she's reliving classes she went to. But she didn't physically leave the house."

"Like when Ruby disappeared the first night we were at Lexington after she scratched Derrick?" she asked, looking at Snow.

"Yes, exactly."

"Who's Derrick?" Mike asked, getting lost as he tried to follow the conversation they were having without him, despite his being in the room. They either didn't hear him or didn't pay attention, however, as his question went unanswered.

"So, if we leave Mike here, he could spill what he knows, and if we take him with us, it's going to send Sandra over the edge. Is that the basic gist of this?" Cade asked and both Sam and Snow nodded. "Great," she sighed. "We're damned if we do and damned if we don't. I hate being in this position all the time."

Snow chuckled lightly at that. "Well, Mr. Caulfield could come with us, and we could bring him back to visit Sandra. He is an athlete and a scholar. Excuses could be made for class, practice, studying at the library."

"It'll hurt her if she finds out?" Mike asked, looking at Sam.

"For now, yeah, it would. For Sandra, ignorance is bliss right now," Sam answered.

"I'll go with you guys. But I can come back, right, as long as I don't give anything away?"

Snow and Cadence nodded in unison. "Yes, until we find out what is going on," Snow replied.

"Fine," he said with a sigh. He rose from the bed, looking sorrowful and haunted. "I can't believe this," he muttered.

Sam and Cadence exchanged a look before Snow and Cadence left with Mike.

CHAPTER 7

Welcome to the Party

They took Mike from the dorm and teleported him to the Guidance office. Mike swayed, a bit unsteady on his feet in reaction to the teleportation. Mrs. Steinberg, the elderly woman who occupied the secretary's desk in the center of the waiting room, offered them a warm smile. She always looked so prim and proper, with her wispy white hair in a bun and high-necked blouse with ruffles. "Officers Snow and Riley," she greeted them in her New York accent. "I take it you are here for Miss Saxon?"

"We are, yes," Snow said. "Would you be so good as to let her know?"

"Certainly." The old woman nodded and picked up her desk phone.

"Thanks, Mrs. Steinberg," Cadence called.

"So, what happens now?" Mike looked between Snow and Cadence as he spoke, taking a seat on one of the couches.

"We'll talk to Miss Saxon and see about setting you up with a place to stay," Snow replied. "We'll also ask her if she has run across any cases like yours."

"We'll get it figured out, Mike," Cadence assured him.

"Yeah, right." Mike snorted. "I'm sure you're really anxious to help me. If I recall, the last time we spoke, you threatened to kick my ass for glitter bombing Sam's closet."

"Mike, that was ten years ago for me. Being angry at you for pranks you pulled a decade ago is just a huge waste of time and energy." She did not add that, in retrospect, it was kind of funny.

Bethany stepped out of her office and lifted a curious brow as she saw Cadence, Snow, and another sitting in the waiting room. She crossed the room, making her way to them. "Hello," she greeted them in her usual soft voice.

"Hi, Bethany," Cadence returned the greeting.

The petite blonde woman paused, looking over the three of them. "What is it? What's wrong?"

Snow and Cade exchanged a look before Cade nodded to Snow. "Go on," she said. "I'll sit out here with him."

"I don't need a babysitter," Mike said, once more grumbling.

"No, you don't," Cadence agreed as she sat down on the opposite end of the couch he was on. "But I'm willing to bet you don't exactly want to be alone right now. Finding out you're dead is hard enough; believe me, I know. Finding out that nothing is as you thought it was, though? I can't even imagine how hard that is. We may not have always gotten along great, Mike, but I'm not the kind of person that is going to turn my back on someone in need."

"What am I in need of?" he asked with a bitter laugh. "I don't even know what I need." He lifted his eyes to search her face for any signs that she was mocking him.

"Answers," she replied quietly. "You need answers and closure."

Meanwhile, Bethany closed the door to her office after letting Snow in. They each made their way to their respective tapestry-covered chairs on either side of Bethany's mahogany desk in her forest-green office. "What's going on?" she asked with concern.

"Well, at the very least, we are hoping you can help to arrange temporary lodging for that young man until we can puzzle out what is going on with him," Snow said.

"Of course, I can arrange a room for him. Does he need guidance as far as how to move on?" she asked as she sat down.

"Not until we figure out exactly what he is," Snow said, taking a seat across the desk from her.

That took Bethany by surprise. "What do you mean?"

"It's a bit of a puzzle, you see. We were wondering if perhaps you had come across anything like this before. Apparently, this poor young man spontaneously showed up at a haunt where the spirits have all been in residence for a decade. He lived in the house at the time of the massacre, but he was not among those dead. In fact, according to Cadence, he was the one who found the bodies and called the crime in to the police."

"Cadence worked the case?"

"No, she was still in college at the time. To be perfectly frank, this is the college dormitory where her brother was killed. Now she knows this young man survived the tragedy at the dorm, and she believes he has gone on to lead his life. But today, his spirit, or what we are assuming to be his spirit, showed up at the dorm, as he was ten years ago, not knowing anything after the day before the murder happened. To him, it is October 28, 2012."

Snow frowned, still trying to work out an answer for the enigma himself. Bethany sat forward a little, her brow creased as she thought it through. "Could it be he died, and his spirit reverted to the way it was in his glory days, before the tragedy? It isn't uncommon for humans to block tragic or painful memories. Perhaps his spirit did just that, taking him back to before life was so cruel to him."

"I hadn't thought of that," Snow conceded. "It is possible, I suppose. We'll do some research to make sure. You're alright with putting him up until then?"

"Sure." She smiled.

"Oh, and we may need to take him back to the dorm once or twice. Apparently, there is a volatile spirit there that was his girlfriend in life. She saw him today and Sam is concerned she might make trouble if she misses him again."

"Of course," she said with a nod. "I'll do whatever you need to help ease the situation. If you think I can help with the girl, too, just let me know." She smiled.

Snow rose and smiled at the young woman. "As always, thank you for your help, Miss Saxon."

She chuckled and shook her head. "Anytime, and please, you can call me Bethany."

Snow nodded and gestured for the door. "Shall I introduce you to him, then?"

"Lead the way," she replied, rising from her seat and stepping around her desk.

Mike had fallen into a sullen silence and was busy staring at the floor when the door opened. Cadence looked over, saw them coming, and rose to her feet, which caught Mike's attention. He came to his feet, too, when he saw the older man and the young blonde coming their way.

"Mr. Caulfield," Snow began. "Allow me to introduce you to Miss Bethany Saxon. Bethany, this is Mr. Michael Caulfield."

"Mike," the young man said as he reached over to shake hands with Bethany. "Call me Mike."

"It's nice to meet you, Mike. I'm Bethany. I'm going to get you set up with a place to stay for the time being." She took his arm gently and led him away.

Snow and Cadence left Mike in Bethany's capable hands and made their way back to their office. Once they were back in the office with their door closed, Cadence flopped into her chair.

"What the fresh hell was that all about? Did Bethany have any ideas?" she asked in exasperation.

"I've never seen any kind of situation like this before," he said. "Bethany did have one possible idea—that it is a form of spiritual amnesia. That he has died, and his spirit has taken him back to before real horror entered his life."

"Do spirits do that?" Cadence asked.

"I have to admit, I've never heard of it happening before, but that doesn't necessarily mean it cannot happen."

"Well, how the hell do we go about figuring this one out? Because I'm fucking stumped." She sighed in frustration.

"We'll need to do some research," Snow said.

"Of course we will, because we're not already trying to do any of that." Her tone was sour as she spoke.

"Yes, well, we need to look into the boy himself now, not just what is prompting the reopening of the dorm." He frowned, thinking to himself. "Why don't you go to Aiden?"

"I'll have to wait for him to be asleep, and he stays up very late."

"You know, we can communicate with him in other ways. He does have access to EVP equipment."

"Thought we weren't supposed to sit down to a cup of tea and have a chat?" she asked, using the phrase he had used once upon a time when she had just crossed over. "Besides, wasn't Croft just warning us about our outside-of-the-box methods?"

"I think, in this case, it might be warranted. You go to him and I'll go to your former partner to see if he found out anything."

"Are you sure? You aren't usually the one to suggest rule-breaking. Usually, it's me," she said.

"As I see it, there is no sense in both of us covering the same territory and taking twice as long to do it when we can split up and cover twice the ground in half the time on our own. And I am beginning to believe that time is becoming more and more of the essence in this case."

"You do realize that in just about every horror movie ever made that splitting up is usually what the plan is before everyone gets sliced and diced, right?"

"I'm afraid I'll have to take your word on that. I was never a great fan of that genre of films."

"Let me guess, drama fan? The more historical, the better?"

"I prefer comedies, actually, and the raunchier, the better."

"I am surprised. Remind to introduce you to Judd Apatow when he dies. You two ought to get along great."

"Who?"

"Never mind." She shook her head, chuckling. "I guess I'll head for Aiden's apartment, then. I wonder if he is there."

"Let's check before you go roaming off." Snow rose, and Cadence followed him out into the observation bay. He went to the nearest person, an older woman who looked about sixty.

"Edna, would you be a dear and pull up Aiden Perkins, 9501, please?"

The woman gave Snow a smile and a nod and punched a few things into her keypad. On the screen, Aiden popped into view in a store with Lauren and Derrick. Cadence recognized the store from the time she had spent watching over Aiden on her television at home. It was Lauren's New Age shop.

"Can I get the address?" she asked Edna. It only took a moment for Cadence's phone to beep that she had received a message. She pulled it out and found the address had been texted to her.

"Do you know the place?" Snow asked.

"Yeah, I do." She nodded.

"And you can get there alright on your own then?"

"Yeah, I'll be fine. When and where are we meeting back up?"

"I'll find you when I'm done with Mr. Halleran, alright?"

"Sounds good," she said with a nod. "Good luck." She and Snow exchanged nods, and she teleported to the shopping area that Lauren's shop was in.

She had been dreading this. She knew Lauren was still angry with her for what had happened with her ex-husband, Dan. She didn't want to reach out to the woman to be rejected. But then, Aiden was always willing to talk, so even if Lauren refused the simplest way of communicating, Aiden would likely figure something out.

She slipped through the glass storefront easily, though her passage caused a few crystals that were hanging in the front window to clink together, chiming. The store was nicely arranged: a case with stones, jewelry, and other accessories was off to the left. A few shelves in the middle held books, statues, and other assorted items. The wall to the right held candles and incense, as well as containers of various herbs and oils. In the very back was a round table, which was where Aiden, Derrick, and Lauren were sitting, but they all looked to the front when they heard the chimes.

"Hello?" Aiden asked, looking side to side and seeing no one.

"A spirit is here," Lauren said quietly, closing her eyes. The woman seemed to be getting much better at attuning herself to the spirits, sensing them when they were around her. Of course, this was something of a double-edged sword for Cadence and Snow, since they had to be around and monitor the paranormal group's activities when they were working.

Cadence made her way to the back of the shop, finding that the closer she got, the less she wanted to do this. She'd already faced rejection the night before, in the least expected of places. While that had ultimately turned out for the better, she wasn't thrilled at the prospect of further rejection from someone who was angry with her.

"Hey, you wanna try out the Spirit Box?" Derrick asked eagerly.

Cadence stopped and blinked. She remembered the spirit boxes from various episodes of the ghost hunter shows she had watched now and then when she was alive. A round thing with a speaker that basically flipped through unused radio stations creating white noise for ghosts to speak through. Would it work? More importantly, since when did they have one? She had never seen them use one before.

"Sure," Aiden said, unfolding his tall body from his chair and heading behind the counter, pulling out the thing.

"The spirit feels … apprehensive," Lauren said with a slight frown before adding, "and familiar."

Aiden slipped back into his seat and put the device on the table between the three of them. He flipped it on and the loud static sound filled the shop as he made his way back to his seat.

"Who is here?" Lauren asked, though she had a feeling she already knew.

Cadence frowned for a moment, wondering if she should answer or stay quiet. Well, hell, she decided,

Snow had sent her here to talk to them. "Cadence," she said and was almost as stunned as they were when she heard her voice come out of the box a moment later.

"Woah!" Derrick exclaimed, and Aiden went fishing in his pockets while Lauren frowned as her suspicions were confirmed.

Aiden put the slightly crumpled felt clover on the table. "If this is you, then you know what to do," he said.

Cade reached out and knocked the clover to the floor.

"You've been communicating with her?" Lauren asked, and her tone was accusatory.

"No, they haven't been around much since we haven't been going out on cases. I just set up a system so I would know when they are around. It's only worked a couple of times when they've come around while we were working a case. They do that so I know they're here."

"They?" Derrick asked.

"Yeah, hey Riley, Snow with you?" Aiden asked, setting out the snowflake as well.

The snowflake remained untouched on the table as Cadence answered. "No. I'm alone." It was almost disconcerting to her that she would speak and then a moment later, like a 5-second live TV delay, she would hear what she had said coming out of the speaker in a staticky voice.

"I'm sorry you're still mad at me, Lauren." She waited for that message to go through before continuing. "But we need your help."

"This is so surreal," Derrick said with an excited grin.

"Sorry, none of us will be dying for you today," Lauren said curtly and moved to shut the spirit box off. Aiden caught her hand and shook his head.

"No, it stays on," he said, barely hiding his anger at her. "They need our help. This is why we do what we do, Lauren. Dan's death was not her fault. You need to move on and stop being angry at everyone and everything. I know you, Lauren, and I know you can hold a grudge with the best of them. But I also know that at your core, you want to help people, alive and dead. That's why you have this shop. That's why you and Dan started this group. And that's why I'm not going to let you let your grief get the best of you. You aren't going to turn away from someone in need. That's not you, or at least it never used to be."

Lauren glared at him for a moment, meeting his challenging gaze head-on. At length, Lauren frowned and reluctantly nodded. "You're right, Aiden. You're right. What do you need, Cadence?" she asked in a resigned voice.

"Research," Cadence replied. "I need someone to look some things up on a computer for me."

"I've got my laptop!" Derrick offered, moving to his messenger bag to pull it out. At least two out of the three people here seemed happy to help.

"Thank you, Derrick," Cadence said.

"She knows my name! This is so cool!" The kid was practically beside himself with glee.

"Yeah, it's when the bad ones know your name that you have to worry," Aiden chuckled.

They waited while his laptop booted up and he connected to Lauren's wi-fi. "Okay," he announced. "What do you need?"

"Michael Caulfield. Please look that name up," she said, once again hearing her voice a few seconds later.

Meanwhile, across town, Snow was lurking in Andy Halleran's apartment. The detective was already asleep, but Snow had been pacing for a few minutes. He didn't think it was proper to go into the dreams of a man he did not know. He had never been comfortable with dream-walking, anyway. But doing so in a stranger's dream seemed overly invasive to his sensibilities.

With a sigh, he sat down on the bed. They needed the answers, and if Snow was honest with himself, he had a few choice words for the detective. While he under-stood Andy's desire to heal and move on, he thought that the man's way of speaking to someone he had once confessed to loving was a little cold. But then perhaps he had just thought he was talking to a dream figure of Cadence.

He found Andy dreaming of a carnival. The detective was on a ride, and as Osmond made his way to the railing around the ride, he saw that Andy was not riding alone. He was with Cadence. Snow frowned, finding this in bad taste given what he had told the woman just the other night. But then people often can't control their dreams. The couple laughed as the ride spun on. Cade had a stuffed animal tucked safely under one arm. While the couple on the ride might be having a good time, Snow was not. He removed the extraneous people from the dream, from the carnival workers to the crowds. Finally, he even removed the dream version of Cadence.

Andy panicked when she suddenly disappeared. His eyes fixed on Snow as the silver-haired Englishman made his way to the ride's control box. Snow stopped the ride and Andy jumped from the seat to confront him.

"Where did she go?"

"No one else was important, were they? So why bother asking about them," Snow said, keeping most, but not all, of his anger at bay. He could feel the wall that he kept his anger behind melting away. "As for her, last night you told her to not come back to you. So, to find you enjoying a carnival with a dream version of her is somewhat distasteful. You get the fun; meanwhile, she was crying her eyes out last night."

Andy seemed at a loss for words for a moment. "What are you talking about?"

"Last night, Cadence came to you asking for help. She needed you to look some things up regarding her brother's murder, the massacre at the dormitory house, and the reopening of that house. You said you would do the research but that she should send someone else to talk to you because you couldn't keep seeing her. Do you have any idea how much that hurt her?" Snow surprised even himself with the anger in his voice.

"I … I'm sorry," he said, taken aback. "I …" He floundered for something to say, but the dreamscape around them shattered. Snow hadn't done it. They were suddenly in a rainy graveyard, in front of a headstone that Snow was not surprised to see bore Cadence's name.

Snow felt like a heel. The guy wasn't coping as well as he had thought. He was trying, but Cadence's death obviously still haunted him. Andy hadn't known that when he had talked to Cade last night, it had been her. He was asking his dreams to leave him alone, to stop haunting him.

Snow took a deep breath, his anger beginning to abate a little as if it were washing away with the rain. "Did you investigate what she asked you to look into or did you just think it all a dream?" he asked, knowing very well that the man might have thought it was his subconscious and nothing more.

"I did check into it," he said, furrowing his brow, as if unable to understand why he followed up on something from a dream. "That … that was really her?"

"What do you think?" Snow asked, trying to hedge around the topic.

"I think in all my dreams these past several months she's never once brought up her brother, or the college dorm." He turned to look at the grave, wiping his face with his hands. "Fuck, that was her," he groaned. "And I told her to go away … How was I supposed to know?" Andy asked, turning to look plaintively at Snow. "I didn't know, I thought … I'm always dreaming of her. I'm trying to do what she said, to move on, but I'm always dreaming of her."

Snow sighed, his anger gone as he faced a man who was obviously miserable. "I know it's hard, especially when the loss is so sudden. Keep doing what you've been doing. Keep on dating, move on with your life. It will get easier in time. But if she comes to you again, not simply a dream but like last night, truly comes to you because she needs help with something, don't turn her away. Last night hurt her more than you know."

"She seemed fine." Andy tried to defend himself.

"Since when have you known Cadence to act on an emotion other than anger when in the moment?"

"Shit," Andy said, his voice hissing through clenched teeth. "I fucked up."

"That all depends," Snow said, trying to get this situation back on track.

"On what?"

"On what you have to tell me," Snow said. "She asked you to research some things for her. Those things are actually quite important to our case."

"Case?" Andy asked.

"The information please," Snow said, phrasing it as a request, not feeling enough of a kinship with the man to let him cry on his shoulder.

"There's been nothing new on the college massacre for a decade. As for the dorm reopening, the college is planning to reopen it as a dorm next year. The movement to do so started about three years ago when Mike Caulfield, who lived in that dorm, got on the board of directors for the school. I don't know why he's so hot to reopen it, though."

Mike Caulfield was spearheading the campaign to reopen the dorm? It seemed that the more they tried to unravel their present case, the more questions they came up with. "Thank you, Detective Halleran, for following your gut instincts and not dismissing her request as simply a dream," Snow said.

"Sure." He nodded. "Could you, uh … Could you tell her I'm sorry for the other night? I didn't realize at the time … I didn't even know she could do that. Visit me like that."

"It's not something we do lightly. But when we have a need, we can communicate with the living through their dreams."

"Is she … Is she okay?"

"She's happy." Snow nodded, smiling a bit.

"Good. I hope she does come back if she can."

"We'll see. I'll pass along your apologies, but I won't lie, your words took a toll. She was very hurt. But she has recovered a bit with the help of her friends."

His words stung Andy, and Snow knew it. He felt bad for the man's grief and for his completely realistic belief that Cadence hadn't been there. But he still didn't like the hurt the man had caused in his partner. He turned and left Andy to his grief and his dreams.

Back in the New Age store, Derrick had punched in the name Cadence had requested. Meanwhile, they all moved nearer to him, living and dead alike. It took a moment for the search engine to process the request, and then, of course, several listings came up.

"Let's see," the young man said. "We've got Facebook, Reddit, MySpace … Who has MySpace anymore?"

"The second link below the Facebook one," Cadence said, frowning. "The news article." Derrick clicked on the article Cadence requested.

"Michael Caulfield," Derrick said, reading. "Member of the Board of Directors for the local college." He scrolled down slowly, not sure how fast Cadence read, or what she was looking for.

The article was from the local paper. Caulfield was indeed the same Mike she had known. He was slightly grey around the temples now, and a little heavier, but there was no denying it was the same person. The article mentioned him as having graduated from there, surviving the massacre, though how you survived something you simply weren't there for, she didn't know. He had left athletics and gone into education, specifically anthropology. He had been a member of the college's board for three years and was currently spearheading the campaign to get his old dorm reopened.

"Oh my God," she murmured, surprised when the spirit box picked even that up. "Jeez, that thing is sensitive."

Aiden laughed. "Yeah, now we can have normal conversations."

Cade grinned a little at that.

"So, what is going on?" Aiden asked. "Why are we looking this guy up for you?"

"I'm not sure what is going on," she said, giving time for the box to translate for her before continuing. "I am hoping it is nothing weird or dangerous this time. I'd like to avoid a repeat of six months ago."

"You and me both," Lauren said, muttering under her breath.

"Lauren, anytime you want me to come to your dreams so you can beat the shit out of me, just let me know. I'll gladly do it. I felt awful about what happened to Dan. I was hoping we could somehow get him out of there before the creature did what it did. Unfortunately, we couldn't. Life sucks, and sometimes that doesn't stop just because you're dead, trust me.

"Now we can work together and help each other out from time to time, or I can fly the coop and you guys are on your own again." She hadn't intended to go off on Lauren, but she was tired of the snide remarks.

"So far, we've helped you," Lauren shot back, looking at the spirit box, as that was her only real way of focusing on Cadence. "What have you done for us?"

"Irene Woods ring a bell?"

"What? How do you … What about her?"

"We helped you get her out of the house for that family. We could have just left her there, for you to deal with on your own. One very pissed-off old woman who didn't believe she was dead and was getting more and more violent about trying to get everyone else out of her house. In fact, when Derrick started to get the EMF spikes and temperature fluctuations, that was me, holding her off from hitting you with a spirit-made baseball bat. You would have felt it, trust me."

Lauren paused, uncertain.

"Say thank you to the nice ghost, Lauren," Aiden prompted.

"I didn't know. Thank you," she said, seeming to genuinely mean it.

Cadence took a deep breath to calm down. "You're welcome," she said. "Thanks to you guys for helping to look this information up. We may need more help. Can we come back to you for it if it is needed?"

"Absolutely." Aiden nodded.

"Sure!" Derrick chimed in.

"Yes," Lauren said at length; all the anger seemed to have left her. "Yes, you can. Anytime."

"Thank you, Lauren," Cadence said, knowing what a huge thing that had to be for her. "And you guys, too. Please tell me this isn't being recorded."

Aiden laughed. "No, no recordings here. We were just hanging out, not investigating."

"Thanks. I'd appreciate it if you guys could keep this conversation and our arrangement between us. Don't tell anyone."

"Got it," Aiden said, having already known that. Derrick and Lauren nodded their agreement, too.

The chimes at the front of the store went off again, and Lauren frowned. "Another spirit."

Cade turned and smiled. "Snow," she greeted him, wincing when she heard her voice come from the spirit box.

Snow's eyes went wide as he heard Cadence's voice come out of the speaker on the table. "What on earth was that?" He looked positively stunned when he heard his own voice come from the thing.

"Can you guys turn that off for a minute?" Cadence asked. "I'll let you know when to turn it on."

Aiden reached across and turned it off. He set his felt objects on the table. "Knock them off when we can talk to you again."

Cade drew Snow out to the front of the store to talk to him, away from the three ghost hunters who were excitedly talking around Derrick's computer.

"What on earth was that thing?" Snow asked.

"It's a spirit box. It picks up our voices so they can communicate with the dead."

"Obviously," he replied, a little irritated.

"You're the one who said it was okay to talk to them."

"I thought you would communicate through Lauren like you did when we closed the ritual circle. I didn't think you would be on the bloody telephone with them!"

"It's not a telephone," Cade said, her voice defensive. "Technically, it's a radio."

"I don't care! Are they recording? Please tell me they aren't recording."

"They aren't recording," she replied.

He looked at her suspiciously. "Are you saying that because I asked you to or because it's the truth?"

"Both," she said with a laugh. "Now come on, they already swore to keep this to themselves, and after a little arguing, even Lauren has calmed down. So, what did you find out?"

"Hmm? Oh, right. There has been nothing new in your brother's case in a decade. However, there was one gem of information. Interestingly enough, the movement to reopen the dorm is being headed by one Michael Caulfield."

"I know," she said with a sigh. "That's what Derrick pulled up on his computer."

"Do we think Mr. Caulfield is still alive, then?"

"Unless he died today, and it didn't get reported? It looks that way."

"Shall we have them look up his address so we can check?" Snow asked.

"Sure," Cade replied, turning to head back to the table the ghost hunters had gathered around again. "Just do me a favor, and don't freak out about the spirit box." She knocked both the snowflake and the clover off of the table. Aiden saw it and picked them up, then reached over and switched the box back on.

"Derrick, can you get an address for Mike Caulfield, please?" Cadence asked.

"Sure, one minute."

"Snow, you okay?" Aiden asked with a laugh. "You sounded like you were having a heart attack about the box."

"Fine, thank you," he replied, keeping his conversation short. Cade grinned at the fact he seemed so uncomfortable around the equipment.

"Here it is. He lives at 229 East Hampton Street. Not far from the college campus."

Cade frowned a bit. "Thanks, Derrick. Goodnight." Cadence and Snow both turned and headed out of the shop, the hanging crystals chiming at their passage.

CHAPTER 8

The Conundrum

The early December cold didn't bother them as Cadence and Snow moved through the streets unseen by the waking world, even if most of that world was currently asleep since it was past midnight. Some houses they passed had Christmas lights sparkling in their yards and on their eaves, trees twinkling in the windows. Some had decorations that had been turned off before the residents went to bed for the night. Other houses were dark and undecorated as they passed through the neighborhood.

There were some patches of snow that had become dirty, frozen over slush. Someone's attempt at a small snowman had half melted away, leaving a roundish lump with twigs that had once served as arms for the snowman sticking out at odd angles and a wet scarf in the snow. A car passed by, music thumping loudly from within, the driver and passenger obviously college kids. They passed by a home where a woman in fuzzy pajamas, a puffy winter coat, and boots was stamping her legs to stay warm while her dog, at the end of its leash, decided whether or not it had business to do as it sniffed around the ground.

Snow eventually broke the silence. "What are you thinking?" They had been walking in silence since leaving the shop, but Cade had a look that he recognized. It was the look that meant she was thinking about something that bothered her.

"Caulfield's address isn't far from the college," Cade said.

"Well, given he is a professor and a board member, that hardly seems suspicious."

"It isn't far from the dorm, either."

"It's possible that the event has haunted him. You have to remember that everyone deals with things in their own way. Some people want to get as far away from the trauma as they can. Other people deal with it by facing it head-on."

"Yeah, but that's not what bothers me the most about all of this," she said as they turned onto East Hampton Street.

"What is bothering you, then?" he asked.

"Why was Mike Caulfield's ghost in the dorm today?"

"Well, that's why we're going to the man's home. To confirm he's died," Snow said, curious as to why he had to explain this at all.

"And if he hasn't?"

"Honestly, Cadence, he must have. The man we dealt with today was no residual haunting or psychic trauma impression. This visit is simply to dot all the I's and cross all the T's."

The house had Christmas lights on in front. Icicle lights hung from the eaves of the front porch, lights were in the bushes, and there were some white wire and light figures of reindeer in the yard. The lights were on in the living room.

"Awfully awake and festive for a dead man," Cade said dryly.

"He could have passed last night, and no one found him yet," Snow suggested.

The door opened, and the Michael Caulfield from the newspaper picture stepped out onto the porch in a robe and slippers. He went to the electric outlet and bent down, unplugging the outside lights. He then went back inside and the living room lights went off, too.

"Yep, he's obviously very dead. No one's found him. Nothing to worry about at all," Cade said in a dry, sarcastic tone, her eyes glued to the house.

"While sometimes I hate being right, I think I'm finding I hate it more when you are."

Cade gave him a slight grin. "That goes for both of us. So, what now?" she asked.

"Now, I think it is time to give Agent Whitfield a call."

"Whitfield? Are we still allowed to talk to him? I mean, this isn't an NHD case."

"It may not be an NHD case, but it is a strange case. I can think of no person better equipped to help us figure out the strangeness than him."

The partners teleported back to the office and closed the door behind them. Cadence flopped into her chair. "Well, I sure can't say it's been a boring week."

"I rather like boring at times," Snow said as he frowned and pulled out his phone. "Speaking of which, you still have your paperwork from last night to take care of."

"Ah, shit," she said with a heavy sigh. She leaned forward and grabbed her pen, opening the file of paperwork while Snow made his call.

"Agent Whitfield, it's Officer Snow," he greeted the man on the phone. "Yes, yes, I'm good, and yourself?" He paused as he was answered. "I was hoping if you had a few moments, you could hop over to our office for a chat. We've got a situation that we're a little puzzled about." Cade shot him a look. "Wonderful, we'll be here!" He hung up and pocketed his phone again.

"Hop on over?" Cade questioned, trying to stifle her laughter but not entirely succeeding.

"What?"

"You said, 'hop on over.' No one talks like that!" She dissolved into a fit of giggles that lasted until Whitfield knocked.

"I'm glad you find my speech that amusing," Snow said in an annoyed tone as he arched an eyebrow. He then turned to the door. "Come in."

Agent Whitfield, looking slightly rumpled and perplexed, walked into the office and closed the door behind him. "You needed to see me?"

"Yes, yes, do sit down." Snow gestured for Whitfield to take the chair they had stowed in the corner of the office for when they had visitors. Whitfield brought the chair over to the two desks and took a seat, rubbing his eyes.

"Did we wake you?" Cadence asked.

"No, I've been doing research for another case for a while, is all. I was on my way home. But I've got some time; what's going on?"

"We found the ghost of a man that is still alive today," Cadence said bluntly.

Whitfield sat for a moment, looking between them. He then blinked and asked, "What? I'm sorry, I must have misheard you."

"We found the ghost of a man today, but the man himself is actually still alive," Cadence repeated.

"Yes," Snow said, supporting his partner's words. "The man in question is a Mr. Michael Caulfield. The monitor from one of the houses we cover called today saying that this spirit had just shown up. This spirit, by the way, still thought it was 2012 and looked as he did at that time. We did a little research of our own and found out that the mortal man is still alive. Can you please tell us how this is possible?"

"It's not," Whitfield said, confident as he shook his head.

"Well, it has to be," Cadence argued as she tried to make sense of it. "I mean, Mike had no idea of anything that happened after he went into the basement over ten years ago. Is it possibly a psychic trauma or something that could gain intelligence to become a haunting spirit?"

Whitfield frowned. "You're telling me the guy is alive and ten years older in the flesh? But his spirit showed up today randomly, with no knowledge of the last ten years and looking like he did back then?"

"Yes."

Whitfield rubbed his face tiredly. "Okay, I'm sorry; I need to get some sleep soon. Before I go, write down his name and the address where the spirit showed up. I'll do some research in the morning, okay?"

"Is this gonna get you into trouble?" Cade asked, while Snow began writing down the name and address.

"I doubt it. Did the spirit have any connection to the place he showed up at?"

"Kind of. It's a dorm house on a college campus. The guy lived there for a couple of years before he graduated."

"Why is a college dorm haunted enough to get a monitor spirit?"

"There was a massacre there," Snow explained, handing Whitfield the paper as he tried to save Cadence from having to say it.

He took it and rose with a tired smile. "Alright. I'll call you in the morning with what I find."

"Thank you very much, Agent Whitfield," Snow said. "As always, we appreciate your help."

Whitfield disappeared from the office and Cade looked over to Snow. "It's been a rough couple of days. Why don't you go get some rest?"

"What about you?" Snow did feel tired, and he had a nagging feeling that things were only going to get more hectic as this puzzle continued.

Cadence tapped the open file of paperwork on the desk in front of her with the pen she was holding. "I have some things to finish up here. Don't worry; I'll get some sleep, too. I just don't want this piling up on me. I have a feeling we're going to be running from one fire to another for the next few days," she said, voicing the same worry Snow had about how the next few days were going to be.

Snow nodded and rose from his chair. "Then I bid you goodnight, Cadence. I'll see you in the morning."

"Night," she said with a smile. She then bowed her head to the paperwork in front of her as Snow disappeared from the office.

CHAPTER 9

Truth

Cadence had only been asleep for a couple of hours when the shrill ringing of her phone woke her. She rolled over in her bed and fumbled for the phone on her nightstand. She managed to find it without opening her eyes, but had to squint to see the green button to answer the call.

"Riley," she said as she answered, noting how sleepy her voice sounded.

"Hey, sis, sorry to wake you," Sam said.

Cade opened her eyes and sat up in bed, suddenly wide awake. It wasn't like Sam to make a call in the middle of the night or the early morning. "No problem; what's up?"

"Can you bring Mike back?" he asked, sounding a bit harried.

"Sam, what's going on?"

"Sandra is going apeshit, that's what. She accepted football practice and study and class, but she has started throwing things around, pitching a fit. If she's still like this when the construction workers get here … It could get ugly."

"I'll call Snow and we'll be there in a few."

"Thanks, Cade." He sounded very relieved.

Cade swung her legs out of bed as she dialed Snow. It rang three times before he answered, sounding very groggy.

"Snow," he said, answering the phone. He then promptly yawned.

"Hey, it's me. There's a problem."

"What problem?" he asked, the sleepiness vanishing from his voice.

"Apparently, Sandra is going apeshit at the dorm and wants Mike back. Think we can get him?"

"Apeshit?" Snow questioned.

"Going off the scale like in Poltergeist proportions, according to Sam. She wants Mike back, and Sam said if she is still like this when the construction workers get there, it won't be good."

"I'll contact Miss Saxon and we'll bring Mike to you. I want you to go ahead to the dorm and see if you can calm her. You've been good at that and she knows you."

"It's not like we braided each other's hair, Ozzie. She and I didn't get along."

"Well, then try to get along now, damn it. Talk her down from this before people get hurt." With that, he hung up.

Cade dressed easily enough and pulled her hair back into a quick ponytail. She slipped the knife that Whitfield had given her months ago into her jacket so it wouldn't be noticeable. Just in case, she told herself. The knife was for if things got dangerously bad. Then she grabbed her phone and was gone from her apartment.

Dawn was just beginning to lighten the sky as she appeared on the corner where the Victorian house stood and she could hear the screaming from inside while still on the street.

She ran into the house and headed straight for the living room in the back, where the yelling was coming from. Julie and Nelia were cowering in a corner of the room as Sam and Sandra seemed to be facing off, with Sam having a hold of one of Sandra's arms.

"Let me go, Sam; this has nothing to do with you," Sandra said, her voice loud and full of anger.

Sam, who was blocking her exit, shook his head. "No, Sandra. I'm not going to let you go over and start trouble in someone else's dorm."

"What's the problem?" Cadence asked sharply; Julie and Nelia looked relieved that someone had come to try to handle the situation.

"Oh, of course, I should have guessed," Sandra said in a voice that dripped venom. "I yell at baby brother and big sister comes running to protect him."

"Oh, cut the shit, Sandra." Cadence rolled her eyes. "What the hell has got you so worked up? I could hear you screaming from the street corner."

"Why the hell are you even here?" Sandra asked. "It's not like you run the place."

"I joined campus security," Cade lied. "They got a report of a disturbance, and like I said, I could hear you yelling from the street. Now what the fuck is going on?"

"My phone is gone." She frowned.

"Your phone?" Cadence asked, looking at the girl incredulously. "All of this is over your damned phone?"

"Well, I have to call Mike!" Sandra protested, trying to defend herself. "He wasn't here when I got back from class, and he hasn't been back."

"So, this isn't about your phone; it's about Mike?" Cadence clarified.

"He could be hurt!"

"Or he could have become a sane person and be avoiding your crazy ass," Sam interjected, earning glares from every woman in the room, including his sister.

"Look," Cadence said, turning her attention back to Sandra, "I'm sure he'll be back soon. You need to be patient, and you need to try being a little less insecure."

"I'm not insecure. I'm worried about him."

"Worried about him being with someone else?" Cadence asked pointedly.

Sandra looked down at the floor and frowned. "It feels like it's been forever since I'd seen him. Then he was here, and now he is gone again."

Cade threw a look at Sam, who shrugged. Where the hell is Snow with that boy? she thought to herself. "Look, Sandra, I know we aren't exactly the best of friends, but I think I'm safe in telling you that he isn't going anywhere. You have nothing to worry about. He's an asshole and a moron, but he's not a cheater." Cade frowned as the truth of what she had just said hit her. To her knowledge, Mike had never been a top scholar. He went through school on an athletic scholarship. When did he suddenly get smart enough to be an anthropologist?

Before she could follow that train of thought any further, Mike came in. He moved to Sandra and hugged her close. Cadence fell back a step or two to stand by Snow and Bethany, who had followed Mike in. Sandra was all smiles, happy to have Mike back, until she caught sight of Bethany.

"Really, Mike?" she said, her tone accusatory as she slapped his arm with force. "That's where you've been? With her?" She pointed an accusing finger at the poor guidance counselor.

"What? No, baby. She's with the old dude."

Score one for Mike, Cadence thought to herself. At least he was quick on his feet with that one. For his part, Snow quietly bristled at being called an "old dude." Meanwhile, Bethany was blushing. Sam relaxed from guard dogging the living room door and joined the three of them.

"Can we just tell her?" Sam asked under his breath to Snow and his sister. "Have her move on? She's a pain in the ass."

Cade couldn't help but grin a bit, but Snow shook his head disapprovingly. "No," the silver-haired officer said.

"Come on," Sandra said. "Let's go to get breakfast. I'm dying for some pancakes and bacon." She took Mike by the hand and began to lead him out of the room, but he stopped.

"I was thinking we could go upstairs and get some sleep," Mike said. He was following the directions he had been given to try to calm her down and keep her in the house.

"We can sleep after. I'm starving!" she protested as she tried to pull him along.

"You've been pitching a fit all night because I wasn't here, and now you want to go out?" Mike asked.

"How do you know what I've been doing?" She stopped pulling on him and turned to regard him suspiciously. "And where's my phone? Did you take it?"

Mike cast a glance at Sam and the others. Snow pulled Bethany aside to talk to her, to plan in case they did need to take Sandra with them when they left. That left Cade and Sam in the doorway, standing between Sandra and everything else.

"Why the hell are you looking at them?" she demanded, catching the glance. "See, I knew something was going on. I know you're up to something, Riley," she said, looking at Sam and accusing him. She moved again, trying to leave the room.

"Sandra, please. Just wait for a minute." Mike reached out for her.

She shook off his hand and moved to the door, but Sam got in her way. "Sandra, you need to calm down. You're being paranoid, and honestly, you're scaring the others," he said, gesturing to Julie and Nelia.

Without warning, she hauled off and punched Sam, full force, in the gut. He doubled over in pain and Sandra ran, taking advantage of the distraction. Mike and Cade ran after her, out into the hallway, where she had stopped. Workmen were pulling up in trucks outside, the morning light shining in the glass panels on the door, and she was looking around, confused.

"Why is everything gone?" she asked. A cold sliver of panic went through Cade as she realized Sandra was now seeing things as they were and not as they had been when they had died.

Sam came lumbering up behind Mike and Cade, an arm across his stomach. "Because you're dead, Sandra," he said, his voice quiet so it wouldn't carry. "Is that what you want to hear?"

"I want the truth." She looked uncertainly from face to face as Snow and Bethany now joined them in the hallway.

"No, you don't, Sandra," Mike said.

"Yes. I do. What is going on?"

Sam stepped forward. He was the monitor for this place, so he felt it was his job to tell her. "We died, Sandra. Though I've been the only one here who knew it for a long time."

She blinked, frowning. She didn't want to believe it, but it made a certain amount of sense. It had been a long time since anything had changed in the house. She had been becoming more and more aware of it, though, and it had been bothering her. Mike coming back just happened to bring those vague feelings of something being off into sharp focus. "How?" she finally asked.

"You don't need to know—" Mike started to say, but she interrupted him.

"Yes. I do. I need to know."

Cadence knew the scenario best, so she answered Sandra. "Someone opened the sliding glass door behind you while you were sitting on the couch, watching TV with Julie and Nelia. He slit your throat and then proceeded to kill them, too."

"You said there were others. Who else?"

"Sandra …" Sam started.

"No, I want to know." Things were finally making sense, and she wasn't about to let them snowball her or hide things from her anymore. "I need to know. You, us, and who else? Because, at this point, I'm not sure who I've seen recently and who I haven't."

"You, Julie, Nelia, Chase, Adam, Bridgette, Greg, myself, and Eri," Sam said.

"You forgot Mike," Sandra said, her eyes fixed on the floor and her arms wrapped around her middle as she listened to them.

"No, I didn't. He didn't die with us."

Sandra's brow furrowed. She knew she had seen Greg and Chase, and of course, Julie and Nelia. "What happened to Adam, Bridgette, and Eri? They haven't been around."

"They moved on," Sam answered with a shrug.

"Which is something you can do," Bethany said, coming forward now. "Why don't we go talk?" She offered her hand to the confused ghost. Sandra looked at the hand hesitantly, unsure if she should take it or not. She didn't know what was going to come next if she agreed to go with the woman, and that scared her.

She looked over at Mike, who nodded to her. "Go with her, Sandra. She's a nice person. It will be okay." Finally, she looked over at Sam.

"Sorry," she said after a moment, "for hitting you."

"It's not the first time you've hit me, Sandra," he said with a bit of a grin, rubbing his stomach where she had hit him. "Though it is the first time since we died," he added, trying in vain to lighten up the situation.

Sandra took Bethany's hand; the guidance counselor nodded to the others and teleported them both back to her office. The tension seeped out of the room after they left, and all of them seemed to sag a little as if they were puppets whose puppeteers had taken a break. Snow rubbed a hand over his face and leaned against the wall.

"Well, I have to say that went better than I thought it would," Sam said as the door opened and a construction worker came in.

"Is she going to be okay?" It was Mike who asked.

"Miss Saxon will help her. She will be fine." Snow assured the young man.

"I hate that I called you guys in for nothing," Sam said.

"It wasn't for nothing, Sam," Cade said. "The way she was when I got here, it was going downhill fast. This could have ended up going either way. Mike and Bethany were the ones who turned it toward the better ending, I think. Even if we did finally have to tell her she's dead. Not to mention it's best we were here in case she tried more violence." She hugged her brother loosely. "But we should get going," she said with a sigh.

Snow nodded. "Yes, we should be getting a call in a few hours."

"Will Nelia and Julie be okay after all of that?" Cade asked her brother.

"They should be, yeah. Nelia and Julie pretty much inhabited their own world when they were alive; it's kinda the same now. I bet they won't even notice Sandra not being here."

"Okay then. We'll take Mike back. If you need us, call us, okay?"

"You got it," he smiled at his sister.

CHAPTER 10

A History of Horror

Snow and Cadence had taken Mike back to his temporary room and then gone into their office. Neither one felt particularly like going home, though both were tired. Cadence was aware she still had paperwork to get through, even though she had finished most of it last night. She wanted to get it off her desk as soon as possible, however. Snow didn't want to be selfish and go home to sleep when his partner was stuck doing work, so he stayed to keep her company.

He sat back in his chair, debating how to broach the subject of Andy with her, or if he even should. While still debating it in his mind, having gone around and around but coming to no conclusion, he fell asleep. Cadence didn't notice her partner leaning back in his chair with his eyes closed; she was focused on staying awake and getting through the paperwork. It wasn't long, however, before her head was too heavy and she rested it on her arm. Then the pen slipped from her fingers as she, too, fell asleep.

A knock on their door woke them both with a start, Snow jumping and nearly tipping himself out of his chair in the process. The knock sounded again.

"Come in," Snow called, making sure he was settled in his chair.

The door opened and Agent Whitfield walked in. His messy curly hair had been tamed somewhat by a comb, and his clothes were far less rumpled and wrinkled than they had been the other night. He blinked when he saw them. "You two okay?" he asked as he closed the door.

"Fine," Snow answered with a smile. "Just a little tired, is all. I take it you've found something out?"

"Yeah, it's actually a good thing you called me; this would have ended up in my division anyway," he said, taking a seat.

"Huh?" Cadence asked. "How is it NHD? I mean, last I checked, it stood for Non-Human Division. While I'll be the first to put out there that Mike is an asshole, he's not a non-human creature."

Whitfield chuckled lightly at that while Snow gave her a disapproving look. "Normally, I would agree with you," Whitfield said. "But if we take into consideration the history of the house itself, we might be able to explain your strange situation with this guy."

"Oh?"

"Yeah, and it's not good."

"Because that would be such a change for us." Cade sighed as she slumped back into her chair with a roll of her eyes.

"Please, Agent Whitfield," Snow said, shooting Cadence a look, "explain to us what exactly you are talking about."

"Well, this situation is beyond strange on the surface. Someone who is still alive having an intelligent spirit from ten years ago? To my knowledge, an instance like that has never happened. Not ever. But then I started looking at the address you gave me. This college dorm of yours? Its history is a little darker than just the one massacre."

"What do you mean?" Cadence asked as she sat up straight, suddenly feeling wide awake.

"Back in the 1920s, it was owned by a man named Overton. Marcus Overton. Back then, interest in the spiritual had kind of come to a head. Lots of people were into it. Séances, Ouija boards, the beginning of more scientific ghost hunting, though their methods would be laughed at by scientists now. Even magic. Hell, Houdini was really big on the paranormal stuff.

"With all of this interest in the spiritual and occult at a peak, we have Marcus Overton. He was an evil man, and I don't say that lightly. He was a surgeon whose patients had a fifty-fifty chance of surviving his procedures. He loved cutting people open, and sometimes he would deliberately let them die on the table so he could do whatever twisted experiments he wanted. Sometimes he would be kind and anesthetize his patients. Other times, that wasn't a priority. Neither was making sure his instruments were clean."

"Good God," Cadence said softly.

"Yeah," Whitfield agreed. "The man was not challenged by an overabundance of ethics. Of course, he got into the national paranormal pastime like a lot of others did, but because he was a darker person, the places he went to with it were dark. Instead of benign séances or magic acts, he delved more into the occult. And I mean the dark side of the occult.

"Now, you need to understand that the NHD is sometimes a misnomer. We deal with non-human creatures, but we also deal with the spirits of people who are just rotten. People who were evil in life and remain so after death. These spirits get imprisoned, in a sense. Sometimes they are jailed on this side and sometimes in the mortal world. It depends on the spirit and on the circumstances. However, there are ways in which these spirits or creatures can get released.

"Mr. Overton got a hold of an artifact that had a particular non-human creature attached to it. He became a kind of acolyte to this creature, worshipping it since its philosophy of pain, blood, and destruction mirrored his. He wanted to release this non-human into the world, which would have been cataclysmic had he been successful.

"The NHD was just getting its footing as more than just a jailing entity, and the force that you two serve on was also just getting started. They decided that a combined effort between the world of the spirits and the world of men would be needed, much like what we did at Lexington, where both sides worked together to stop that creature. Both sides worked together to stop Mr. Overton because what he was planning would have broken laws on both sides of the veil. Releasing this particular non-human takes a lot of pain and a lot of blood. He had been planning to host a party at his house, inviting practically everyone from the town, and he planned on murdering them all. That's when we knew we had to put a stop to it. That we had to cross lines in order to keep everyone, both sides, safe."

"How did they do it?" It was Snow who asked.

"I looked over the case files this morning. Turns out, one of us went to the breather police and got them investigating the not-so-good doctor about his mortality rate and body disposal methods. Mr. Overton had absolutely no intention of being arrested, though. He killed two of the police officers sent after him initially. When those officers didn't come back, they sent practically the entire force to the house and surrounded him. He started shooting; they shot back. He was killed, and that's when our side took over and imprisoned his spirit. The officer we had been working with helped with the physical needs of the ritual. He then took the vessel that we had put Overton's spirit into and hid it. The officer also took the ritual objects, including the non-human artifact, and hid those as well."

"Okay," Cadence said as she nodded slowly. "I see why the house has bad mojo. However, I'm not getting the connection between everything you just told us and why there is suddenly a ghost of Mike Caulfield from ten years ago."

"I can't see any connection either," Whitfield said. "But I do have an idea. Can we take Mike back to the house so he can retrace his steps? Maybe I can find something there related to all of this that would let us know," Whitfield suggested.

"We can call Miss Saxon and have him brought to the house, yes," Snow said.

"Wait, did you just volunteer to go back in the field?" Cadence was grinning as she asked this. He had always struck her as a deer-in-headlights kind of guy when faced with a situation that didn't involve straight research.

Whitfield grinned back. "I know, not my kind of thing. Six months ago, I would never have volunteered for something like this, but after we worked together on that case … It's kind of exciting." He chuckled, although the laugh sounded nervous. "I mean, I wouldn't go looking to square off against a shadow creature again anytime soon, but it was a nice feeling to be involved in the solution."

Snow smiled and nodded. "We'll make a field officer of you yet, lad."

"You might want to include Miss Saxon as well," Whitfield said. "If this Mike guy gets upset about what we find out, she may be good at calming him down."

"I'll contact them and we'll arrange to go soon," Snow said with a nod.

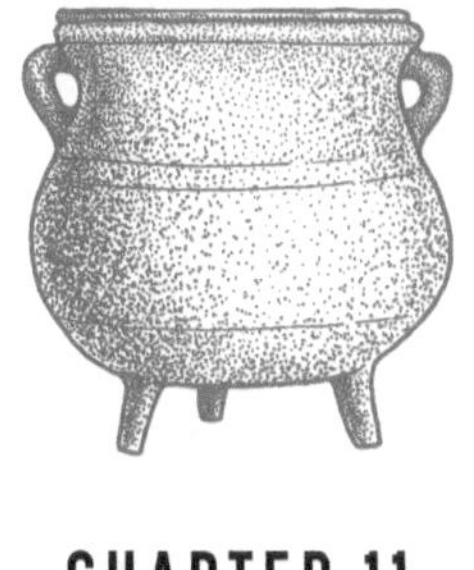

CHAPTER 11

Retracing Steps

Bethany and Mike had been able to get more sleep than Cadence or Snow. They were ready to go when Snow called. Mike especially was anxious to get out and start figuring out what was going on. The group of five made their way to the Victorian as the vibrant colors of the sunset were painting the sky. Cadence had called Sam, letting him know they were coming. He was waiting for them in the front hall, pacing back and forth.

"Hey," he said by way of greeting as they came in.

"Hey, Sam," Cade smiled as they all filed in.

Whitfield looked around the hallway. He noted the paint cans and ladders, as well as the tarps on the floor. "There's construction?"

"Yeah," Sam said. "The college is going to reopen the dorm."

"What?" Whitfield couldn't believe that a responsible college would be willing to reopen a place with such a dark history.

"First of all, Agent Whitfield, this is the monitor for the dorm, Sam Riley. Sam, this is Agent Whitfield," Cadence introduced them.

"Riley?" Whitfield looked between the siblings as he asked. "As in ..." He trailed off, pointing to Cade, who nodded.

"Yeah, he's my brother."

"Really?"

Sam laughed at the surprise. "Yeah, really."

"Why so shocked?" Cade asked.

"Oh! No, no, sorry. It's just that you both died so young. It's kind of a shame. Anyway, let's see what we can figure out here. Sam, are we going to disturb anyone here by going into the basement?"

"No, even if you walked in where the rest of them are, they may or may not see you. Most of them just relive the day we died."

Whitfield nodded and frowned, then turned to Mike. For his part, Mike was standing next to Bethany, looking worried and a little scared. "Uh, Mr. Caulfield? If you could, please retrace your last steps before you woke a couple of days ago?"

"Well ..." Mike said, frowning as he began. "I was up in my room. I had some time to kill between class and practice, and Sandra was in class, so I was alone. I was thinking about the Halloween party we were gonna have. We always have the best parties here. Legendary, ask anyone. Well, I guess not anymore. Anyway, I remembered we had boxed up the decorations from last year and tossed 'em in the basement. So, I decided to go down and get the box so I could go through the stuff to make sure we could still use it all. See if anything needed new batteries or needed to be replaced."

"Okay, let's go down to the basement, then." Whitfield gestured for Mike to lead the way.

Mike walked past them and headed to the basement door. He was followed by Sam, then Whitfield. Bethany, Cade, and Snow took up the rear. Down the wooden steps they went. A forgetful worker had left the basement lights on, making it a little easier for them. There was a small square landing, then a left turn, and three more steps down into the basement proper. Cream-colored paint covered the wood paneling of the walls, and dull gray concrete served as the floor. High on the wall opposite the stairs was a small rectangular window, and beneath that were the hookups for a washer and a dryer. The smell of fresh paint was still strong.

"Where was this box?" Whitfield asked.

Mike frowned again as he tried to remember. "I got down here," he muttered. "Then ..." He turned and moved to the small storage closet under the staircase. "I think it was in here."

"The fuses are in there, too," Sam offered.

"Didn't you say the electricians had been down here working on the wiring when Mike came up?" Cade asked. Sam nodded.

Whitfield nodded and looked into the closet. Directly in front of him was the fuse box. The storage area was empty, though, no boxes. Looking down, he noticed a panel of wood on the wall seemed off-kilter. He bent down and, sure enough, he saw that the panel in question had been kicked in about an inch. He mustered his energy and pulled the panel out to see what, if anything, was behind it.

"Son of a bitch," Whitfield cursed, then immediately looked embarrassed. "Oh, uh, sorry for the language, ladies."

"What is it?" Snow asked.

Whitfield reached in and pulled out what looked like a small, very dusty urn in one hand and what looked like a top to it in the other. It looked like the top had been sealed onto the vessel with wax, but that the wax had cracked, letting the top fall off. "It's the prison that they sealed Overton's soul into."

"And they thought it was a good idea to just leave it lying around in the house he had lived in?" Cadence was incredulous that they had treated the prison of someone so dangerous so carelessly.

Whitfield could only shrug. "I don't know what they were thinking, honestly." He looked down at the porcelain in his hands and then he looked at Mike. "Did you happen to kick the wall when you were looking for the box of decorations?"

"Um … I guess? I … I went in there. The box I wanted was on the bottom, so I had to move a couple of other boxes on top of it. I was taking the top one down, bitching up a storm cause it was heavy …" He frowned and moved past Whitfield into the closet. He stood about where he thought he had been, and no one missed the fact that his foot was right beside the false panel. When he turned, pantomiming bringing down a heavy box, the back of his foot hit where the panel would have been if it were closed.

"When did this happen?" Whitfield asked.

"October 28th of '12," Mike said.

"When you woke up a few days ago, you were down here?"

"Yeah, right about here," he said, standing just inside the closet. "Some guy was working on the fuse box. I tried to ask him what was going on, where everything was, but he wouldn't answer me. I tried to grab his arm to get his attention and my hand went through him. That's when I went upstairs."

"And the massacre was on the 29th of '12, correct?" Whitfield was piecing something together. Cadence could see on his face that the gears in his mind were working.

Sam nodded. "Yeah."

"Did you see who did the killings, Sam?" Whitfield asked, turning to him.

"No," Sam said as he shook his head. "The guy wore a face mask."

"Like a ski mask or a Halloween mask?"

"Halloween."

"What kind?" Whitfield continued his questioning. No one interrupted, since he seemed to know exactly where he was going with it.

"A clown," Sam replied, not sure why that mattered. "Not a happy circus clown either, but one of those twisted, out-of-a-horror-movie-type of clowns. It was something that went over the whole head, not just the face; it had its own hair and everything."

Mike looked sick all of a sudden. "The make-up on the mask's face ... Was it like, black diamond shapes around the eyes? And the hair was green and purple?"

Everyone in the room went still. Sam looked at Mike, his eyes reflecting the memory of the horror he had died in. "Yeah," Sam said, his voice barely a breath.

Mike closed his eyes and his knees buckled, no longer supporting him. "No, no, no, no, no. This isn't possible. It can't be." He rocked back and forth on his knees, cradling his head in his hands. Bethany knelt down beside him, placing a calming hand on his shoulder.

"That was your costume for Halloween that year," Cadence said, stating the conclusion that all of them had come to. "Wasn't it?"

Mike nodded. "Yeah, but I didn't do it! I came down looking for Halloween decorations. I wouldn't kill anyone, especially Sandra." Bethany comforted him while Snow, Cadence, Whitfield, and Sam huddled together, a little bit away from the confused and grieving man.

"Okay, genius, what happened?" Cadence asked Whitfield.

"Look at the vase," he said, holding the century-old porcelain vessel out for inspection. "You can see there are two layers of wax. The bottom layer is yellowish-white, like a tallow or beeswax candle. You can see the top layer is red. I think what happened is that Mike here kicked the panel accidentally. When it came loose, it knocked the vessel over, which broke the old, and by then, brittle wax seal. I think Overton escaped his imprisonment and possessed Caulfield. That explains why you still have a physical man walking around today. He took possession of the kid's body, imprisoning Mike's soul in the vessel in return. All he had to do was reseal the wax and put it back and no one would be any wiser."

"So, this maniac possesses Mike's body, kicks his soul out, and commits a massacre the next day. Then he lays low, drops out of football, becomes a scholar, and works on the college board? This doesn't make sense," Cadence said, confused.

"Who is this Overton guy?" Sam asked, having not been privy to the meeting between Snow, his sister, and Whitfield.

"A guy from the 1920s who played at being a doctor but was a full-time sadistic ass-wipe," Cade said. "He wanted to free some non-human creature from its imprisonment, but got himself imprisoned instead."

"Great," Sam said with a sarcastic roll of his eyes. "You know, Mike may have been a dick to me most of the time, but no one deserves that."

"Still here," Mike said, both his face and voice full of misery. He hated that they were talking about him like he wasn't there.

"He and I should go back," Bethany said, rising from the completely defeated-looking form of Mike. "It would be best if he's not here right now," she added quietly.

"Of course," Snow said with an understanding nod. "Would you like me to go with you?"

"No, I can manage," she said with a soft smile. "Thank you, though. Call me if you need me." Mike rose, looking numbly at the floor. He didn't look at anyone or anything as Bethany led him off. Once they had gone, the three investigators and the monitor resumed their conversation.

"Sam," Whitfield said, his brow furrowed as he tried to think things through. "Did you see anything odd on the clown?"

"Did I see anything odd about an evil clown with a knife coming to kill me? Care to be more specific?" Sam asked and Snow noted to himself that both Rileys seemed to share the same dry, sarcastic sense of humor on occasion. Sam was generally a brighter, happier person. In this instance, however, the similarities between the siblings shone through.

"Were there any symbols that might not have been part of the costume?" Whitfield clarified.

"Kinda hard to tell. I mean, it's a clown; weird and creepy is normal. Plus, there was a lot of blood on him by the time he got to me and Eri." Sam paused as he thought about it, trying to remember in detail things he would prefer to forget. "Maybe … I mean, Mike said he was going for the creepy clown thing. But there was some symbol on the forehead of that thing, and Mike didn't mention it when he was listing off the major descriptors of the mask. It looked like it had been drawn on after the mask had been made."

"Could you draw it for me?" Whitfield pressed his lips together in thought after asking the question.

"I think so," Sam said with a nod.

Whitfield handed Sam his phone, along with the stylus. Sam took it and closed his eyes for a moment, thinking. He then drew a small half circle facing down on the bottom with a line going up from the middle of it. Then he drew a larger half circle facing up, with the line going through it and stopping at the ends of the half circle. It looked like some weird trident.

"That's what I was afraid of," Whitfield said with a sigh as he took back his phone and stylus.

"What?" Cadence and Snow said in unison.

"This is the symbol for the non-human that Overton was trying to release."

"So, we weren't a random massacre. We were a ritual sacrifice," Sam said, unable to keep the bitterness from his voice.

"Apparently," Whitfield said with a nod.

"Son of a bitch," Sam said, his voice just above a murmur. Cadence lightly threw an arm around her brother, giving him a half hug.

"We should probably head back," Snow said quietly. "This throws the reopening of the dormitory into a whole new light. We can almost guarantee he's planning a new bloodbath. Plus, we're likely going to have to coordinate an effort to stop him again."

"Do I get to be involved in this?" Sam asked, anger burning in his eyes. "This asshole killed me and my girl-friend. The least I can do is to return the favor."

"We're already taking huge risks by involving others—" Snow started, but Cadence cut him off.

"We'll have to see, Sam. But I promise you that if we have a place for you, we will definitely ask for your help," she said. She was not about to let Snow get all uptight about the rules now. Her brother had a right to his vengeance if he wanted to help dole it out. Snow shot her a quick look, but she ignored it as Sam hugged her gratefully.

"Thanks, Cade," he said. He then reached out to shake Snow's hand. "And thanks to you as well, Officer Snow."

"I think, at this point, you can call me Osmond or just Snow if you prefer," he said with a smile.

Insane Ideas

Cadence sat down at her desk with an irritated sigh. "We have to stop this. We can't let the college reopen the dorm just so that this psychopath can hop right back on the bloodbath train, right?"

"Well," Snow sighed, "we obviously have to do something. We cannot sit by and knowingly let it happen, especially as it does concern a non-human and its follower. A follower who had already been imprisoned by the NHD for the egregious crimes he committed while trying to bring about the non-human entity's resurrection. But as Whitfield has already gone to his bosses to tell them about what this Overton guy has done, there is very little we can do ourselves now."

"What about Aiden and his group? Or Andy? I mean, if this guy is as sadistic as Whitfield was saying, then surely he hasn't been keeping his hands clean for a decade. There must be some skeletons in his closet, real or figurative. Whitfield even said they had to get the living involved with this the first time."

"But you know as well as I do that someone like Andy is going to need evidence in order to get a search warrant. He's not going to be able to arrest the guy for crimes some ghosts say he committed. Even if that ghost is you, otherwise, his captain will have him committed," Snow added with a chuckle. He was glad to see that the topic of Detective Halleran wasn't making Cadence flinch. Perhaps she was beginning to move on.

Cade chuckled and nodded. "Yeah, he would need evidence. I do have to say that I would love to be a fly on the wall in the courthouse if he did try to put that down as a reason for a search warrant." She then sighed and rubbed her eyes. She was feeling the effects of the last few stressful and mostly sleepless days. She pulled her ponytail down to let her dark gold hair spill over her shoulders. "God, why do these things have to get so complicated?" she groaned.

"We do seem to be getting more than our fair share of strange happenings, don't we?" Snow commented.

"You would be the expert. You've had years of experience, after all, old-timer," she teased.

"Yes? Well, perhaps you're the culprit. After all, things were fine and normal until you got here," he joked back.

"Better be careful, Ozzie," she warned with a grin. "Keep it up with the joking around and you may have to turn in your snooty British guy membership card."

"I suppose you're just rubbing off on me." He laughed.

They laughed for a few minutes, then, as their laughs subsided, they sighed and looked at each other. "Seriously, though," Cadence began again, "where do we start?"

"For now, we wait for Whitfield," Snow advised. "It is possible we could put a bug in Detective Halleran's ear to maybe look into our hijacked Mr. Caulfield."

"You'd have to do that, though," Cadence said, sobering.

Snow shifted in his chair and frowned. "Cadence," he began, but she interrupted him.

"No, Snow, it's okay. I get it. I do. It's probably best, he and I can both move on."

"No, you don't understand." Snow paused, wondering if he should even say anything now that the subject had been brought up. It would be all too easy to remain silent and let Cade think her former partner simply didn't want to see her anymore. However, Snow had been around long enough to know that when you keep secrets, they eventually get spilled, and then things are usually worse. She deserved the truth. "When Mr. Halleran said that to you, he thought you were a dream, something that happens a great deal according to him. When the good detective realized that it had been you the previous night, he was quite apologetic." Snow held his breath, hoping that he hadn't just undone the healing she had managed to do since Andy's refusal to see her again.

Cadence frowned. "Andy apologized, huh?"

"Numerous times." Snow nodded.

Cade's brow furrowed and she fell silent for a time. Snow let her be for a moment, but when the silence stretched on, he became concerned. "Cadence, what are you thinking?"

"I'm wondering if we're going about contacting him the wrong way."

"What do you mean?"

"Well, if Andy's subconscious is giving him such a hard time about me … Let's go another way."

"Cadence, you can't appear to him mid-day in the precinct."

"I don't intend to," she replied, a slow smile spreading on her face.

"Why am I suddenly terrified of whatever it is you have rolling around in your mind?" Snow said in an apprehensive tone.

"Because it's a good idea," she said. "And you despise my good ideas."

"No," he said, correcting her. "I like your good ideas; it's the insane ones that I despise." Cadence just grinned at him in reply. "This is going to be one of your crazy ideas, isn't it?" he said with a sigh.

"Probably," she said with a nod.

Snow sighed in resignation, putting a hand to his forehead as if he were nursing a headache. "Alright, let's have it."

"Lauren and Aiden."

"I'm sorry? I thought we were talking about Detective Halleran."

"We are. We ask Aiden to take Lauren and go to Andy. We go, too, and I talk to Andy through Lauren, or hell, maybe even that box thing they have. This way, he isn't confused about whether it is a dream or not, and he can ask questions to them that only I would know the answer to, so he knows they aren't trying to cheat him. It also gives him a paranormal expert for the weirder cases that might involve us, and it gives them further credibility in their field."

"You forgot one tiny, teensy, niggling, little, minute detail. We're not supposed to confirm life after death."

"We've already confirmed it to Aiden and Lauren when we worked with them on the shadow creature case. Besides, to those who believe in the existence of ghosts, every single EVP that's caught is confirmation. Whitfield said already that it was a cooperative effort between our side and theirs that took down Overton and stopped his freeing the imprisoned non-human. We've already proven that we can handle that kind of cooperative effort when we took down the shadow creature. Let's face it, getting Aiden, Lauren, Derrick, and Andy on the same page as us, Whitfield, and Bethany … It seems like a win/win situation all around."

"Except for the fact that's against the rules," Snow said, reiterating that point.

"Do you see a better way? If you do, please tell me. I'll be happy to hear it."

Snow frowned and turned over her proposal in his mind. If he set aside the fact that it was so very blatantly against the rules, it was a perfect solution. It would help the police solve a cold case and prevent another massacre. It would give credence and prestige to a group that had already helped them and whom they owed for sitting on very compelling evidence. Lastly, and likely most importantly, it would help them keep an imprisoned non-human from getting free.

"You're right." He sighed in defeat.

"Besides, Croft already likes the way we're doing things, he said so himself. As long as we don't go around advertising what we're doing, we should be fine," Cadence said.

He gave her a skeptical look, but nodded. "Alright then, how do you think we should go about setting this up? Do we go to Detective Halleran and try to have him go to Aiden and Lauren? Or go to them and have them go to him?"

"Go to them; it'll be easier. Then they can go to him, and we'll tag along."

"This is your brainchild; I'll let you take the lead. I have just one favor to ask of you, however," he said.

"What's that?"

"Let's try not to get into too much trouble for this?"

Cadence grinned and they rose. They left their office and a few moments later, they were in front of Lauren's shop. The lights were on and there were a couple of customers inside. Derrick was sitting at the back table and Lauren was helping the customers. Aiden was nowhere to be seen. Lauren looked up when the crystals chimed, marking the entrance of the two ghosts. She cast a glance back to Derrick, but then had to go back to helping the customers. Cadence and Snow passed her by and went straight to Derrick. The kid had his laptop set up and was on a social media website.

"With customers here, it's not like we can make use of that voice box thing they were using last time," Snow said, sounding almost grateful, and Cadence nodded.

"They don't have it on right now anyway, but I think I can get his attention. I just hope he doesn't freak out too much."

"Cadence, what are you planning?" Snow said with a frown.

"Relax, Ozzie, I can do this." She reached toward the computer and used her energy as she touched the laptop's mousepad. She did circles with her finger, making the cursor move in circles.

"What the ..." Derrick frowned. He touched the mousepad, his finger passing through hers, feeling icy cold as it did. He looked around, frowning. He turned and rummaged in his messenger bag, coming up with a sheet of paper and a pen. He tore off a square from the piece of paper and wrote down Cade's last name on the square.

"If this is you," he said quietly, not wanting to be heard by the customers toward the front, "knock this paper off the table."

"He's a quick study," Cade said, looking at Snow with a smile. She then knocked the piece of paper off the table.

Derrick grinned happily. "Awesome!" He breathed. He picked the piece of paper up and tore off a few more squares from the larger sheet. None of the customers paid him any mind. He scribbled on both torn-off squares and set them on the table beside him, a few inches away from each other. One said, "Just visiting," and the other said, "Need help."

"Okay, now, which of these is the reason you're here?" he asked. He kept his eyes on the computer screen as he asked this, so as to not seem suspicious or crazy to anyone who happened to look his way.

"Let me do this; otherwise, you'll end up using all your energy playing twenty questions with the boy," Snow said. Cadence stepped back and gestured for him to go right ahead and he reached forward, knocking off the "Need help" piece of paper.

"Okay," Derrick said, picking up the piece of paper from the floor and then tearing three new squares from the now-diminishing piece of paper and writing on them. He set them on the table, a few inches away from each other again. "Which of these three?" he asked, sitting back. The first piece of paper said "Derrick," the second said "Lauren," and the third said "Aiden."

"I give the lad credit; he is managing this reasonably well," Snow remarked as he brushed all three pieces of paper off of the table. Derrick picked up the pieces of paper and then grabbed his cell phone, dialing.

"Hey, Aiden, it's Derrick," he said into the device, pausing for whatever the other man had to say. "Good, good, yeah. Hey, can you come down to the shop? No, everything's cool, just want to have a meeting." He nodded along to what Aiden was saying. "Sounds good, man. See you in a few." He grinned as he hung up. "He's on his way." He breathed.

Lauren locked the door as the last customer left. "Derrick?" she called as she turned off the "Open" sign.

"Yeah?"

"One sec," she said, deciding she didn't want to be yelling across the store. She finished with the locks and lights and made her way back to where Derrick and his laptop sat with the ghosts. "Hey, everything okay?"

"Yep!" He smiled. "They're here."

"Who? Cadence and the other one?" she asked.

"Yeah! Well… I know she is; I don't know about the British dude."

"I've been relegated to some random British … dude … now?" Snow's annoyance was almost palpable.

"Relax," Cadence said with a chuckle. "I think she'd welcome you more than me."

"I think they're a team," Lauren said. Cadence relaxed as she noticed a distinct lack of anger on the middle-aged woman's part this time.

"Oooh, maybe she's not so pissed off at me anymore."

"One can dream," Snow said with a soft chuckle.

"Well, they want to talk to all three of us, so I called Aiden. He's on his way," Derrick told Lauren as the woman took a seat at the table.

"You've been talking to them?"

He nodded and showed her the pieces of paper. "I didn't think it would be a good idea to pull out the spirit box in the middle of the store with customers here. So, I tore off bits of paper and wrote things on them. If the paper is right, they knock it off the table." Derrick was so proud of himself that Lauren couldn't help but smile.

"You did well, kiddo," she smiled, and Derrick grimaced.

"I'm not a kid."

"I'm sixteen years older than you. To me, you're a kiddo," she chuckled. A knock on the front door drew the attention of everyone, and Lauren got up to let Aiden in.

"Hey, hey," he said, greeting them as Lauren locked the door again. "What's going on?" His long legs made quick work of the distance to the back table, and he folded himself into a chair, looking between Lauren and Derrick. "Why the sudden meeting?"

"Lauren, wanna get the spirit box?" Derrick asked her, since she was still on her feet.

"Sure," she said, and went into the office behind the counter.

Aiden arched an eyebrow at Derrick. "What's up, bro?"

"Your friends are here, and they need our help," Derrick said.

"Are they? Wonder what's up now," he mused.

Lauren returned with the spirit box and turned it on, setting it in the center of the table. "Okay," she said, seating herself once more at the table. "We're all here. What do you need our help for?"

Cadence looked to Snow, who nodded his encouragement. "This is going to be a long story, so bear with me, and thank you all for being willing to listen." She let that message pass through the box, then frowned, trying to think of how to start.

"The last time Snow and I were here, I asked you to look up Michael Caulfield. I thank you for doing this because it has been helping us piece together something of a mystery. It turns out that Mr. Caulfield is possessed by the spirit of a crazy mass murderer who is trying to summon a non-human creature."

"Like the one we helped you get rid of?" Derrick asked.

"Worse than," Cadence said, not putting too fine a point on it. "Let's put it this way: the one this guy wants to release would make that one look like a sugared-up toddler."

Lauren winced and Aiden whistled. "Ouch, that's not good," Aiden said.

"No, it's not," Cadence responded. "When this guy possessed Caulfield, he turned around and killed nine people at Caulfield's dorm."

"That was your brother's murder, wasn't it?" It was Aiden who asked, remembering the details he had dug up regarding her brother's murder when he was trying to verify that she was real and not a dream the first time she had come to him.

"Yes. It was. Now the possessed Caulfield is planning another bloodbath. He's behind the reopening of the dorm."

"The kids that would move in there would be sitting ducks," Derrick said, protesting the ludicrous idea.

"Which is why we're trying to stop it," Snow finally spoke up. He hated hearing his voice come out of the spirit box, but he wanted to try to keep this question-and-answer session from going off track. "We have a solution we think may be beneficial to everyone involved.

"We want you to go and talk to Cadence's old partner, Detective Halleran. We'll be with you. We need him to look into a few things on the criminal side of this, to see if we can make any headway with a police investigation against Mr. Caulfield. This could benefit you lot because it is possible you could become paranormal advisors to the police precinct. If they have odd cases, you could possibly be of use to them. I know the police have used psychics before to find children and such. That would help them and lend you guys some credence and prestige in your own field. It helps the police solve a cold case from a decade ago, prevent another one from happening, and keep a non-human creature from being freed while imprisoning his henchman."

"Cadence, when you first came to me," Aiden said, "you told me you didn't want me checking with the cops about you. That doing so would hurt people. I'm assuming you meant Halleran."

"I did; he was my partner and had been for a long time," she said with a nod, not that he could see it. "But this goes beyond personal feelings and mourning. This is trying to prevent another massacre and bring someone who has committed terrible crimes to justice."

"You seriously think the police are going to let us talk to the detective with no problems and no questions?" Lauren seriously doubted it would be that easy.

"No, I don't," Cadence said and paused before continuing. "As uncomfortable and awkward as I know this is, I want you to go to his home. Bring the spirit box with you. And Aiden, please bring the tape from the first time you saw us."

Snow's jaw dropped in shock, and everyone began talking at once.

"When you were attacked?" Aiden couldn't keep the surprise from his voice.

"What tape?" Lauren and Derrick asked in unison.

"Yes," Cadence said in reply to Aiden.

"Now, wait just a minute!" Snow said in protest.

"What tape?" Lauren asked again.

Aiden opened his mouth to reply to Lauren, but Cadence's voice coming out of the spirit box silenced him for the moment.

"Snow, I know Andy. That tape and my voice will be worth more to Andy than any random question-and-answer session. Trust me, he won't do anything with it. It will prove that even though I'm a ghost, I can be hurt, torn up. Believe me when I tell you that notion will motivate him," Cadence said.

It was silent in the room for a moment, the ghost hunters letting the ghosts have their argument without interruption. After a few moments of a stare-down between the two, Snow nodded, though the only one who could see the nod was Cadence. "Fine," Snow finally said with a sigh, relenting. "The tape and this infernal voice box."

"You got hurt dealing with the shadow creature?" Lauren asked, her mind sidetracked from finding out about a tape she had no knowledge of by this new tidbit.

"Yes, she was," Snow answered for her. "Do you remember when the creature threw the door over your heads in the kitchen at Lexington Hills? Right after that, it grabbed her and tried to tear her into pieces. It damn near succeeded."

"But I've had plenty of time to heal," Cadence added.

"I had no idea you had gotten hurt," Lauren said, her voice quiet and apologetic. "I had no idea spirits could get physically hurt."

"You're going to have to tell us how to get there," Aiden said.

"But what is this tape you are talking about?" Lauren looked to Aiden as she asked this, back on track now that her curiosity about Cadence being hurt had been satisfied.

Aiden shifted uncomfortably in his chair underneath her scrutiny. "Yeah, so … there is a tape from that night at Lexington. You see the door go flying, the creature in the doorway, but then you can see it attack. As they are trying to fight it off, you can actually see them, damn near clear as day."

Both Lauren and Derrick were looking at Aiden with wide eyes, but it was Lauren who spoke. "And you never bothered to bring this up before now?"

"That's our fault," Cadence said, not thrilled at giving Lauren a new reason to be angry with her. "Crystal clear evidence like that is what Snow and I are charged with keeping from happening. When we saw that you all had captured it on the dropped camera left in the room, we had no choice but to go to Aiden and ask him to bury it. He very kindly agreed." Cadence didn't bring up the fact that it had been a trade. He sat on the evidence in return for being able to say a belated goodbye to his almost fiancée, Bethany.

Lauren frowned and looked over to Aiden. "We're going to need to have a long talk about this relationship you have with these ghosts."

Aiden nodded to Lauren, understanding why she would be upset about finding out about the tape. "Will do," he said, promising her that discussion. "But Riley, we will need directions to this cop's place." He repeated the request, as it had likely been forgotten in the hubbub about the buried tape.

"Just give me the address, and I can look up directions," Derrick said.

CHAPTER 13

A Meeting of the Minds

Cadence gave him the address and it took Derrick only a few moments to plug the info into his phone and pull up the GPS directions. Derrick packed up his laptop and Lauren turned off the spirit box and grabbed her purse. She would have to tend to the register before she opened for business tomorrow, but it could wait for now. They all piled into Aiden's van and made a pit stop at his house to grab a camcorder and the tape that he had never even told his companions held such evidence. Then Aiden drove them to the apartment building of Detective Halleran, following the directions voiced by Derrick's phone.

"Is anyone else nervous?" Derrick said on the elevator ride up to the tenth floor. Both Aiden and Lauren smiled and nodded.

"They aren't the only ones," Snow said. "Are you sure bringing the tape out is a good idea? We had Aiden bury it for a reason."

"I know Andy. He won't cross any lines, and it will show him that I can still be in danger."

"You're manipulating him into helping us," Snow said with a mixture of trepidation and wonder.

"I think after the last time I spoke with him, I get to kick him in the knees once or twice. Metaphorically speaking, of course."

Snow chuckled and then the elevator dinged, announcing that they had reached the floor. They all filed off of the elevator and headed down the hall to Andy's apartment. Aiden had somehow been elected to be the one who knocked, so he did.

"Yeah?" came Andy's voice from inside after a moment.

"Detective Halleran? I'm Aiden Perkins. I'd like to talk to you, please."

The door opened, but the chain remained in place. "If you need police help, you can contact the station," Andy said.

"No, you don't understand; we need to talk to you specifically," Aiden said as Andy looked behind Aiden and took in Lauren and Derrick. "I know this is weird, but can we come in?"

Cadence moved through the door and put a hand on Andy's arm. "Let them in," she said. She knew he couldn't hear her. However, she was hoping the intention would be conveyed.

Andy paused, thinking it over, then frowned and closed the door, unchaining it and reopening it. "Not sure why I'm doing this," he said as he grumbled in a quiet voice, gesturing for them to come in.

"Thanks," Aiden said, aware of his heart pounding and his palms sweating. "This is Lauren Kurtz and Derrick Getty."

Andy nodded a greeting to them and then frowned, seeing the camcorder in Derrick's hand and the strange speaker-like device in Lauren's. "What's this all about?"

Aiden took a deep breath, suddenly acutely aware of how preposterous this sounded. "Cadence Riley asked us to come and speak to you."

Andy arched an eyebrow and looked at them for a moment, then shook his head. "I'm afraid I'm going to have to ask you to leave."

"No, we can prove it!" Derrick said, piping up and trying to salvage the situation.

"Oh, really?" Andy asked, his voice dripping with sarcasm so thick it bordered on venom. "How?"

Lauren turned on the spirit box and the sound of static filled the apartment. "Because she can actually talk to you with this device and prove it to you herself."

"Hi, Andy," Cadence said quietly, the spirit box conveying her words to a suddenly stunned and speechless detective.

He shook his head after a moment. "No. This is a trick or something."

"It's not, detective. It's her, I swear," Aiden said.

"Really? Cadence, what's your dog's name?"

"No dog, just a cat. His name is Darwin. Thanks for taking him in, by the way," she replied, having expected the interrogation to prove she was real.

"And your sister's name?" he asked. Cadence rolled her eyes. Expected or not, this was going to get tiresome.

"Brother," she sighed. "Samuel Patrick Riley and he died at age 19 while attending the college in town. But why don't you ask me a tougher question, Andy? Like what you said to me after I died when I came to say goodbye to you. Or what you said to me the last time I visited your dream, or where that dream happened to be. Or should I just gloat about the waitress at that terrible coffee shop we were last at and how she just wasn't that into you?"

Right before they got the call to back up Keller and Saddiq on the Scott Sage arrest, Andy had insisted on them stopping at a specific coffee shop. It was done by a designer who thought retro 70s design was going to be the next big thing. The place was all mid-century furnishings in orange and almond. The coffee had been awful, but Andy had wanted to ask out one waitress there. She shot him down in one fell swoop by showing him a picture of her girlfriend.

That stopped Andy in his tracks, and he shook his head, moving to the couch and sitting down hard. "Shit," he said as he tried to wrap his brain around all of this. He even went so far as to pinch his arm to make sure he wasn't dreaming.

Lauren moved over to him, the spirit box in hand as it emitted its loud white noise. "I know this must be hard for you," she said gently. "But she came to us asking us to help her get in touch with you. She needs your help. Our help, I suppose."

"Help with what?" Andy had no idea how to take any of this. It was almost too much for his mind, and so he was snapping and talking a bit more loudly than usual. "She's dead, so how the fuck am I supposed to be able to help her?"

"Which, by the way, is still not your fault," Cadence said through the spirit box, trying to calm him. Then she added, "Aiden, show him the tape. Lauren shut the box off so he can hear, then turn it back on afterward, please."

"Tape?" Andy asked. Meanwhile, Lauren did as Cadence asked and shut the spirit box off.

"Yeah," Aiden said, opening up the camcorder and turning it on. "About six months ago, we had an investigation at Lexington Hills. Some other people had been in there and had summoned a shadow creature there." Aiden noted the perplexed look on Andy's face. "Kind of like a demon," he said by way of explanation. He then continued. "We didn't know about it at the time. This is what we caught on video." He hit play and handed him the camcorder.

Andy sat there and watched the tape with the volume turned up. It played through the beginning, going through the lobby and the dining hall. Derrick and Lauren moved in behind Andy to see, as they hadn't seen the footage yet, either. Dan could be seen on the film, crouching by the door, trying to jimmy the lock with his knife. Then he cut his thumb, the door swung open, and Dan went running.

Cadence and Snow watched the breathers in the room as, other than Aiden, who was used to the footage by now, they all began to get wide-eyed at what they saw. The shadow creature appeared in the doorway and tore the door off its hinges. Derrick and Lauren went running after the door sailed over their heads to crash on the other side of the kitchen. They could all clearly hear the voices of Cadence, Snow, and Ramon as they tried to get Cadence free of the creature. Andy watched the unmistakable form of Cadence as she fought back against the shadow and its tentacles.

Aiden reached over and hit the stop button as the tape ended. Derrick, Lauren, and Andy sat there in silence, eyes wide as they digested what they had just seen. Aiden gave them a few minutes and then said, "Cadence came to me in a dream that night, asking me to bury the tapes. She gave me information to look up and verify, to prove I wasn't just dreaming it. We've kind of been working together with her and her partner ever since."

"Partner?" Andy's voice was sharp as he said the word, looking up at Aiden.

"Yeah, the English guy on the tape. His name is Snow. They work together."

"It ... It looked like that thing hurt her," Andy said, frowning.

Lauren nodded. "It did, from what she said." She then flipped the spirit box back on.

"It did hurt me," Cadence said, echoing what Lauren had said. "It could have ended me if Snow and Ramon hadn't been there, helping me fight it. With the help of these three, we managed to get rid of it. Aiden is right. I did ask him to bury the evidence. It needs to stay buried, but I needed you to see that. Because I thought it would help you decide your answer to what I am about to ask you."

"And what's that, Cade?" he said with a sigh, rubbing his temples. He could feel a headache coming on.

"I have information on the college massacre and that someone is planning to do it again."

"Oh? You know who did it?"

"Yeah. Michael Caulfield."

"Caulfield? He's the one who called in, finding the bodies. Hell, now he's on the fucking board of directors. Cade, we can't just go slinging mud at him without evidence. You, of all people, should know that." He rubbed his hands on his pant legs, a habit he had when he was agitated.

"I don't expect you to arrest him or get a warrant based on what I'm telling you. I just want you to hear me out. It's not Mike Caulfield, or at least not the real one. The real Caulfield was possessed by an evil spirit, for lack of a better term. The spirit of a guy named Overton. Marcus Overton, who owned the dorm house back in the twenties. He did a lot of killing back then and the cops tried to nail him for it. Things went a little sideways and it ended in a shoot-out between Overton and the cops. Overton ended up dead. Guys on my side of things imprisoned his spirit. The living person they entrusted the physical prison with was stupid enough to hide the artifact in the house. When Mike went into the basement to get Halloween decorations, he accidentally knocked it over in its hiding spot, releasing Overton. Overton, in turn, promptly kicked out said college kid's soul and imprisoned it in his old cell.

"Overton went on a killing spree the next day, wearing the freaky clown costume that Mike had bought. He did those killings to try to earn favor with this non-human creature that he is trying to free. Like I told these guys, that non-human creature is going to make the one we handled at the asylum, the one you saw on that tape, look like a walk in the park. So, you have Overton's soul in Caulfield's body. Look at missing persons records, Andy, or for any John Does that were found mutilated surgically. This guy was a shady surgeon back then and has a hard-on for that shit. I highly doubt he's been sitting idly on his hands for ten years, just biding his time."

Andy had leaned forward and begun taking notes, putting down names and relevant details. "I'll see what I can find out, but what good is it going to do you?"

"Well, if you get actual dirt on him, you can arrest him. Enough evidence to get the warrant and then getting his ass in a cell would be a help. It would discredit him, get him kicked off the board, and hopefully get this initiative to reopen the dorm stopped. Also, getting this guy put away will keep another massacre from happening. I'd call that a win."

"And if I can't arrest him?" Andy asked, looking at the spirit box. "What then?"

"Well, we're working on it on our end, too. To see if we can figure out a way to get this solved without any bloodshed."

"Can you guys keep me informed?" Andy looked from the spirit box to the trio of ghost hunters as he spoke. Movement caught his eye, and he saw Darwin circling around a spot as if he was rubbing against someone's legs. He arched an eyebrow but said nothing about it.

"If you guys find a way to take care of things from your side, let me know. I'm not a big fan of sticking my neck out on a wild goose chase."

"No, but you are a fan of sticking your neck out when the cause is just, Andy," Cadence said. "This is one of those times. Like I said, I'm not looking for you to go in front of a judge for a warrant based on what a dead woman is telling you. I'm just asking you to do a little digging when you have time."

"Alright," he said with a sigh, running his hands through his short brown hair. "I'll do it."

"Thank you. Thanks to you guys, also," she said, looking at Aiden, Lauren, and Derrick, not that they could see her. "We couldn't have done this without the three of you helping."

"You're welcome," the three said, practically in unison.

"Could I ask a favor?" Andy asked, looking at the paranormal group. "Give me five minutes with that box thing. Alone?"

They exchanged looks as Snow shot one to Cadence. "Tell you what," Aiden said. "We're gonna go down and hit the coffee shop across the street. Bring the box back over to us when you're done."

Snow arched an eyebrow at Cadence, hesitating to speak because of the spirit box. He didn't want the box to convey his presence to Detective Halleran. Cade shrugged at Snow. She was actually okay with this, and she didn't mind if Snow stayed or went. She knew at this point she had nothing to hide from him. Besides, it never hurt to have moral support.

The three ghost hunters left the apartment and Andy closed the door behind them, then turned to where the box was. "Cade?" he asked.

"I'm here," came her reply from the spirit box.

"Your friend … partner, I guess. Did he tell you …? Did he tell you I'm sorry?"

"He did, and thank you, but it ended up being okay. I can understand how my popping up would kind of make it hard for you to move on. I'm sorry for coming tonight, but we need help with this, and you are our best choice."

"No, it's okay. So, you're some kind of cop for the supernatural now?"

"Old habits die hard, right?" she said with a chuckle. "And just to be clear, you do know you can't tell anyone about this, right? About me being a ghost or that there even is such a thing as the afterlife. It's kind of one of the big rules, and I'm pretty much downright smashing that rule to bits by doing this."

"You? Flip the bird to the rules? Never. I get it, don't worry. No one would believe me, anyway. I just think it sucks that you got stuck as a ghost," Andy said. He sat down on his couch, facing the box that had been left on his coffee table.

"I made the choice," she said. "I was given a choice and I could have moved on. But Andy, you know me. I had a chance to help, to continue helping. This is what I want to be doing."

Snow wasn't sure what to do as he watched and listened to the conversation unfold. He hadn't wanted to leave with the ghost hunters, as the last time these two had spoken, it had ended with her more despondent than he had ever seen her. But he didn't want to be standing in between them either. He could tell that Cadence was more relaxed than he had thought she would be, which relieved him. He finally opted to stand behind Cadence, a little to one side, a kind of physical statement of his having her back in this.

"You always were a workaholic," Andy said with a wistful smile. His brow furrowed for a moment and he looked like he was going to say something, but then he stopped.

"What is it, Andy? You wanted the box here so we could talk, but you're not saying anything. Not anything of value, anyway. You forget I know you. I know the difference between your real talk and your small talk."

"I'm dating someone," he said, the look of guilt heavy on his face.

"I know; you told me in that last dream when you told me not to come back to you. And before you say it, stop. No more apologies. I told you I wanted you to move on with your life, and I meant it. Did you ever stop to think the reason the timing was never right for us was that we weren't right for each other? Much as we liked each other and enjoyed spending time together, I'm not sure we were meant to be anything more than best friends. I love you as a friend, Andy, and I always will, and I'm sure you'll always love me as a friend, too. Anything else just isn't going to happen, and it's best we both accept it and move on and stop feeling guilty for trying to move on, because as much as Hollywood may romanticize things, I'm not about to go possess Whoopi Goldberg to kiss you."

That made Andy laugh, which was what she had been hoping for. She smiled as he did. "Hey, don't knock the

Whoopi. Jumpin' Jack Flash was Oscar gold," he said with a chuckle.

"I always preferred her as Guinan in Next Gen myself," Cadence shrugged, amazed at how easy it was to fall back into the banter with him.

"You just have that preference because you were crushing on Wil Wheaton. Though how you could have liked that character is beyond me."

"Hey now! No hating on the Wheaton."

"Geek," he teased.

"Jock," she threw back. They laughed and even Snow smiled, enjoying seeing the two of them relate without the heartbreak that had always seemed to be an undercurrent between them before.

"Feel better now?" Cadence asked.

"Much, actually," Andy nodded.

"Good. Now, you go do your thing. When you give them back this contraption, tell them that we've gone, but we'll be in touch. If you get anything, give them a call. Aiden knows how to get a message to me if it's an emergency. Otherwise, give them the info and they can get it to us when we check in with them."

"The tall guy knows how to get in touch with you?" Andy looked almost insulted. "How come I don't?"

"Not a good idea just yet. Maybe in time, we'll see. I have rules I have to go by, too. Though, according to my partner, I only remember the rules so I can break them."

Andy snorted in laughter. "Yeah, that sounds about right." Andy sighed and rose from the couch, picking up the static-spewing box. "See ya, Cade."

"See ya," she said, and then, just before he switched off the box, she yelled, "Jock!"

"You are such a brat!" He shook his head as the box was turned off and fell silent.

"You handled that superbly," Snow said as they watched Andy leave his apartment.

"Thanks," she smiled.

"I know he said he felt better, do you?"

"You know what? I do. We've got him researching Caulfield now. So hopefully, he can dig up dirt that will put the guy away and prevent another bloodbath from happening."

"You know I didn't mean about that."

"I know," she said, conceding he was right as she turned to look at him. "And yes, I do feel better. Stronger even, which is weird since I have no actual muscles. But it was nice to fall back into just joking around with him again."

"It's a combined emotional and mental strength," Snow said with an understanding nod. "I know, and I'm very proud of you."

"Thanks," she said as she smiled. They then headed back to the office.

CHAPTER 14

Test Program

Cadence and Snow teleported into the observation bay in front of their office door. Snow had his hand on the handle of their door when one of the ladies from the observation bay stopped them. She looked as if she had been waiting for them to come back.

"Officers Snow and Riley?" she asked; they turned to face her.

"Yes," Snow confirmed.

"Captain Croft would like to see the two of you in his office," the woman said. Once her message was delivered, she turned and went back to her station. Snow arched an eyebrow and looked at Cadence.

"I take it this isn't good." She feigned ignorance.

"I doubt it," he affirmed. "Usually, when he wants to see us for the less important things, he comes to our office."

"Well, yeah, but maybe he came by here, and since we weren't here, he left the message."

"Or he came by to see us, and we weren't here, so he decided to look into what we were up to. If that's the case, I doubt what he saw pleased him."

Cadence gave her partner a long, hard look and then shook her head. "It must be exhausting for you," she said at length.

"What?"

"Having to put so much time and energy into finding the pessimistic side of everything."

"Not nearly as exhausting as always looking for ways to circumvent the rules, as you do," he jibed back.

"Ooh, score one for Mr. Stuffy Pants." She grinned. "Come on, lead the way." She gestured.

Snow led her through a corridor and they came to a waiting room in front of a large oak door. There were a couple of small sofas there and a desk with a happy-looking plump woman seated behind it. She looked like her hair had been dyed or frosted a platinum blonde, and it was done up in a kind of beehive hairdo. Wide horn-rimmed glasses framed her brown eyes and were not going to be lost with the chain of pearls attached to the earpieces. She smiled as she saw Snow.

"Osmond!" she said greeting him in a breathy, high-pitched voice. "It's good to see you. How are you?"

"Bonnie!" he returned the warm greeting. He moved over to the desk she sat behind. She rose and they hugged, which brought a raised eyebrow from Cadence. "It's good to see you, too," he continued. "How have you been?"

"Good, good," she said, nodding as she reseated herself. "I hear you and your new partner are getting along well." She nodded a hello to Cadence, who returned the gesture with a wave.

"We are. But I'm wondering … why has he called us up here?"

"I don't know, dear," she said with a shrug. "You'll have to wait until everyone gets here to go in and find out." She gave Snow a smile, eyes sparkling with mischief. Her expression said that she knew damn well why they were here, she just wasn't saying.

"Everyone?"

"Yes, there's two more expected."

He frowned, his brows furrowing as his forehead creased. "Two more," he said, pondering.

"You worry too much, Osmond," Bonnie said.

"See?" Cadence said, speaking up. "I'm not the only one who thinks so. Thank you, Bonnie."

"You're welcome," Bonnie said with a laugh, though her laugh was more of a titter.

Footsteps brought everyone's attention around and they saw Bethany come in. She looked both perplexed and apprehensive. She stopped short as she saw the three of them. "I'm sorry. Am I in the right place?"

"I guess that depends," Cadence said. "Are you here to see Captain Croft?"

"Y-yes. I received a message to meet him at his office."

"Wonderful! Come on in, honey, and have a seat. We're just waiting for one more, then." Bonnie gestured for Bethany to get comfortable on one of the couches.

Bethany offered a shy smile and nodded, moving to sit next to Cadence. Snow had perched himself on a corner of Bonnie's desk and looked entirely comfortable being there. "Do you know who else we are expecting?" Cadence asked, although she was pretty sure she knew.

"Just one more," Bonnie said with a smile that conveyed her enjoyment of keeping a secret. Apparently, she was not about to give up the information. The three of them didn't have long to wait, however.

Agent Whitfield of the NHD came in, looking nervous as he always did. He blinked when he saw Snow, Riley, and Bethany waiting there. "Uh …. Hi," he said with a frown, afraid that nothing good was about to happen. "What's going on?"

"Wonderful, everyone is here," Bonnie said with a smile. She pressed a button on her desk phone. "Mr. Croft, they're here."

"Send them in," Croft's voice said over the speaker. She rose and gestured everyone toward the door. The tension in the room seemed to heighten as everyone, including Cadence, was nervous about why they had been called to the captain's office.

The office was larger than Cadence had expected. One wall was entirely comprised of bookshelves, which were full of different tomes of varying thicknesses and even some scrolls. There was a comfortable seating area in one corner of the office with two couches making a right angle, with a coffee table in front of them. The captain's desk was a large wooden affair with two comfortable chairs in front of it. There were some files on the desk, a potted plant in one corner, and an antique-looking set of scales with a white feather in one of the bowls in the other corner. The wall behind him looked almost like a forest, as he had so many potted plants and trees back there. Centered behind the desk was a painting of an Ibis.

"Ah, yes, good, please, have a seat," he said, his deep, warm voice welcoming them. He gestured to the two couches as he rose from the chair behind his desk. Cadence and Snow took seats on one couch, while Bethany and Agent Whitfield took a seat on the other. He paused for a moment, looking between the four of them.

"Now, first of all, I don't happen to have a knife on me, so if you could drop the tension level so that I don't have to cut through it, I would appreciate it. I'm sure you're all nervous. Everyone always is when they get called in here." He paused, pulling one of the chairs from in front of his desk over and sitting down so that he wasn't looming over them.

"Here's the issue. I know what you all have been up to. I know of Miss Saxon's going out into the field, of Agent Whitfield helping out when he is not explicitly authorized to do so. I know about the two of you conversing with breathers. All of it is against the rules, but all of it has been done for the right reasons.

"Now, if others knew, I'm sure that they would disapprove. However, I'm more of a results man and I like the results that I'm seeing. As most of you are aware, the NHD is being bogged down with a lot of cases. In fact, they have been dealing with a lot more than usual of late. I have spoken with the NHD captains and some of the other captains in this region. Some areas, like ours, are seeing a large upswing in non-human activity. In response to this, we're putting together a few test groups.

Groups that seem to be very capable of working together and getting the job done instead of turning tail and running the moment they get a whiff of a non-human or think they might have to bend the rules a little. You lot are my group."

He paused for a moment, letting that sink in. "Agent Whitfield, you've been temporarily reassigned under my command, as have you, Miss Saxon. Miss Saxon, you'll still work with your office, but if Snow and Riley need you in the field to help someone, they have the authority to call on you." He then turned his attention to Snow and Cadence.

"As for you two ... you now have as much authority as an NHD agent. You have access to their arsenal and more leeway with the rules. This is excellent news for the two of you, considering the relationship you have developed with that paranormal group. Add in the tie Officer Riley has to her former partner and the introductions you have made between the detective and the paranormal group this evening ... Yes, I am aware of it ... and I would say you have one hell of a team at your disposal.

"Your duties will vary a bit from now on. You will still have your usual duties of monitoring your region," he said, looking at Snow and Cadence. "All of your usual duties still apply. However, you will now be tasked with dealing with non-human entities or evil entities in your area, whereas before you would have passed those up the line to the NHD." He looked over all four of them, then leaned back in his chair. "Questions?"

Everyone sat in silence for a moment as they processed what had just been said. Eventually, Bethany leaned forward a little bit. "So, I'm not going to get into trouble for going to houses to try to coax spirits to move on, then?"

"No trouble at all, if that's what Snow and Riley deem necessary," he assured her.

"Am I still reporting to NHD?" Whitfield asked.

"If there are no current investigations or cases that need your help, then yes. But you will first and foremost be working with Snow and Riley. This is an association that has proven itself to be worth its weight in gold. In just six months' time, you three have dealt with two non-human cases, and yes, I am counting the case you are working on now. Most territory officers don't see that many in a decade's time.

"Now, Whitfield, you will need to show them the closet so they know where to go for any items they may need." He continued addressing Whitfield. "Paperwork will be turned in to my office instead of your previous superior's office. When not busy with this team, you can then go to NHD and offer them your services. But this team comes first in your duties. Am I clear?"

"Yes, sir," Whitfield said; he was cautiously optimistic now that he was not about to be reprimanded.

"Excellent," Croft nodded. "Now, then … onto your current case of Mr. Overton. Though I suppose it's Caulfield now, isn't it?"

"Yes, he possessed a young man about ten years ago named Caulfield," Snow explained. "We think that the vessel Mr. Overton's soul had been imprisoned in was accidentally knocked over by the real Mr. Caulfield. That caused the seal to break and Mr. Overton to become free. He took Caulfield's soul and imprisoned it in his old cell. He then inhabited Mr. Caulfield's body and went on a killing spree the next day as an offering to the non-human he was seeking to release."

"Shaldoxz," Croft said.

"Sorry?" It was Snow who said it.

"Shaldoxz. The name of the non-human Mr. Overton is after."

"Wait, he's trying to free Shaldoxz?" Whitfield couldn't keep the shock from his voice or face as he sat forward on the couch. Croft nodded. "That's worse than I had thought."

"Yes, I know," Croft said. "I was part of the initial team that imprisoned him."

"You were?" Cadence questioned.

"Yes."

"Then answer a question for me, please. Why the hell did you all not think to remove the vessel from the house? Or put a better seal on the vase, like crazy glue, instead of wax? Or put him in titanium instead of porcelain?" Croft chuckled, which irked Cadence.

"All good questions," he said with a nod. "But you see, for this particular incident, we were in charge of imprisoning, not the disposal of the physical trappings. The breathers were in charge of keeping the vessel hidden."

"They did a bang-up job," she said in a dour voice.

"That is exactly why I am thrilled that you have such a good working relationship with those ghost hunters. Perhaps this time we can seal Mr. Overton away for good," Croft said.

"We absolutely cannot let him free Shaldoxz," Whitfield said, shaking his head.

"Please explain this Shaldoxz thing to me," Cadence said, looking at Whitfield.

"I don't have the entire file, but I have looked him up before. Shaldoxz is a non-human of incredible power. He feeds on blood, which is why so much blood has to be shed to free him. The trickiest part of him, though, is that he imbues the one who summons him with his power, as he partially possesses them."

"More possession," Cadence said. "That seems to be this month's theme."

"No, you don't understand," Whitfield said, his tone one of urgency. "Do you remember when you possessed Lauren? When you and she had to occupy the same space to perform the ritual to banish the shadow creature?"

"That was possession?" she asked, surprised.

"Yes," he said with a nod. "Or at least it was a kind of possession, the same kind of possession that Shaldoxz does. They share a body, they share minds, and they share powers. It's not like what Overton did to Caulfield, kicking the original soul out to completely take over the body. This way, you have the strength, the intelligence, and the senses of two people in one; only one of those people happens to not be a person at all."

"So, it seems you were right in telling Aiden and the others that this scenario will make the Lexington Hills case look like a walk in the park," Snow said.

"I'm beginning to hate my being right about things as much as you do," Cadence said to Snow.

"I can have the old files of Overton's case dug up so you can go over them if you think that will help," Croft offered.

"Please," Whitfield nodded. "It's better if we have too much information than too little."

"Officer Riley," Croft began, looking at her. "Are you still comfortable with the idea of working with Detective Halleran?"

Cadence blinked, having not quite expected that topic change. "I … Yes. I'm comfortable working with him."

"Good," Croft nodded. "There may come a time when we'll have need of a contact on the breather police force."

"You do understand that he can't go and have someone arrested on the word of a ghost, right?"

"Of course, of course," Croft said, waving away the idea. "I wouldn't expect such a thing. But like now, when you are using him for research into Overton's activities for the last decade, it can be quite useful. Now you can all go. I'm glad you've all agreed to be part of this team. I'm sure it will be more than successful," he said with a smile, rising to his feet, making it clear that the meeting was over.

Everyone followed suit, rising and moving to the doors. Croft got there first and opened the door for them. A man in the waiting room who had been talking to Bonnie looked up and nodded to them as the four exited. Croft gestured for the man to come in and then closed the door behind them. Bonnie offered them all a bright smile.

"Not as bad as you all had thought, then?" She noticed that the four of them were far more relaxed than when they had entered Croft's office.

"Nothing bad at all, Bonnie," Snow said with a smile. "Have a good night." They all offered Bonnie a parting wave as they left the office. Bethany went back to her office and Whitfield went back to his department, saying he needed to refresh his memory on Shaldoxz. Snow and Cadence meandered back to their office and shut the door behind them.

"Hell of a development," Cade said as she sat back down.

"Very interesting, yes," Snow said, nodding in agreement.

"What do you make of it?"

"Well, it's obvious that he's impressed with how we have been working with Miss Saxon and Agent Whitfield, and that he likes the success we've had so far."

"It sounds like there is a 'but' in there somewhere," Cadence said.

"I've just never heard of this happening before. A territory officer being promoted to NHD, for all intents and purposes, is quite rare."

"Well, he did say this was a kind of test program. But you are right; it almost seems too good to be true," Cadence said with a frown.

"How so?"

"We retain our territory duties, yet get the authority of the NHD and access to their toys? It's like we get to play in our sandbox and other people's sandboxes. Plus, we get the best shovels and pails to do it with."

"Interesting analogy," Snow chuckled. "Do keep in mind, though, that we are not just playing in sandboxes. We're monitoring the activity in all of those sandboxes and are responsible for the maintenance of them as well."

"Ah, gotcha," she said with a nod of understanding.

"It's been a long day. Why don't we see if we can take an evening off, hmm? It will be tomorrow at the earliest that we can expect to hear from Detective Halleran."

"Good point," she said as she stretched her arms up above her. She was exhausted and beginning to feel a bit silly. She knew the events and lack of rest had to be wearing on Snow, too. They both rose and headed home for the evening.

CHAPTER 15

A Small Respite

Cadence felt better the next day. She had gotten some sleep and replenished her energy. There had been no overnight or early morning emergencies. She even got into the office before Snow and was working diligently on her paperwork by the time he got there.

"I'm sorry, I must have the wrong office," he said as he opened the door.

Cadence looked up, confused. "Huh?"

"Well, you see, normally, when I come into the office, I'm the first one here. Not to mention the fact that I ordinarily need to prod my partner into doing the paperwork. Though you do resemble my partner to a remarkable degree, she has never beaten me here, let alone voluntarily done the paperwork. So, I assume I must either have the wrong office or you must not be Cadence Riley."

"Yeah well, you know what they say about people who assume." She chuckled.

"I take it you're feeling well?" he asked as he sat down.

"I am, yes." She smiled. "If bored by this crap." She gestured to the paperwork. "How about you?"

"Quite well, thank you."

Their chit-chat was interrupted by a knock on their door. "Come in," Snow called.

The door opened and Bonnie poked her head in. "Excuse me, sorry for the interruption."

"Come in, Bonnie, come in," Snow said warmly, waving her in with a smile. She entered and closed the door behind her. "What can we do for you?" Snow asked.

"I just came to tell you that Mr. Croft is arranging a new office for you. It will be ready later today."

"A new office?" Cadence asked. "Why?"

"This office would be a bit too small for three desks. Agent Whitfield will be joining you in the office, after all. You will also need room for a conference table for when the four of you are meeting on a case. I think you'll like it." She smiled. "So, if you need to pack anything up, you might want to go ahead and do so."

"Thank you, Bonnie We'll see to it," Snow assured her. Bonnie smiled and left the office. Cadence arched an eyebrow at Snow.

"What?" he asked.

"We have to pack? Seriously? Are metaphysical movers coming in to take our boxes?"

"No," Snow chuckled. "The only thing we'll need to take will be the map."

"I thought everything was based on mental image or mental projection. Can't we just envision it there?"

"Sometimes doing things the more mundane way is easier, especially when it involves a change to your surroundings. Like when we hung up the map together. Doing things mundanely can make them more real, and it requires little to no actual energy expenditure from you."

"Okay. Where do we get boxes, then?"

Snow went to the office door and opened it. He bent down for a moment and picked up two empty cardboard boxes. "Ask and ye shall receive," he smiled, closing the door. He handed her a box and kept the other for himself. "Help me unpin the map?"

They went through the motions of packing up what few things they had in the office. Cadence took her colored pins out of the various locations on the map after writing a note to herself to remind her where they all went. They took it down from the wall and folded it. There were a few case files they had kept in the filing cabinet in the corner that they put in their boxes and the potted plant from Snow's desk.

"Wow, we didn't personalize this place much, did we?" She chuckled.

"Perhaps that's something we can work on in the new office," he suggested. "Though, to be fair, we've been partnered only a few months."

"How do we do that, anyway? I mean, it's not like we have family photos. How do you guys get the plants, for that matter? Is there a florist I don't know about around here? Or do the ghosts of dead plants just suddenly appear in random places?"

Snow laughed and shook his head. "Plants have life energy the same as people. If you want, I can show you how to get some plants for yourself."

"Yeah, sure, once we get settled in the new office. Assuming I can't kill it again. I was never very good with plants. My apartment tended to be where plants went to die."

"No," Snow laughed. "You can't kill it again."

Cadence shrugged. "Okay then." She sat back down and pulled a file from her box, determined to try to finish her paperwork since they seemed to have a brief lull. She had finally finished when Whitfield knocked on their door and entered.

"Hi," he greeted them. "Ready to go?"

"Go where?" Snow asked.

"Well, I thought while they were moving our offices around, you might want to come and check out the closet."

"The NHD arsenal?" Snow asked as he rose to his feet.

"If we go there, does that mean I have to give back the dagger?" Cadence asked as she, too, rose.

"You still have that?" Whitfield asked in surprise.

Cadence froze and pressed her lips together. Then, after a moment, she gave him a wide-eyed, innocent smile. "Maybe?"

Whitfield laughed and shook his head. "Keep it. You have every right to it now." He gestured for them to follow him. They turned a corner and went up a flight of carpeted stairs. Reaching the top, they turned and went down a hall to the door at the very end. It was labeled "Supply Closet." Whitfield paused to grin at them and then opened the door.

Calling the NHD's arsenal a closet would be like calling Buckingham Palace a quaint cottage. The room was huge and well-lit, with a lot of glass, chrome, and white. Cadence instantly felt the hairs on the back of her neck rise in response to the white walls and floor.

Inside the room, cases of artifacts and weapons could be seen, from simple daggers and swords to things that Cadence couldn't make out. She crossed the room to a piece that looked like a white plastic "S" and picked it up.

"Careful!" Whitfield said, his tone urgent as he followed her. He ducked when she turned, as if she were going to cut his head off with the handheld device.

"What is it? What does it do?" Cade asked as she examined it. A click sounded from beneath one of her fingers and a bolt of energy shot out of one end, hitting the wall to her left. "Oh," she said, her eyes wide.

Whitfield ran his hands through his hair in distress. "Cadence, I appreciate your curiosity, but if you don't know what something in here does, for God's sake, don't pick it up."

"Yeah, got it, sorry." Cadence turned around and set the item back down on its shelf next to an item that looked as if a stapler and a teddy bear had a child together. As she released the bolt thrower, the other people in the room, who had turned to see what the commotion was, turned back to their work. Cadence returned to looking around the room, with her eyes instead of her hands.

There were drafting tables set up in the middle of the room and people sat at them with pencils and other drawing tools. There were also workbenches set up with what looked like several different projects in various stages of construction. Cadence kept her hands clasped behind her back as Whitfield showed them around.

"If we need something for a case, this is where we'll come for it," he said, leading them to different shelves to show off finished products. "They have weaponry, trapping devices, everything you can imagine and probably quite a lot you can't."

"Trapping devices?" Cade asked, images of the ghost trappers used in that old Bill Murray movie going through her head.

"Something we may need soon with any luck," Whitfield nodded. He pointed to the various people at their drafting desks. "They design this stuff, and it's meant to function as easily as possible. I'm not an engineer; I don't know how they make it all work, especially some of the newer stuff."

"You get a lot of the newly dead to do this, don't you?" Snow asked, looking with some awe at the sheer number of things in the room. "In order to keep up with technology."

"Yes, we do," Whitfield nodded. "We trade off with the Lifestyles Department on getting the engineers."

"There is a Lifestyles Department?" Cadence asked.

"They handle the televisions, phones, and computers, things like that," Whitfield explained.

"Ah, I see." She nodded, looking around the room. The number of items in the numerous glass cases and shelves was impressive, to say the least. She wasn't sure how some of the things she saw were supposed to work, or what they were supposed to do, but no doubt if she needed them, she would learn.

"Well, thank you, Agent Whitfield; now we know where to come should we have need of supplies," Snow said.

"I'm just glad you two have access now. Your territory seems to have a lot of dangerous issues," Whitfield replied.

Cadence was very relieved when they made their way back out of the arsenal and into the gray hallway. She relaxed perceptibly when the door closed behind them. This was not something that went unnoticed by Snow, who lifted an inquiring eyebrow at her before returning his attention to Whitfield. "So, when do you think the new office is going to be ready?" she asked her partner, ignoring his look.

"It should be ready now, I would imagine," Snow replied.

"Let's go check." Whitfield shrugged.

"Do we even know where it is?" Cadence asked.

"We can ask Bonnie. She'll know," Snow offered. The three of them traipsed back down the stairs and made their way to the waiting room in front of Croft's office.

Bonnie looked up and smiled at them. "Good timing, we just got the message that they are done with your office."

"Wonderful!" Snow smiled.

Bonnie rose from her desk and led them a short way back down the hall, and opened a door. Cadence let out a whistle. The room was done in rich hardwoods and blues and greens. It had some bookcases, presumably for Whitfield and his research, as well as filing cabinets for case notes. Just inside the door and to the left was a round table with six comfortable chairs arranged around it. Three hardwood desks were arranged in a

U-shape in the middle of the room. Wall space was open on the wall opposite the bookshelves, with a perfect place to hang their map and a table beneath it. There was even a small bank of monitors on the back wall so that they could keep tabs on things personally.

"Wow," Whitfield said as he let out a breath.

"I'm glad you all seem to like it so much," Bonnie said with a chuckle. "I'll be sure to tell Alistair you're pleased. Have fun settling in." She turned and left, closing the door behind her.

"Holy crap," Cadence said. "This must be one hell of a promotion." She crossed the room to the desks. Each one had a black enamel nameplate with a name engraved in gold lettering. Snow had the desk in the center of the U, while Cadence had the desk to his right and Whitfield had the desk to his left.

"Indeed," Snow remarked. He pulled the map out of his box and walked to the space of wall that was above the table. "Cadence, give me a hand?"

"Sure," she said, pulling her box of colored push pins from the cardboard box on her desk. They began putting up their territory map while Whitfield began unpacking his boxes. In no time at all, they had settled into their new office.

"This, I could get used to." Cadence smiled, sitting back in her comfortable desk chair.

Snow chuckled, then paused when his phone began to ring. He pulled it from his coat pocket and answered it. "Snow." He paused, listening and nodding. "Yes. Yes, we're on our way."

"Problem?" Whitfield asked, standing up.

"No, not at all, actually," Snow said. "Simply something Cadence and I need to see to; follow up from an old case." Whitfield nodded and sat back down, going through some of his own paperwork. Cade arched an eyebrow, but rose to her feet and followed Snow out the door.

"What's up?" Cade asked.

"Nothing to worry about," he said, leading her down the hall.

"Well, what old case needs following up on?"

"You'll see," he said with a hint of a smile, heading down their hall of doors. He stopped at one she knew well, and she gave him a suspicious look. He opened the door and they stepped into the lobby of Lexington Hills.

"Snow, what are you up to?" Cade looked at him with narrowed eyes before looking around the lobby. It wasn't that she minded coming to the asylum at all. Her issue was that Snow was acting suspiciously, like he had something up his sleeve.

"You'll see," he said again.

As always, it never took long for Ramon to pop into the lobby when he sensed new people in the building. Cadence did a double take when she saw him, however. She had always seen Ramon in his orderly uniform, clean and white. Tonight, he was wearing black dress pants and a white button-down shirt with a black blazer over it and a black tie with a silver pattern.

"Damn, you clean up nice," she said with an appreciative smile. "What's the occasion?"

"I believe they call it a date," Snow said.

"A date?" Cadence turned to face Snow, her jaw open in disbelief. She couldn't believe Snow had arranged a date for her without her knowledge. She was torn between being furious with him for it and just enjoying the time with Ramon. Of course, she decided she could always enjoy the date and then be angry with Snow later.

"You didn't tell her?" Ramon frowned at Snow.

"I wanted it to be a surprise," her partner said with a slight shrug.

Ramon frowned and turned to Cadence. "I'm sorry. Snow and I arranged for him to stay here this evening so I would be free to leave the grounds. That way, we could spend some time together away from the hospital. He had said that he had spoken to you, and you had agreed. I had no idea that he hadn't even told you."

Cadence looked at Ramon while he was speaking, but once he was done, she turned again and looked at Snow, narrowing her eyes. "Tomorrow, you and I are going to have a long talk about personal boundaries, along with what is and is not cool to do." She then turned to Ramon. "Since you two have already arranged this, I would hate for your night out to go to waste." She looked him over again, then looked down at her own attire, feeling terribly under-dressed. "Give me a couple of minutes?"

Ramon smiled and nodded. "Of course."

Cadence nodded and went into the dining hall, which no longer had any doors separating it from the lobby, and ducked into a corner. "Mental image." She sighed to herself, closing her eyes and mentally cursing herself for her sudden case of nerves. He had dressed nicely, so Cade wanted to as well, except that dressing like a cop was so much easier. Makeup, jewelry, heels, and dresses weren't part of her everyday attire. Cadence focused her mind and remembered the dress that she had worn to the last Christmas party she had attended at the station. The dark blue velvet dress that was off the shoulder, how the bodice hugged her slender curves, the feel of the hem as it hit the back of her calves. A hairdresser had worked magic and pinned up Cade's dark gold hair with hair combs that had sapphire-looking jewels on them. Cadence had worn a necklace that had been her mother's, a teardrop pendant that was an actual sapphire, as opposed to the fake ones in her hair. There were modest heels on her feet instead of the usual flats, and the stylist had done her makeup for her as well. Cade had to admit that as much as she loved being considered one of the guys by the other cops, she had loved the double takes of the guys she worked with when they realized it was her.

When Cade opened her eyes and looked down at herself, she saw that it had worked. She was in the heels she remembered, wearing the dress. Her hair was off her neck, replaced by the cold feel of the necklace chain, and she could even feel the rarely worn makeup on her face. She didn't need a mirror to know she looked as good as the night of that party. It was then that Cadence realized exactly how nervous she was. A deep, unneeded breath was taken, and she smoothed the velvet dress down her thighs.

When she stepped around the corner, through the doorway that had housed actual doors until six months ago, she saw both men turn toward her. Cade smiled as, in unison, their jaws dropped. Snow's look of shock was especially rewarding.

"You look incredible," Ramon said as she rejoined them.

"Yes, speaking of cleaning up well," Snow said. "You look lovely."

"Thanks." She smiled. "So, how long has it been since you got to leave the hospital?"

"This will be my first time leaving since I died."

"Guess we'll really have to live it up then. Um … no pun intended," she added, then looked to Snow. "So, when is pumpkin time?"

"Pumpkin time?"

"When do we have to be back by?" she rephrased, not feeling like explaining the story of Cinderella to him since he likely knew it and just didn't understand her phrasing. Besides, she was still somewhat annoyed with him.

"Oh, I'll call you when I need you," he said, waving them off. He then disappeared as he presumably teleported upstairs.

"So," she said, turning to face Ramon. "Where are we headed?"

"You tell me. Remember, I've not been outside for a very long time."

Cadence nodded and thought for a moment. "You like Christmas stuff?" she asked.

"Yes, I do," he replied.

"Perfect." She smiled. She reached out for his hands, and once he had taken hers, she teleported them.

The usual black of night was replaced all over by streetlights, store lights, and Christmas lights. She had taken him to the part of the city that played host to the annual city Christmas tree, with a nearby ice skating rink and Christmas village. The tree was about twenty feet tall, and its lights and decorations were always breathtaking. The air was cold; the people walking around had their breath billowing like steam from their mouths, and they were bundled in hats, coats, scarves, and gloves. The streets and sidewalks were clear but wet, and there was snow on the ground in the grassy areas. The cold did not bother the two of them as they passed unseen among the bustling people.

"It's gorgeous," Ramon said, looking at the tree, then at the area all around them. "This is a place you like to come to?"

"I used to," Cadence said as they walked hand in hand over to a vacant bench. "We lived in this area when I was in high school and college. Back then, my folks would bring us here every year. They would shop and leave me and Sam to skate. Then, we'd all go for coffee and hot chocolate at that place over there," she said, pointing.

"Sounds nice," he said with a smile.

The smile she gave as she nodded was a bit wistful. "It was. We stopped after Sam died, though. I don't think any of us could face it that first year. By the next year, my dad was overseas. When he didn't come home, it was just me and Mom. I don't think either one of us wanted to try to keep up the old tradition." She shrugged.

They got up and began walking as a couple of breathers made their way to what they thought was an empty bench. "Did you and your mother make any new traditions after that?" Ramon asked as they walked along, taking their time and looking at all the Christmas lights.

"Other than the new tradition of pretending everything was normal? No. She would bake, I would decorate. We both tried to keep things going for the other one, I think. We would watch the movies and try to pretend that the memories didn't hurt. But it just was never the same after that. When she died, I didn't even bother trying to do Christmas anymore. I'd work to give the cops who had families a shot at a day off."

"That was nice of you. It must have been very lonely, though."

Cadence shrugged as if it didn't matter. "I had friends."

"Friends aren't family, though, I know. My family lived in Florida. I came up here for medical school."

"You came all the way up here for medical school?"

"It was one of the best schools that would accept people like me at the time," he said with a shrug. "I got the job at Lexington, worked, went to class. I always missed my family, though. Especially at the holidays. That was the worst time for me to be away from home."

"What traditions did you have?" she asked as they walked along the path. She did her best to ignore the "people like me" comment Ramon had made. America in the 40s hadn't exactly been known for its racial or cultural tolerance. A snowball sailed through her as a few children had a snowball fight nearby. Usually, she complained about things like that and how weird they felt. This time, she didn't even notice as she and Ramon walked hand in hand.

"Well, we didn't have the weather," he said with a chuckle. "Snow was something we saw on Christmas cards or in the movies. I think we celebrated a little differently, too. We still exchanged gifts, and it was a time for friends and family, but Christmas Eve was a huge thing for us."

"How so?" They stopped once more under a tree that had twinkling white lights strung up in its bare branches.

"We call it Noche Buena, or Good Night. It is this huge family celebration," he said with a smile. His eyes grew a bit distant as he recalled his childhood. "Mama, Abuela, my sisters … they would spend days cleaning the house, shopping, and making food ahead of time. Papa would get a pig from one of the farmers who would butcher it. We would roast the pig over a fire pit, and oh my." He smiled, his eyes centering again on Cadence. "You could feed an army with what our family would put out for Noche Buena. The kids would play and sing songs; the adults would talk and laugh. Then around midnight, we all went to church for mass."

Cadence smiled, but then a thought occurred to her. "Was this a mistake?" she asked, afraid that maybe it had been a bad decision to bring him some place that might highlight things he missed. She couldn't ignore the phantom pangs of heartache she was feeling either at the memories.

"Not at all," he said with his usual warm smile. "I've dealt with my death and the things I left behind. Besides, I enjoy getting to see you like this. I wouldn't trade it for anything."

"It's the dress, right?" she said, making the joke as an automatic defense mechanism against compliments.

"Not the dress," he said, still smiling, "the woman in it." With that, he released her hand, only to slip an arm around her, and they continued walking.

CHAPTER 16

An Urgent Move

"How are things going?" Snow asked Bethany as the four of them sat in the new office.

"Fine, I suppose," the petite blonde answered. "Michael is a little anxious, but Sandra being with him is helping out a lot. Do we know what is going to happen to him yet?"

"Sadly, no," Snow replied. "It is all dependent on how this case turns out. If we're able to pull Overton from his body and leave the body alive, then he gets his body back. But if the body dies, he'll have to move on like every other soul."

"Maybe it would be best if he moved on now." Cadence shrugged.

"Cadence, really," Snow said in an admonishing tone. "I know the man was not your favorite person due to his treatment of your brother, but—"

Cadence cut him off as she shook her head. "It's not that. Think about it. I mean, would you want to go back to your body knowing someone else had taken it for a ten-year spin and committed unspeakable acts of violence against your friends? Your girlfriend? Not to mention if the cops ever come up with evidence against him for the massacre or whatever else his body has done in the last decade. He could end up in jail for something he didn't do. Pleading that his body was possessed might get him knocked down from jail to a mental asylum, but still, it's not a happy ending. Moving on might be the better way to go."

"I can see your point," Snow said with a frown. "Especially given that we've pointed the local law enforcement in his direction."

"Bringing us to another question," Whitfield said. "Has there been any word from Detective Halleran?"

"None yet, but we should probably check in with him tonight," Cadence replied.

"I agree." Snow nodded. "We've given him a day to do a little digging. He'll either have an inkling of something, or he'll have turned up nothing."

"Which means we should get in contact with our paranormal buddies," Cadence said, then paused as her phone rang. "Riley," she said, answering it. She paused, listening and frowning. "Yeah, no problem. We'll be right there."

Everyone rose as she did. "That was Sam," she said, as she pocketed her phone. "Apparently, Caulfield is poking around the dorm."

"Michael?" Bethany asked, surprised.

"Not the spirit, the body," Cadence said.

"Good luck," Bethany said, waving to them, then leaving the office as the three of them teleported to the dorm.

It was mid-afternoon and sunlight was streaming down through the patches in the clouds. Most of the snow that had fallen the days prior had melted, but there were still a few white patches of snow under the eaves and in shadows where the sun didn't fall. They walked through the yard and into the dorm building, where Sam was waiting in the lobby.

"He's gone to the basement," he said with a worried look as Cadence, Snow, and Whitfield entered. "I think he's after the vessel."

"We put it back, didn't we?" Cadence asked, looking to Whitfield.

"Yeah, but," the Agent started to answer. He was cut off by a loud, angry bellow from downstairs. "But the seal was still broken, the cap was off, and he'll know that Michael escaped," he finished with a grimace.

Footsteps pounded angrily up the stairs, and then the door to the basement was thrown open. The body of Michael Caulfield stood there, breathing heavily, eyes full of anger. He looked around wildly for a moment, as if trying to find the person responsible for breaking the seal on the bottle. The four ghosts stood there, watching. His hands were trembling with anger, and in them, he held the vessel and its top.

"I know you're here! I know you can hear me!" he bellowed. "Enjoy your parole because you're going back to jail, son." Caulfield's face was red and the vein in his forehead was standing out. "You're going back," he whispered. He looked around again, then ran out of the house as fast as his formerly athletic legs would carry him.

"Mike's got to move on," Cadence said. Her tone was quiet, but urgent.

"Before Mr. Overton has the chance to once again seal his soul away, yes." Snow nodded as he spoke, agreeing with Cadence.

"Go, we'll be fine," Sam said. "He's gone now."

"Call us if anything else happens," Cade said, giving her brother a concerned look. "Be careful." The last thing she wanted was for Caulfield to come back and go through some ritual, thinking he was sealing Mike away again, and accidentally imprisoning her brother instead.

Cadence, Snow, and Whitfield teleported back to the office. They made a beeline through the observation bay to the guidance office. Mrs. Steinberg looked up in surprise as they burst through the door and made their way to Bethany's office.

"I'm sorry, Miss Saxon is with someone."

"This can't wait," Whitfield said, flashing his NHD badge. Although she looked a little shaken, poor Mrs. Steinberg didn't protest.

"Hey, how come he gets a badge?" Cadence asked as Snow knocked perfunctorily on the door, then opened it.

A man sat in the chair in front of Bethany's desk, looking slightly dazed and confused. He had no visible trauma that Cadence could see, so she assumed he had died of some kind of medical condition. Bethany looked concerned, if somewhat annoyed, that they had just burst in on her.

"I'm sorry for the interruption, Miss Saxon," Snow said. "And my apologies to you as well, sir. However, something of the utmost importance has come up. We need you. Now."

Bethany frowned. "But I'm in the middle of—"

"Bethany, Mike is in danger," Cadence interrupted.

Bethany nodded and came around her desk. "Mrs. Steinberg? Could you see if Gregory is able to take Mr. Park? An emergency has come up." She then turned to Mr. Park. "I'm sorry, sir. I know this horrible timing." The man, who was very obviously of Asian descent, bowed his head.

"It's fine. Apparently, I'm not going anywhere," he said. Cadence hid a smile. At least the guy seemed to have a sense of humor about it.

"If you'll wait in the lobby, Mrs. Steinberg will take care of you until Gregory can help you," Bethany said, ushering the man out of her office as politely as she could. He nodded and went to have a seat in the lobby.

"What kind of danger?" Bethany asked as she closed the door.

"Overton found out that Mike got free. He's currently working on trying to put him back in the bottle," Cadence explained.

"Oh!" Her eyes widened as she realized the danger.

"Yeah, so we need to get him moved on," Cadence said.

Bethany turned to the door that was on the back wall of the office. She gestured for them to follow her. "Let's talk about this with him." She led them through the door and into the temporary apartment that Mike was using.

Mike and Sandra were in the living room. Sandra was sitting on the couch, Mike was sitting on the floor, and they had the coffee table between them. They were playing cards. Both looked up when the door opened, though, and they set down their cards and rose.

"The gang's all here," Mike said quietly. "This can't be good." Sandra moved around the table and slipped an arm around Mike.

"It's not," Cadence said with a sigh, feeling no need to beat around the bush. "There's a problem."

"Can't get my body back?"

"It's a bit trickier than that, actually," Snow answered. "The man who possessed your body and consigned you to the imprisonment vessel is aware you have escaped."

"How?" Mike asked, confused as to how the man could have found out.

"He went to the dorm," Cadence explained. "He apparently went looking for the vessel. Maybe to make sure nothing had gone wrong with all of the construction, I don't know. But he found the vase thing with its top off. He was less than amused."

"And now he's looking to put you back in your prison," Whitfield finished.

"But you're not gonna let that happen to him again, right?" Sandra asked.

"No, we won't," Bethany replied as she closed the distance between herself and the young couple. "But in order to not let that happen, we have to secure you in your afterlife. You cannot continue to wait around here, or he could imprison you again."

"But what about my body? I mean, what if you do manage to get him out of me?"

"I hate to be the bearer of bad news, Mike, but let's look at this practically for a minute," Cade said. "Do you want to be in control of that body anymore? The hands that were used to kill your friends, girlfriend, and God only knows how many other people in the meantime. The police could dig up evidence linking you to crimes you didn't commit, but your body did. Do you want to go to prison for things you didn't do but your body did while someone else was at the wheel?"

"I … I didn't think about that." Mike frowned.

"I know this sucks," Cadence said; she moved to stand next to Bethany as they spoke to the couple. "I also know you may not believe me, given our history, but try. Neither of you asked for this, and neither of you deserves this. But you have to make your decision now, or you risk ending up like a genie in a bottle again for who knows how long."

Bethany moved forward, looking at both of them. "Sandra, if you still need time, you can have it. Unfortunately, I can't in good conscience risk Michael getting caught up in the prison again. Michael, I'm sorry, but we need to come to a decision for you."

Mike sat down heavily on the couch and Sandra sat down beside him; both were frowning. "I was hoping I could go back. But Cade makes good points. I hadn't thought about it, but she's right. I don't think I could live with knowing what had been done. So, I guess I'll be going on."

"The option we spoke of?" Bethany asked, clarifying.

"Yeah. You okay with that?" he asked, turning his head to look at Sandra.

Sandra leaned against Mike and put her head on his shoulder. "That's fine," she replied.

"Hey, Cade?" Mike said, looking up. "Tell Sam I'm sorry for all the shit I gave him. He was a good kid."

Cade gave Mike a soft smile in return. "I'll tell him. I know he's sorry for what's happened with you."

Mike nodded and sighed, then looked at Bethany. "So, what now?"

Bethany moved over to the wall, where the front door was. She put her hand on the door and whispered to it. The door shimmered and changed. One moment it was a regular-looking door with cream-colored paint; the next moment, it seemed to be made out of something other than wood and looked opalescent. Bethany turned back and gestured for Mike and Sandra to join her.

They crossed the living room hand in hand. Cadence, Snow, and Whitfield stayed back by the couches, letting the couple have their privacy as they moved on. Bethany opened the door for them and stood aside. Blinding light spilled from the door as if there were several spotlights on the other side, all pointed at the doorway. Snow turned aside, and Cadence threw up a hand to shield her eyes. Then the light was gone, and the door was closed. The four partners stood in the living room of the temporary apartment, and Mike and Sandra were gone.

"They left their cards," Whitfield said quietly, looking at the coffee table where the playing cards lay.

"They won't need them," Bethany said.

They all seemed glad that Mike and Sandra had moved on, but there was an air of somberness in the room, as well. For Cadence, it was the first crossing she had seen. Snow was a bit upset that things hadn't been able to work out better for Mike. Bethany was always a little saddened when people moved on. She was happy for them, but it was always so final. As if by some unspoken agreement, the four turned and left the room, heading back to their office, leaving the cards as they were on the table. No one said a word.

CHAPTER 17

Calling Card

"**I** can't believe you have kept in contact with them," Whitfield said as he, Cadence, and Snow entered the New Age shop together. Their entrance was followed by the familiar sound of the crystals chiming together at their passage. Lauren was in a discussion with a middle-aged woman at the counter while a couple of other people were browsing the shelves. Lauren looked up at the chiming and glanced over her shoulder to the back table, where Aiden was sitting with Detective Halleran. The two looked deep in conversation.

"Why would we not?" Snow questioned, saving Cadence the trouble of replying. "They are a good group of people, and they have proven themselves quite adept."

Cadence made her way to the table in the back room. Aiden had set out his little felt shapes: the clover and the snowflake. She chuckled softly upon seeing them.

"It's not like they have a phone I can call," Aiden was saying. He hadn't noticed the crystals chiming out front. "I mean, I can go somewhere and talk and hope the message gets to them, but ..." He shrugged.

Andy frowned. "Where's a good ghost phone when you need it, right?" Cadence took that as her cue and brushed the clover and snowflake off the table.

"Christ, talk about timing. Guess we don't need that phone after all," Aiden said with a chuckle, keeping his voice low. Andy's eyes went wide.

"She's ... they're here?"

"Yeah, it's this system we worked out. See, I have the snowflake for Snow and the clover for Riley. It's an Irish name," he said with a shrug. "When they're around, they knock them off, so I know they're here."

"Maybe I should start doing that, too," Andy said with a bit of a smile.

"Unfortunately, since the shop is still open, we can't exactly bust out the spirit box," Aiden said.

"These people are coming to a New Age store; they don't expect this kind of stuff?" Andy asked.

"Nah." Aiden shook his head. "Mostly, the people who come here want candles and crystals, things like that. This kind of stuff would be way out of their comfort zone."

"It's kind of out of mine, too," Andy said as he shifted a bit in his chair. "So, how do we talk to them?"

"Oh, they can hear you just fine. The issue is we can't hear them. Without the equipment, there is no way to have a live conversation."

Andy frowned, but nodded. "Fine, I guess I'll talk for now."

Aiden noticed that Andy looked uncomfortable. "You don't have to look like you're talking directly to them. Just tell me. They'll hear you." He shrugged.

Andy nodded. "Fine, I researched Caulfield a bit more. Turns out he didn't get the best of grades in school up until the, uh, incident at the dorm. After that, he was stellar scholastically and passed tests with flying colors, but he dropped football. I guess his professors must have passed it off as a change of heart brought about by the killings.

"Now, we've had quite a few John and Jane Does turn up over the last decade, but I wasn't able to put together any kind of particular pattern or find any way to tie the more gruesome ones to him. Even if one out of every five or ten was because of this guy, it would be hard to find it, given the sheer number. We're talking needle in a haystack. At least without anything more definitive, like a preferred area to hunt in or a preferred victim type. We'd need some kind of calling card to mark the kill as his."

"That's it!" Whitfield exclaimed.

"Huh?" Cadence turned her attention from Andy and Aiden's conversation to the NHD Agent.

"What's it?" Snow asked.

"The calling card! He had put the glyph for the non-human he wants to free on the mask when he did the dorm killings. He was known to have carved it on his victims back in the twenties. He might have carved it on the victims or even tattooed himself with it."

"Yeah, but a random tattoo isn't concrete evidence," Cadence argued. "No one reported seeing the symbol other than Sam, and let's face it, ghosts aren't exactly thought of as credible witnesses in a court of law."

"No, but it is something we could give to Mr. Halleran as a way of honing his research," Snow pointed out.

"Okay, now to tell him somehow." Cade frowned, turning back to the conversation.

"So, other than the admitted bad taste of trying to reopen a murder scene as a college dorm, I don't have anything on this guy." Andy sighed, leaning back.

"Fingerprints," Cadence murmured.

"What about them?" Whitfield asked.

"He was at the dorm today. He left his fingerprints."

"True, but it isn't precisely illegal for him to have been there, Cadence," Snow said.

"No, but it is suspicious. Especially since he removed something from the place that had been stored there for eighty-some-odd years."

"But again, the trouble comes with telling Detective Halleran." Snow frowned. "We may simply have to stay until the store closes and they can bring out that infernal spirit box."

"You really don't like that thing," Cadence said with a small chuckle and a smile.

"Given how sensitive it is to our presence and our voices, no, I do not. I have no issue with them using it to communicate with us. But if they use it elsewhere … I shudder to think what kind of evidence they could gather."

"What things?" Whitfield looked between Snow and Cadence, having no idea what they were talking about.

"Spirit boxes, or so they call them," Snow said with a sniff of disdain.

"Relax, Ozzie, those things are used by all kinds of paranormal groups, even the ones on TV."

"It's a miracle the officers in those territories have managed to keep a lid on their charges. Do you think someone like Ruby would be compelled to keep quiet?"

"Well, then, let's just be thankful that the TV crews haven't descended on Lexington Hills yet."

"Good God, I don't know why I didn't think of this before," Aiden said with a grumble in his tone. "Hold on a sec." He got up and went to the back office. Lauren shot him a quizzical look as he passed her by. He came out of the office a few moments later with the spirit box in hand. He went back to the table and grabbed his felt shapes. "We can do this in my van."

Andy jumped to his feet and the two men quickly made their way out of the shop and to Aiden's large van. The ghosts followed along, as eager as the breathers to have this conversation. Aiden and Andy got into the two front seats and the ghosts easily passed through the walls of the van and sat in the back. It didn't take long before the loud static of the spirit box filled the van.

"Are you guys here?" Aiden asked.

"Yes," Cadence said. Snow shuddered at hearing her static-laden voice come through the device after she spoke, and Whitfield's eyes got as big as saucers.

"Cade," Andy said with a smile. "You guys hear what I said in there?"

"Most of it, yes. That it's like a needle in a haystack. But we have a couple of things for you. The first is that he actually might have a calling card. Whitfield said that back in the twenties, Overton would sometimes carve a symbol on his victims. It's the symbol of the creature he wants to summon, the one that requires the blood offering. I … I don't know how to draw it for you, though."

"Tell me what to draw," Andy said, pulling out a notepad and pen from his pocket.

"Okay. At the bottom, draw a half circle, like an upside-down bowl." She watched him draw it. "Only it doesn't have a rim. It's just the open half circle facing down." He scribbled through the line he had drawn on the bottom of the half circle. "Okay, now draw a line straight up, starting through the bottom of the half circle and going up … A little higher … Good. Okay, now a wider half circle facing up with the line you just drew going through the bottom of the half circle, and the ends of the half circle being as tall as the line."

Andy drew the half circle, then looked at the symbol as a whole. "It looks like a kind of chalice with a spike through it."

"Kind of," Cadence said, agreeing with him. "Sam says he had that symbol on the clown mask when he did the killings, and Whitfield says it is possible that he continued his habit of carving the symbol into his victims. See if the coroner can pull any records with that symbol on any of the bodies in the last ten years."

"Who's Whitfield?" It was Aiden, who asked though Andy looked like the question had been on the tip of his tongue as well.

"He works with me and Snow," Cadence said, not wanting to get into the whole NHD thing.

"The coroner is going to love me, asking him to look through ten years of worth of records for the second time this week," Andy said with a sigh. "Most recent should be easiest, though, and we can backtrack from there depending on what we find. You said you had a second thing to tell me?"

"Yes. Caulfield was in the dorm today. He went to the basement; there's a hidey-hole under the stairs, right under the fuse box near the baseboard. He took an old vase that has a top to it. That's what he was imprisoned in and where he stuck Mike's soul for the last decade. If you need his fingerprints, they will be there on the front door, the basement door, and the wood panel under the fuse box."

"He's a professor, Cade. He was fingerprinted by the college. I have access to his prints if I need them, but thanks."

"Crap, I hadn't thought of that." She felt embarrassed now. She should have known that, but she had been so caught up in trying to find ways to get this guy that it had totally slipped her mind.

"Don't worry about it. This symbol should help, though. I'll get with Naveen down at the coroner's office and get this going."

"Thanks, Andy."

"Are we all good? Should I turn this off?" Aiden asked.

Andy nodded. "Yep, I think so."

"We're good, thanks, Aiden," she said.

Aiden nodded and switched off the box. Andy thanked the man, then got out of the van and headed to his own car. Aiden left the driver's seat and headed back into the store to put the spirit box away.

"I'll follow him," Whitfield said. "I can look over their shoulders while they do their research."

"A good idea. Call us if you have a need," Snow said. Whitfield nodded and headed off to hitch a ride with Andy.

"Think we should go with him?" Cadence looked at Snow as she asked the question. "He doesn't have much field experience if there is trouble ..."

"No, he should be fine with Detective Halleran," Snow said. "Whitfield is an NHD agent, after all, and he has his phone should anything go awry."

"You're right." She nodded. She couldn't shake the feeling of foreboding, however. Overton knew that something was up. She didn't think he was the kind of person to be okay with that, especially if he tried to imprison Mike again and found that he couldn't.

The Coroner's Office

Whitfield rode silently along with Andy as the detective drove to the coroner's office. The detective was drumming his fingers on the steering wheel in agitation as he drove, cursing under his breath at every red light. Whitfield, meanwhile, was feeling pretty good. This was the first time he had gone out in the field by himself—no other NHD Agents, not even Snow or Riley, to back him up. He was thrilled about being trusted enough or thought capable enough to go on his own. But he was also a little scared he was going to screw something up.

Whitfield followed along as Andy made his way into the old brick building that served as the city coroner's office. Past the secured waiting area they went as Andy flashed his badge to the worker there. They went down the corridor and through two swinging doors into a large room. The room had metal tables, scales, and tables of instruments and supplies. Two men in white lab coats were currently investigating the insides of some dead man's stomach. One man had long, dark, curly hair pulled into a ponytail and the tan complexion of someone of Middle Eastern descent. The other man, who was a little taller than his partner, had close-cropped black hair, a pale complexion, and a hooked nose. Andy paused just inside the door.

"Naveen," he called over to one of the men.

"Halleran," the man with the dark ponytail said, his voice accented with a vague European-sounding accent. "I'll be right with you." The man handed an instrument over to the other lab-coated man. "Carry on," he instructed him.

Naveen turned and began stripping the bloody latex gloves from his hands and tossed them in a trash can that was marked with a biohazard symbol. "Still on the Doe hunt?" he asked as he approached Andy. "Or are you here about something else?"

"Yeah, I got new information. I'm looking for anyone with this symbol carved on them." He showed Naveen the drawing he had made in Aiden's van.

"I've seen that before," Naveen said in surprise.

"You have?" Andy was a little surprised at how quickly Naveen answered.

Naveen nodded. "Not in a few months, but I've been seeing it for years. Not often, mind you, maybe two or three per year. But it's something one takes notice of. Hey, Lambert," he called over to the short-haired man.

The man stopped what he was doing and made his way over, tossing his gloves in the trash. "What's up?" he asked.

"This symbol, I know it's come across the slab a few times on different bodies. Have you seen it lately?"

He took a look at the drawing, then looked at Naveen and Andy and shook his head. "No. Why? Is it important?"

"Just curious," Andy answered.

Lambert nodded slowly and shrugged. "I'm gonna go to dinner. I'll be back later." He went to the sink in the room and began washing his hands.

"Don't mind him, he dislikes it when he's interrupted," Naveen said, waving away Lambert's abrupt declaration. He guided Andy into an office off of the examination room. "After the third one, I actually started a file on them and sent a copy of the information over to your people."

"Seriously?" Andy was a little surprised, as he hadn't heard anything about a serial killer. At least he hadn't heard of one that had been going on for years with this type of MO.

"Yeah." Naveen nodded. "You think I'm going to see something like this keep crossing my desk and not think something's odd about it?"

"No, I didn't mean it that way," Andy explained. "I just hadn't heard anything about it on my end."

"Well, you have been a little busy the last few months," Naveen said and pulled up a file on his computer. "Here we go. Not all have been Does, but the majority of them are. Other than the symbol, though, none of them seem to have a connection to each other—men and women, old and young, thin and fat, homeless and middle class.

There haven't been any rich or notable victims yet, though. Whether this killer is staying away from them on purpose or not, I couldn't tell you."

Andy nodded, looking over the pictures of the victims as Naveen scrolled through the information he had collected. Whitfield, who was standing behind Naveen, did a double take when he recognized one of the pictures. Bethany Saxon's face, pale and tinged gray-blue, came on the screen, followed by a picture of the symbol carved into the inside of her wrist.

The men kept looking through the information, unaware of Whitfield's recognition of one of the victims. "You're right," Andy said, annoyance clear in his voice. "Nothing connects any of these; not location, type of victim, nothing."

"You'd have to talk to your captain. He's the one I sent the file to, but I don't know if you were in the precinct yet, let alone a detective back then. I'm assuming they didn't go public with the information as they wouldn't want the press to get wind that there was a serial killer out and about that they had no real way of tracking. Has there been another one? Is that why you're asking about these?"

"No, but I may have a lead on the perp," Andy said.

"You do? Well, good luck. I, personally, would love to not see this crap every few months."

"We'll see. It's tenuous at best and nothing concrete."

"Well, good luck anyway."

"Thanks. I appreciate it. Have a good night, man."

"You, too," Naveen said.

Andy walked out of the office with Whitfield hot on his heels. His footsteps echoed off the white linoleum floor and sea foam green painted cinderblock walls. As he neared the heavy metal door, Andy pulled his phone from his pocket and dialed a number.

"Hey, it's Halleran," he greeted whoever had picked up. "Is Captain Rodriguez still in? Good, can you ask him not to leave until I get there? I have to talk to him about a case. Yeah, it's important. I should be there in about ten. Thanks." He hung up the phone and slipped it back into his pocket as he exited the morgue building. Whitfield took the opportunity to teleport back to the office as they exited the building. They had the information now, proof that Overton had been killing. Halleran was on his way to his captain to try to bring down the hammer.

Whitfield didn't follow Andy across the parking lot to his car. He never saw the shadowy figure with the baseball bat get the drop on Andy and knock him out. He never saw the figure struggle to dump the detective's unconscious body in the trunk of his older car, which was parked beside Halleran's vehicle. He never saw him drive off.

CHAPTER 19

From the Frying Pan ...

Snow and Cadence looked up as Whitfield walked back in. Both noticed that he looked a little off and, if possible, more nervous than usual.

Snow was the first to break the silence. "Anything?"

Whitfield nodded as he took a seat at his new desk. "Detective Halleran spoke with this guy named Naveen, who, it turns out, has been compiling information on that symbol being carved into bodies."

"Naveen is the head medical examiner. He's a good guy, and very attentive. I'm not shocked he would notice it and keep a file," Cadence said. "How many victims? Did he say?"

"Two or three a year, at least."

Snow let out a slow whistle. "So that would be twenty to thirty victims over the course of a decade."

"Not to mention the nine he started off with at the college," Cadence said, adding on to the possible total.

"Or any others that didn't bear the mark on their bodies but were murdered in the presence of it, like some sort of graffiti," Snow said, leaning back in his chair.

Cadence let out a whistle that mimicked Snow's. "Overton's a busy guy."

"Yeah," Whitfield said, shifting a little uneasily in his chair and fidgeting with his fingers. "No kidding."

"What's wrong?" Cadence wasn't going to let Whitfield's behavior go unremarked upon.

Snow leaned forward in his chair once more. "Yes, you do seem a bit unlike your usual self."

"It's nothing," Whitfield said, trying to brush it off.

"I'm calling bullshit on that," Cadence said. "Out with it."

Whitfield sighed, then leaned forward and lowered his voice. "They were looking through pictures of some of the victims that had been identified as having the mark." Whitfield shrugged, then glanced toward the door. "One of them was Bethany," he whispered. Both Cadence and Snow sat back in their chairs, momentarily stunned into silence.

"She did say it had been a ritual," Snow said at length.

"Yeah, you're right," Cadence said with a frown. "Back when she was yelling at Dan for getting involved in a cult. We should have asked her if she had seen the symbol."

"It was carved on the inside of her right wrist," Whitfield offered, then shuddered at the image in his mind.

"Well," Snow said, his brow creasing in thought, "I would suggest not bringing it up to her. Not unless we need to."

"Yeah," Cade said. "I don't think we have to make her relive her death. I doubt we'll learn anything new, and honestly, I wouldn't want to do that to her."

"Agreed." Snow nodded.

"So where was Andy off to when you left him?" Cadence asked.

"He was going back to the precinct," Whitfield answered. "He called to make sure the captain was there. Apparently, Naveen has been sending over the information he has been collecting for the last however many years. Andy was a little surprised that he hadn't heard about it."

"Yeah, come to think of it, I didn't know either. But it's possible the captain had a task force on it before I even got there. This guy has been going at it since my junior year of college. So now what do we do? Just wait to see what Andy comes back with?"

"I need to research the imprisoning ritual they used on Overton," Whitfield answered. "We need to be ready if something happens and he leaves Caulfield's body."

"What about some of the traps you guys have upstairs in the closet?" Cadence posed the question, but wondered if any of them would work, or if they would be as useless as the net they had tried to use on the chaos demon at Lexington Hills.

"That would be fine in an emergency," Whitfield said. "And we should probably keep one on us at all times until we have this solved. But he can't be permanently held in one."

"It's like a holding cell versus a jail cell." Cadence nodded.

"Exactly," Whitfield agreed.

Cadence's phone rang and she picked it up from her desk. "Riley," she answered. "Hey, Sam," she said with a smile, but the smile almost immediately dissolved into a frown. She practically jumped to her feet. "What do you mean?" She gestured for the men to follow her and she crossed the room to the door. "We're on our way. Is he alive? Okay, be right there."

"What is it?" Snow had never seen her react like this to a call, so he was hot on her heels as Whitfield brought up the end of their procession.

"Sam says two guys, one of them Caulfield, just brought in Andy and dumped him in the basement. He's bleeding from a head wound and he's tied up and gagged. Sam's staying with him." They opened the door that led to the corner across the street from the dorm and ran across that street and into the house.

Moonlight and streetlights filtered through the newly replaced windows, painting the white-walled hallway in a gray light. Two shadowy forms stood at the base of the stairs to the second floor. The body of Mike Caulfield was quickly recognized by Snow and Cadence, even in the dim hall.

"I know him," Whitfield said, pointing to a thinner man with close-cropped brown hair. "He was at the morgue, working with Naveen. Um … Lambert! Lambert is his name."

"You guys stay with them and see what they say. I'm going down to the basement," Cadence said. She didn't stop to see if they argued with her or not. She just ran.

Sam met her at the foot of the stairs. "How is he?" she asked.

"Out cold," Sam replied with a frown, pointing out to Cadence where her former partner had been dumped. "But alive."

Cadence went over and knelt next to Andy. His right temple and his forehead over his right eye were swollen, and blood had run from the gash to cake down his cheek and even on his shirt. "What happened?" she asked, getting back to her feet once she was satisfied he was somewhat okay. "What did you see?"

"This short-haired guy came in with Andy over his shoulder. I had no idea at the time that's who it was, though. Mike or Overton … whatever I'm supposed to call him, he comes in after this other guy, asking him if he was insane. He said there was no way he was going to use a cop, that it was too high profile. Meanwhile, Short Hair tells Overton that the cop was on to him. That he was at the coroner's office asking about the symbol. They dumped Andy here, which is when I recognized him and called you, and they went upstairs."

Snow appeared by Cadence's side, having come down unnoticed while the siblings were talking. "The short-haired one from the coroner's office has gone. He said he had to get back to work. Overton is on the phone with someone now. Whitfield is up there listening in. Cadence, you have to go get Aiden."

"I'm not leaving him!" she protested.

"You can do more good for him by leaving him here with Sam and me. Get Aiden. Think, Cadence. We cannot untie him ourselves, let alone get him to safety. They can.

You are the one who talks with Aiden the most. He will listen to you."

"What if he won't come?"

"Then we'll work it out from there, but go now and try to get him to come."

Cadence frowned, but nodded and teleported.

Upstairs, Whitfield was following around a pacing Mr. Caulfield. The man had a cell phone to his ear and was furiously talking to the person on the other line.

"You think I don't know that, Wolf?" Overton was saying. "But this is important. You need to get over to the college dorm house that I'm reopening." He paused his talking, but not in his pacing, as Wolf answered. "Trust me. Get over here and come in the back, not the front." He hung up and headed downstairs. Whitfield followed, joining back up with Snow and Sam.

"He's got someone coming over," Whitfield said. "And not just anyone; remember the case six months ago? Dan said someone named Wolf was the leader of the cult. The guy who had the ritual that had supposedly been wiped off the face of the planet, right? Well, our guy here just got off the phone with someone he called Wolf."

"What are the odds it's the same person, though?" Snow asked.

"What were the odds of me finding Bethany's picture on the coroner's computer?" Whitfield countered.

"Good point," Snow conceded.

"Where's Cadence?" Whitfield asked. "The way she was acting before, I didn't think she would leave him."

"She's gone to get Aiden. We can't get Detective Halleran out of this on our own," Snow said.

"Good thinking."

Overton, in his stolen Michael body, pounded down the stairs to the basement and began to pace, agitation evident in his every move. At one point, he paused near Andy and turned to kick him soundly in the gut. "I don't need this shit!" he hissed at the unconscious detective. "Do you have any idea what I went through to get this son of a bitch's life turned around?" he asked, gesturing to his body. "Moron was damn near failing any class that mattered. And now to have someone like you come sniffing around after all this time? Christ, what was Lambert thinking? Attacking a cop? I'll have to deal with him, eventually." Overton grumbled as he continued venting. "That kid's stupidity is causing me more headaches than I need." He gave Andy one last withering look and a final kick, then went upstairs.

"Follow him, Whitfield," Snow said.

"On it." Whitfield nodded.

"Are you okay with the cop?" Sam asked.

"I don't see him giving me any trouble," Snow said. "Why?"

"I want to check on the others here. I doubt they're even registering that anything is going on, but I need to check. I also want to keep an eye out for Cade and these helpers she is bringing. See if I can let them in or lock the other guy out some way."

"Excellent," Snow said. "You have a good head on your shoulders, Sam."

The Cavalry

Cadence ignored the chimes as they sounded at her entrance into Lauren's New Age shop. She had popped into Aiden's apartment only to find it dark. She was excruciatingly aware of the seconds ticking by as she ran to the back table. Aiden, Derrick, and Lauren were all there. The spirit box was not out, let alone on, and she didn't have time to waste. She touched Lauren's arm.

"Someone's here," Lauren said with a frown, feeling anxious suddenly as she picked up on Cadence's emotions. "They're upset."

"I'll get the box," Aiden offered.

"No, there's no time," Cadence said, putting both her hands on Lauren's arm. "Let me talk through you, please, there's no time." She concentrated everything she had on mentally conveying to Lauren what was going on.

"No," Lauren replied to Aiden, shivering at the ice-cold air on her arm. Images flashed through her mind of the old college dorm where the massacre had taken place. An image of a man hurt and tied up in the basement. A feeling of near panic and that time was short nearly suffocated her. The hairs on her arms were standing on end. "It's Cadence. She needs us to go right now. Grab the box so we can talk in the van, but right now, we have to go to the college dorm where the massacre was a decade ago."

"Where her brother died?" Aiden asked, but the other two were already on their feet. Derrick ran to the back office and grabbed the spirit box, and Lauren turned off the lights and locked up the shop as Aiden and Derrick followed her out the door. Aiden took the driver's seat, Lauren was next to him, and Derrick sat in the back. Once the engine was on, Lauren turned the spirit box on and the sound of static filled the car.

"Talk to us, Cadence. What's going on?" Aiden glanced at the box in Lauren's hand as he spoke.

"Andy's hurt. He's in the basement of the dorm house. I think the guy who has him is going to kill him. Please help me get him out of there. He's unconscious and tied up. There is no way I can get him out of there on my own. I need help." She hated being so powerless to help her former partner.

"Wait, so you're taking three civilians into a place where a known killer is?" Lauren asked.

"Maybe we should call 9-1-1?" Derrick said, not exactly thrilled with the prospect of facing off against a killer.

"Yes! Call them, please. Tell them Detective Halleran is injured and possibly in jeopardy."

"Need to turn off the box to make the call." Derrick apologized as he pulled out his cell phone. "It's too loud."

Lauren switched off the box and frowned. "So, yet again, we're going into a situation that's dangerous because she asks us to?" Although Lauren had managed to deal with a lot of her anger toward Cadence, she was resentful at their being put in a dangerous situation again because of this ghost.

"Lauren, I know there is no way you would sit by and let this guy get hurt when we could prevent it," Aiden said.

"No, I wouldn't," she said, agreeing with Aiden even as she frowned. "I'm just not a fan of constantly being put in this kind of situation."

"Constantly? Please. This is the second time in what, six months?"

Lauren continued to frown, but fell silent. Meanwhile, Derrick was on the phone with the emergency operator giving her the location of the officer that was in trouble. Cadence was practically tearing her hair out with worry.

Derrick finished the call and hung up. "They're on their way."

Lauren turned the box back on. Cadence was grateful for the opportunity to speak to them again. "Park a little bit away," she said through the device. "With the cops coming, I don't want you guys to get boxed in."

"How are we supposed to explain why we're there?" Derrick asked.

"Say you saw the guys come in with the cop over one of their shoulders. That you know Andy because he has come by asking you guys for information. You recognized him and became concerned, so you were trying to help him," Cadence said. "Lauren, when we're there, can I talk through you if I need to? You aren't going to be able to bring the box in."

"Sure," the woman said with a sigh of resignation.

"Thank you," Cadence said. "I'm going back to make sure that there's a good way for you to get in. I'll be back with you." She teleported to the front yard of the dorm house. She could hear voices coming from the back and ran around the house quickly. She saw Whitfield standing nearby, as well as Overton and some other man who was wearing a coat with a hood as well as a ski mask.

"We might not be so behind schedule if the nitwits you had sent to the asylum had been able to summon that thing correctly," Overton said to the other man, growling in anger and frustration.

"What they did worked; the entity was summoned," the unknown man said calmly. "I'm not sure what went wrong afterward, but the ritual worked. And my side of the operation is no reason for you to screw up this big now." He gestured to the house. "You think I'm just going to come over here and kill a cop for you?" he said, his voice a mere hiss as his breath was visible in the cold air. "You're out of your goddamned mind!"

Cadence went to Whitfield, who had his phone to his ear. "Everyone else still in the basement?" she asked him.

"Snow is. Sam is waiting for you in the front hall."

Cadence nodded and teleported into the house, enjoying for once the fact that she didn't have to bother with doors or walls. Aiden, Lauren, and Derrick had just opened the door as Cadence entered the foyer behind Sam.

"Hey, I'm here," she said to him.

"I see you got help." Her brother looked relieved.

"Yeah, here's hoping this works."

"I locked the back door behind Caulfield when he went out to talk to that guy," Sam said with a bit of his old mischievous grin. Derrick closed the door quietly behind him as they tried to sneak in as noiselessly as they could. Sam went over to the door and closed his eyes, using his energy to lock the front door, too. "There. Front and back are locked. He has keys, but it will slow him down a little."

Cadence grinned at her brother. "Good thinking." She reached over and touched Lauren's arm. "The basement," she told the psychic, showing her a mental image of the path she would need to travel to get there.

"Basement," Lauren said in a hushed whisper and edged around Aiden to take the lead.

They crept through the house, making as little noise as possible as they made their way to the open basement door. Aiden moved around Lauren and took the lead as the three began to creep down the stairs. Sam went over to the sliding glass doors and peeked out.

"The second guy is walking away. You don't have too long before Caulfield gets back in here," Sam warned.

The shadow of Overton came to the door and tried to open it. The door banged as he pulled on it. Whitfield came through the wall, looking very worried.

"Wolf told him to call him once he had taken care of this mess or not to call at all," Whitfield said. He then glanced at the door. "Locked?"

"Yeah, I locked the front and back," Sam explained. "The ghost guys are here now." He pointed to the basement.

"Let's get down there," Cade said and teleported without waiting for agreement from the other two.

They went down into the basement and found Aiden and Derrick working to free the still-unconscious Andy from his bonds. They were cutting through the plastic zip ties on Andy's wrists and ankles. They had already removed the bandanna that had served as a gag. Cadence went to Lauren and touched her on the arm. The psychic closed her eyes to better attune herself, to hear more clearly.

"Right now, the guy has been locked out of the house, but he has keys. I want you guys to wake Andy up, then get into a corner of the basement, so you aren't directly in this guy's line of sight."

"Okay," Lauren said, her voice barely a whisper. She then looked at Derrick and Aiden. "Wake him up if you can. Then we have to hide. The guy is locked out right now, but he can get back in. He has keys." Lauren didn't wait; she moved to a far corner of the basement.

"Detective," Aiden hissed, gently shaking the unconscious man. "Detective, you need to wake up."

Andy groaned weakly and moved a little, but didn't seem to come to. Sam looked up suddenly and a terrified look crossed his face. "He's in."

Cadence touched Lauren on the arm. "He's inside, in the hall." They could hear the man's heavy footsteps on the floor above them and knew they were out of time.

"The guy's in. Hide," Lauren said in a hiss to Derrick and Aiden. Though where they were supposed to hide in an empty room, none of them knew. The alcove under the stairs would only keep them obscured for so long.

"Detective, we need you to wake up," Derrick whispered, patting Andy on the cheek that wasn't caked with blood. "Dude, what if he's in a coma or something?" he asked, looking at Aiden.

"No coma," Andy croaked. "Where am I?" He opened one eye to look at Aiden.

"You got your gun?" Aiden replied.

Andy reached into his jacket. "No." Aiden and Derrick were helping him to his feet when two things happened at once. The door to the basement, that Sam had closed behind the ghost hunters when they went down, slammed open. Simultaneously, sirens could be heard wailing in the distance as they approached the house.

"Well, well, what do we have here?" Overton questioned, his voice a growl, as he came down the steps and noticed Andy was not where he had left him. Overton stood at the base of the staircase and used his cell phone as a flashlight, sweeping it over the room. He stopped when it fell on Andy, Derrick, and Aiden, who had moved to the wall opposite the stairs, opposite from the corner Lauren had hidden in. "It looks like my one hostage has multiplied to three. My hat's off to you, detective, nice trick."

"Let them go," Andy said, blinking, trying to get his vision to clear, as he was confident there were not three Mike Caulfields in the basement.

"Now, why would I do that?"

"You do hear the sirens, right?" Aiden said. "Whatever you're playing at is over."

"THIS IS THE POLICE," a voice sounded over a bullhorn. "THE HOUSE IS SURROUNDED. COME OUT WITH YOUR HANDS BEHIND YOUR HEAD."

"Kidnapping and assault of a police officer are charges that are going to ruin your career, Caulfield. Don't escalate it to murder, let alone three counts," Andy said, fighting not to slur his words through the fog in his brain.

Overton seemed to pause for a moment, as if considering his options, before he began creeping over to the unsteady officer being held up by Aiden and Derrick. He pulled out Andy's gun, which he had apparently taken from the detective while he had been knocked out. "But you see, only two people have to make it out of here. Then it's my word against whoever survives. Or my word over three dead bodies." He shrugged. "I am a respected member of the community, after all." He sneered.

He might have been about to say more, but for Lauren. She had been slow and silent as she had crept out of her corner. She snuck behind him unnoticed as he spoke to the men, and whacked him as hard as she could on the head with a discarded and forgotten heavy wrench she had found. His eyes widened for a moment at the impact, and then he fell to the ground like a dropped sack of potatoes. His fingers twitched when he hit the ground, and the gun fired. Everyone froze for a moment, taking stock of their bodies and looking everyone over.

"It hit the wall." Aiden breathed in relief.

The report of the gunshot had brought the police inside and the sound of their footsteps overhead in the front hall was thunderous. Men calling "Clear!" as they went through rooms could be heard as well.

"Just stay put until they get to us," Andy said wearily, leaning on the two men. Lauren grabbed the gun from the limp hand of their would-be murderer and handed it to Andy.

"Seems like a good idea if you have this instead of him," she offered with a shrug.

He holstered his weapon as the multitude of heavy footsteps reached the doorway to the basement and flashlights, as well as sight lasers, could be seen illuminating the stairwell. "Down here!" Andy called to them. "Detective Halleran here with three civilians. The perp is down."

Five officers in tactical gear rushed down the stairs. The ghost hunters reflexively threw their hands in the air. Two officers began to secure Caulfield's body. Once the basement had been officially cleared, EMS was allowed to come down with a stretcher. Aiden and Derrick helped Andy over to the stretcher and the EMS guys took it from there.

Cadence walked over to Lauren and touched her arm. "Thank you," she said to the psychic. "You did a great job."

Lauren didn't respond, nor did Cadence expect her to in a room full of cops. Aiden, Derrick, and Lauren were escorted upstairs by officers to get their statements. Snow followed Aiden, Sam followed Derrick, and Whitfield followed Lauren. They wanted to keep tabs on as much as they could. Cadence stayed downstairs with Andy as the EMS team checked him and Caulfield over.

"I thought you said his pulse was strong," one tech said to the other, which caught Cadence's attention sharply. "It's thready and weak. Help me get him on the stretcher."

Shit, she thought. She wasn't equipped to try to trap Overton's spirit now. They had run out of the office so fast at what Sam had told them, they hadn't had time to go up to NHD to get the spirit traps. She pulled out her phone and dialed her partner.

"Snow," said the elegant English accent over the line.

"Overton's pulse is weak, or so say the techs. What if he dies?"

"I'll send Whitfield to get equipment now," he replied tersely and hung up.

"What I wouldn't give for cuffs and a gun," she said with a groan, hoping that the medical techs would be able to stabilize Caulfield's body so that they wouldn't even need to deal with Overton's spirit. Two other techs began moving Andy's stretcher up the stairs, despite his protests that he could walk. As much as Cade wanted to follow along to be sure he was alright, she knew he would be. Her job was to stay with Overton, to make sure he didn't somehow find a way to get out of this.

Her attention was pulled to the downed body of Caulfield again as the EMS tech cursed and began chest compressions. Cadence knew it was too late, though. She pulled her knife as she watched the spirit of Overton rise from the body of Caulfield like someone getting up after a nap.

Overton was a good half a foot shorter than the large, formerly athletic body he had inhabited. He wore a brown suit that looked strange, old-timey. Given that he had died in the twenties, however, that hardly surprised Cadence. Overton took only a moment to orient himself, then began looking around as if searching for someone or something. Then his eyes landed on Cadence.

"Well, hello there, pretty one," he said, then rushed her faster than she had thought possible.

CHAPTER 21

Missing

Snow and Sam made their way down to the basement. Andy had been brought up, but Cadence hadn't followed him up. Assuming that his partner had the sense to stay behind to watch Overton, he and Sam were returning now that Aiden and Derrick were done giving their statements. They were simply waiting for Lauren to be done with hers.

"Oh no," Snow said under his breath when he saw Caulfield's body being put into a body bag. "Cadence?" he called, looking around the basement for her.

"What is it?" Sam was also looking around the room for his sister. Snow's obvious concern made him worry.

"Overton is free. Caulfield's body died, which freed Overton. Cadence?" he called again, pulling his phone from his pocket and hitting speed dial.

"Shit!" Sam swore. "Cade!" he yelled, moving up to the top of the stairs. The EMS techs passed right through him, one shivering and muttering something about a cold draft.

"She's not answering," Snow called up to Sam, who came back down the stairs. Snow began moving slowly, looking carefully at everything in the basement—walls, floors; nothing seemed to be escaping his scrutiny.

"What does this mean? What are you looking for?"

"Ah, here," Snow said, kneeling by a small rippling pocket of air roughly where the stretcher Andy had occupied had been. "He escaped here. You can see the ripples like someone threw a stone in a pond."

"I see the ripples," Sam said, standing behind Snow. "But where is my sister?"

"She's gone. I'm assuming he took her with him."

"What?" The alarm in Sam's voice was unmistakable.

"Well, he's not like a non-human. He can't simply consume her. There's no sign of any kind of a fight and if there is one thing I've learned about your sister in the last six months, it's that she would have put up a fight if she had been able to. If either one of them had bled, we would see it. He took her. He must have somehow surprised her and taken her. That's the only explanation."

"Taken her where?" Sam asked, his voice betraying his anger and alarm.

"I don't know." Snow sighed.

"Got it!" Whitfield called out as he came running down the stairs with some sort of box-like contraption in his hands. He skidded to a halt as he saw the looks on Snow and Sam's faces, then looked around the basement. "Where is everyone?"

Snow rose slowly to his feet with a sigh. "You're too late. Caulfield's body died, Overton has escaped, and it looks like he took Cadence with him."

Whitfield's eyes boggled. "Took her where?"

"Don't know yet," Sam replied, saving Snow the effort of repeating himself. "But you guys have a way to find out, right?" He looked between his sister's partner and the NHD agent. "Right?" he asked again, his voice both sharper and angrier when neither of them immediately offered the assurance he was looking for.

"I … I don't …" Whitfield faltered.

"I don't know, myself. But we know a man who might be able to tell us. Captain Croft."

"Well, let's go then," Sam urged. "Time's wasting."

"Whitfield and I," Snow began, but Sam cut him off.

"Whitfield and you are taking me with you. There are a grand total of three spirits in this dorm left. Everyone else has gone on. The three that are here are so damned far gone in their own routine or reality that they are practically residual at this point. They don't need me. My sister does. An extra set of hands could be the difference between saving her and not."

Snow looked Sam squarely in the eye and saw the same fire and determination there that he so often saw in Cadence. He frowned. "Stubbornness does seem to be a family trait with you Rileys, doesn't it?"

"You have no idea," Sam said in a serious tone, no smile on his face. Had Cadence been there, she would have definitely seen the shadow of their father in her brother's face and tone. It was a voice and look that gave no leeway for opposition or argument. The usually bright and cheerful Riley sibling was grim, serious, and not about to listen to anyone telling him no.

"Fine," Snow said with a sigh, relenting. "The sooner we get moving and stop arguing here, the sooner we find her. Come on then, Whitfield. It's back to the office. Let's hope the captain is in." Snow reached over and took Sam's hand, teleporting them to the observation bay back at the office.

CHAPTER 22

... Into the Fire

Cadence woke up bound to a chair. Her body was sore and the air around her was hot. She lifted her head up and opened her eyes. She was in a square cage that had a solid metal floor, but the walls and ceiling were simply bars. There was a chain that held her cage above the floor, and the cage rocked to and fro gently; as it did, the chain clinked from time to time. The room beyond her cage seemed to be made of dun-colored stone, and it seemed to be a sort of natural cavern. The ceiling rose thirty to forty feet, and along the walls, there seemed to be natural stairways worn into the stone that led to nat-ural-looking archways.

Through one of those archways came Overton, looking nothing at all like Caulfield. He had a pale, almost waxy complexion and pinched features. Small, beady eyes that seemed too close together appeared to smile in cruel delight when he saw her awake. He seemed to have traded in his old suit for a black robe, which made him look like some kind of Gargamel wanna-be. He made his way down the staircase of stone, his black robe trailing a step behind him.

"Ah, good, you're awake," he practically purred. She pressed her lips into a thin line but didn't answer him. Not yet, anyway. He spread his arms and gestured to the room around him. "Not bad for a quick getaway, wouldn't you say?"

He crossed the floor, his eyes fixed on her. He smiled at her silence. "I always did have a thing for the strong, silent types. Always so much more fun to make them scream." Her cage, which seemed to be hanging, swung a little more as he wrapped his hands around a couple of the bars. She struggled against the bonds that tied her arms behind her and to the back of the chair. Her legs were similarly bound to the legs of the chair. It seemed to be no use. There was no give to them at all. She was very securely tied up.

He grinned as he saw her struggle, and as he saw her realize she wasn't going anywhere. He loved that moment when his victim realized that there was no escape. "It's amazing the things you can spend your energy making when you have so many decades with which to make it."

Realization hit her: the vase. "We're in the vase." She broke her silence.

His smile broadened. "Ah, now she understands. It's lucky I had planned for contingencies. So much time imprisoned here gave me plenty of time to think through things that could go wrong and spend my energy making things like those ropes. Though I must say, I had always imagined a man in here, not a lovely young woman like you. I suppose times have changed, haven't they?"

"Why do all of this?" Cadence asked. He felt like talking, so she might as well make use of his mood and see what she could learn. "I mean, are you just psychotic, or is there an actual plan?"

He laughed. "Of course, there is a plan. You don't think a person goes to this amount of effort for there to not be a plan, do you?" He once again gestured to the chamber around them as he asked this.

"I don't know." She sighed, trying to appear bored with the conversation, to perhaps egg him on to try to impress her. "I've seen a lot of different criminals go to a lot of effort when they didn't have much of any kind of a plan."

"Well, I can assure you that there is indeed a plan. A global plan."

"A global plan?" She couldn't help but scoff. "How stupid do you think I am? You were offed in the twenties. You were imprisoned for about ninety years, then only managed a decade in your shiny new stolen body before you were offed again. You seriously expect me to think you're capable of a global plan?" She gave him a highly skeptical look.

Anger flashed in his eyes. "You understand one thing right now, I could have gone on in the great lump's body for quite a while longer."

"Only if you wanted to go to jail, which, believe me, is where you were headed after that stunt with the cop."

"One of my underlings pulled that so-called stunt with the cop," Overton retorted. "Then he saddled me with his mess. A mess I could have handled just fine if those nosey assholes had kept out of it and just let me kill him. But no, they had to play the heroes. So, the choice became simple." He shrugged. "I chose to let the body die so that I could at least be free to work here. This way, I can carry on with my plans, free of jail in either that world or this one, and perhaps whoever hit me will actually take the fall for the murder. I doubt it, though. I will say you were a surprise, but not an unwelcome one." The last sentence was punctuated by a long, leering look down her body.

"In your dreams, rat face," she shot back, but he only laughed.

"Quite the spitfire now," he said with a smile, stepping away from the suspended cage. Cadence got a sick feeling in her stomach at the way he emphasized that last word.

"Let's see how long that lasts." Overton backed over to a lever and pulled it. Something slid open beneath her, a panel in the floor. Suddenly, a yellow-orange glow brightened the room. Cadence saw flames lick up from the floor, curling and caressing the bottom bars of her cage and the metal floor. Her feet were securely fastened to the legs of the chair, so she couldn't pull her feet up.

He watched with a happy smile, looking quite pleased with himself, excited about what he was going to see. The flames moved, creeping ever higher. Cadence flinched from the heat, but there was nowhere for her to go. She tried using her energy to make a knife to cut through the ropes, but try as she might, she couldn't do it.

Overton laughed at her struggles as the flames began burning her feet. The warmth grew and she tried to divert her mind from it, focusing on other things like Snow or Ramon's face when he smiled at her. She grimaced and tried not to give in, but after a few moments, it hurt too badly. She screamed as she felt the heat searing her ghostly flesh through her shoes, tears of pain falling from her eyes. It felt like the soles of her shoes were melting and her feet were sinking into the molten rubber. One scream seemed to be all he wanted, for once she had done it, he pulled the lever and the trap door slid into place again, cutting off the flames.

"So, Spitfire, you were saying?"

Her feet and legs stung with burns and her voice was hoarse as she answered, "I said ... in your dreams ... rat face."

He laughed, delighted. "Oh my, you are going to be so much fun."

"So, what is this grand global plan you have, anyway?" Cadence asked, figuring that if she could keep him talking, then he wouldn't wander back over to the lever that released the fire. She tried to sound as normal as possible as she asked, but her teeth remained locked together against the pain in her feet.

"Do you have any idea the amount of power the spirit has, young Spitfire? The amount of power you have? Well, when not in that cage." He chuckled. "We create things with our minds all the time; our own images, our own realities, items, and equipment. The breathers can't do that."

She waited for him to go on, but he seemed to be waiting for her to ask the next question. "What does this have to do with your wanting to release Shaldoxz from prison?"

"You haven't noticed? I had pegged you as being smart enough to connect the dots."

"Yeah, well, pain tends to interfere with my reasoning," she retorted. "Sorry to disappoint you."

He chuckled and shook his head. "I suppose they call them stupid cops for a reason." That elicited more struggles against the bonds from her and he smiled. "Stupid, but full of fire." He pulled the lever again, and this time it took far less time for Cadence to scream.

CHAPTER 23

Plea for Help

Snow, Whitfield, and Sam ran down the hallway and into the waiting room in front of Croft's office. Bonnie looked up and offered them a happy smile; the smile quickly faded as she saw their expressions.

"What's wrong?" she asked.

"Bonnie, I'm sorry, but is he in? We need to see him," Snow said.

"I'm sorry, but he's …"

"Right behind you," Croft cut in, interrupting his secretary. "What's going on?"

"Sir," Snow said, turning to face his former mentor. "We need your help. Immediately."

Croft frowned as he looked over the three men. "I see you have somehow traded one young Riley in for another."

Sam nodded to Croft as he was noticed and was desperately trying to keep himself still. He didn't like wasting time. All he wanted to do was find out where his sister was and go get her. He wasn't sure he could deal with her not being around in any form anymore.

"Alistair, I'm sorry, but we need to talk to you. We need your help. Cadence needs your help." Snow spoke fast as he pled with him, not making any effort to keep the urgency from his voice or face.

Croft nodded and motioned for them to follow him. He knew it was unlike Snow, who was almost always unflappable, to be this panicked. He opened his door and let them pass into his office, then closed the door behind them. "What's happened?" He gestured for them to take seats on the couches in the corner of the room. Whitfield and Snow sat down. Sam remained standing, leaning against the wall with his arms crossed over his chest.

"Caulfield died, Overton is free, and he's got Cadence," Snow replied, giving his superior officer the shortest version of the story he could.

"And so now I'll ask again, what happened? How did all of this come to pass?"

"Someone who worked for Caulfield jumped Detective Halleran," Whitfield started. "I guess they figured he was getting too close to something. This guy and Overton, or Caulfield, whatever you want to call him, went to the dorm house."

"When they showed up, I called Cade and Snow, letting them know what had happened," Sam said.

"The three of us went to the dorm house," Snow continued. "Detective Halleran was hurt, unconscious, and tied up. Cadence went to get our group of ghost hunters to help free the officer before Overton could kill him. Overton went outside to talk to someone he had called."

"Wolf. He called Wolf," Whitfield interjected, finding this an important point. "Wolf is the same guy that supposedly had the shadow creature creation ritual that was performed at Lexington Hills six months ago."

"So, Overton is in collaboration with this Wolf figure, then?"

"It seems so," Whitfield said with a nod. "He was asking Wolf to kill the cop and dispose of him. Wolf refused, told him to clean up his own mess."

Snow took over once again. "Cadence returned, having roused the cavalry. Sam locked the back door to keep Overton out for a bit longer and then locked the front door once the paranormal team had come in. They got Detective Halleran free, but Overton came in before the lot of them could get out. He was advancing on them when the psychic of the group hit him in the back of the head with a pipe."

"And that killed him," Croft said with a nod.

"Not at first. He was alright for a while but then suddenly deteriorated," Snow said.

"I came back here to get a trap," Whitfield said with a sigh.

"By the time Sam and I got back downstairs, Caulfield's body was being put in a body bag. Overton was nowhere to be found, and neither was Cadence. There was no blood, just a ripple effect indicating a jump to somewhere else."

"And how is it that young Sam comes to be here?" Croft asked, turning his dark eyes to the blonde-haired man.

"I asked them to bring me," Sam said. "Gave them no choice but to bring me is probably more correct. I'm not about to sit on the sidelines while my sister is in danger."

"But your post," Croft began.

"To hell with my post!" he exclaimed. "There are three others there. Only three, and they are all but residual at this point. They don't leave the rooms they were killed in anymore. Sandra was the last one I had that was fully aware and intelligent and argumentative. Now she's moved on. Let me help get my sister back. No, you know what? I am going to help get my sister back." Sam looked at Croft with a determined, defiant expression, as if daring him to say otherwise.

Croft eyed Sam for a moment, pondering this. Finally, he nodded. "Snow, please ask Bethany to go to the dorm. If there is anything left of these spirits there, ask her to help them move on. If not, we'll let them be in peace." Sam relaxed visibly now that he was officially allowed to stay for the time being.

"Do you know where he would have taken her?" Snow asked.

"As a matter of fact, I do. He's very likely gone back to the world he had ninety years to create." That seemed to stun them all into silence.

"He went back to his prison?" Snow couldn't believe that would be the case.

"Well, with the seal broken, it's not a prison anymore, is it?" Croft questioned. "And he's had nearly nine decades to fashion it any way he wanted. That would be a lair worth returning to. The trouble is going to be finding a way into it."

"Sir, I think, given what is going on, we need to know a little bit more about what we are dealing with," Snow said. "Why did Overton want to summon Shaldoxz? He has been moving almost too patiently for someone hell-bent on releasing a non-human creature."

"You are right. Overton isn't someone who is simply maladjusted and who just wants to create a little more havoc in the world. This is something that is turning into a problem that is widespread and has been going on for a very long time. It all started in the mid-eighteen hundreds."

"Overton has been around for that long?" Whitfield asked.

"No." Croft shook his head. "But the plot he serves has been."

"Plot?" Snow asked. "What plot?"

Croft rubbed his forehead. "I'll try to sum this up quickly, as I know we're on something of a time clock here. There is a faction among spirits that believes that we shouldn't simply tease our existence to the breathers. They believe that if we showed ourselves for what we were, that we could be gods. That, in fact, we should be gods."

"That's insane," Sam said in disbelief.

"It is to us. But they believe that we could rule over humans. Not only that, but they believe that they can use non-human and evil human spirits to give them more power to do so. They think they can control these spirits, leash them, so to speak. The more non-humans a spirit controls, the more powerful they would be, the more fearful the humans would be of them."

"But this doesn't make any sense," Whitfield said. "There is no way to control a non-human or bind it to your will."

"Someone somewhere in that group says there is." Croft shrugged. "I don't personally know myself. But that is why the NHD has been increasingly busy. The spirits who are in this sect influence humans, either by appearing to them in dreams or by outright possessing people, like Overton did. Those influenced humans then gather other like-minded people to them to help in the cause.

"Now, I will say that when I influenced Mr. Kurtz to take his group to Lexington Hills, I had no idea he was involved with or going to be involved with such a group. I had merely intended to set up a good, challenging, but normal, run for you and your new partner, to test the pairing out," he said to Snow. "With what happened after and how the two of you handled the case, how you reacted to both praise and censure from your commanding officer, well, that decided it for me."

"Decided what?" Snow asked, almost hesitant to hear the answer.

"I decided that you two would make a wonderful task force for this kind of thing. The case of young Sam's dorm fell in your lap before I could put everything together that I wanted to, but it simply further illustrated my point."

"What was your point, and who were you making it to?" Snow questioned.

"I have superior officers, too," Croft explained. "I had to show them that normal NHD procedures were sometimes not enough. I had to show them that certain officers, if they were the right team, could undertake some of the NHD's cases, if they had proper NHD backup and equipment, of course. Your work on the case with … Irene Woods, I believe her name was? Well, when you brought in Bethany to help the spirit move on before she became too violent or gave up too much information, it was an unorthodox move, but the right one to make. Between your work at Lexington and your work with Mrs. Woods, I was able to bring the four of you together as a team to be able to help with these kinds of cases. Your work with that group of paranormal investigators, a group that does seem trustworthy, only strengthens your ability to be effective in these situations. Add to that Officer Riley's ties to a current detective, and you present yourselves as an almost unbeatable team."

"A team that's currently down one member," Sam reminded them as he shifted against the wall, his patience wearing thin.

"Yes, yes." Croft nodded. "So, let's see what we can do about finding a way into that vessel."

CHAPTER 24

The Offer

Overton threw the lever and the trap door slid shut. He had left it open longer this time, even though she had started screaming earlier. Her pants had been burned off to about the knees, and the skin beneath had blistered and begun to peel. Tears streamed down her cheeks and her face was twisted in a grimace of agony.

He stood there for a moment, just watching her. She was strong; he had to give her that. Many he knew would have been blubbering at this point, begging to be set free and promising him anything he wanted. She cried from the pain, screamed from it even. But no pleas for mercy crossed her lips, no promises, false or otherwise. He rather admired that.

"You know," he said, "you don't have to stay in there."

"But it's so cozy," she said through gritted teeth.

"Mmm, so I can see. You're very strong-willed. I like that. You could work with me. The rewards of such a partnership would be better than what you're getting now."

"How would you know?"

"Please," he scoffed. "When has any bureaucracy ever given any consideration to its civil servants? You would have freedom, power, be revered like a god."

"A god? Too much responsibility," she said in a croak, her voice hoarse.

He grinned, chuckling. "Oh, you do seem to have an answer for everything, don't you, Spitfire?" He had never bothered asking her name. Spitfire seemed an appropriate nickname, given how he was torturing her. "I wonder if you see the whole picture, though. Don't you think it would be nice? You could have the power of a non-human spirit or two at your fingertips. You could own the love and fear of legions of humans willing to do your bidding. You can't tell me you don't see any allure in that."

Cadence opened her eyes and looked at him. She was trying to ignore the searing pain in her legs and feet and concentrate on every little syllable uttered by the madman in front of her. Her gaze was as level and steely as she could make it as she met his gaze. "I don't see any allure in it. All I see is the pitiful attempt of one dead man to raise himself above others."

"Oh, it's not just me," he said, his voice sounding almost like a purr. "There are hundreds of others in the spirit world working with me. Or do you think it is just bad luck that you all have had more non-human entities being freed than normal? No, there are a great many of us working together to bring this to fruition."

"And what exactly is the goal that you're working toward?" Cadence asked with a weary sigh. "Other than being a class 'A' asshole."

He gave her a look, but let the remark slide. "We're going to bring the spirit world out of the shadows. No longer will we have to watch life go on around us and not be able to take part. We can possess bodies and once more partake of what the flesh offers us. Pleasures like food, drink, and sex, all of it. We can use the power of non-human spirits to goad the breathers into fearing and worshipping us like gods!"

"You don't think that whatever gods already exist might have an issue with that?" She gritted her teeth in pain.

"With the power of the non-humans on our side, it won't matter if they do. We'll be stronger than them. We'll rule in the flesh world and in this one. You can't say that doesn't tempt you."

"Um … I can't?"

He blinked. "Are you actually saying you would truly rather things continue as they are?" He shook his head, unable to believe it. "You mean to tell me that you would prefer to remain an unglorified civil servant in the status quo than rising to a heavenly … no … godly status?"

"You really have no idea who you are talking to, do you? I never, ever sought glory for what I did. Not in life, and certainly not now. I do it because it is what is right. It is what is needed, and someone has to do it. I have absolutely no interest in your glory or your version of how things should be or what accolades and worship you want for yourself. I'm more interested in helping and protecting those who need help and protection."

"I see," he said with a frown. "Well then, I guess I'm wasting my time with you then."

"Probably," she said, knowing she was signing her own death warrant by not going along with him.

He started to move the lever again, to open the trapdoor and let the flames creep up and lick at her again. Cadence took a breath and braced herself, but Overton suddenly stopped and turned sharply to look behind him at a couple of other tunnels in the wall. "Damn," he hissed, then turned back to her. "Looks like you may prove useful to me after all, Spitfire. It seems you make good bait." With that, he threw the lever, and in seconds, Cadence screamed again.

CHAPTER 25

Dead Vessel

Snow led Croft, Whitfield, and Sam to the new age shop where the paranormal group seemed to hang out so often. He had never been more relieved to see the three breathers there. Lauren was huddled over the back table, her hands curled around a cup of tea. Aiden and Derrick sat with her. Everyone was silent, but apparently, they were expecting ghosts. They had the spirit box on the table between them.

The crystals at the front of the store chimed together as the quartet of ghosts passed into the shop. Lauren let her head drop a little. Aiden reached over and switched on the spirit box.

"Hey, Cadence," he greeted the spirits. The men shared a look and Croft nodded to Snow.

"Cadence isn't here. This is Snow," he said, feeling a bit uncomfortable as he heard his English accent coming from the staticky voice box. "Cadence is in trouble."

"Did she do something wrong?" Derrick asked.

"Not that kind of trouble, I'm afraid," Snow replied. "When Caulfield's body died, it released the spirit of the man who had stolen the body from the real Caulfield. Overton is his name. Overton has kidnapped Cadence. We know how to find her, but we need your help."

"Gee, this sounds familiar," Lauren groaned.

"Nothing dangerous on your part, I assure you," Snow said. He knew how Lauren abhorred putting their group in danger to assist the spirits. "We simply need some candles lit, a vessel like a jar or a vial with a lid that can be sealed, and to be able to use this space. Agent Whitfield, who helped us with the Lexington Hills case six months ago, will stay here with another spirit. They will be performing the ritual to imprison Overton's soul once more. Will you help us?"

"Sure," Aiden replied without hesitation. He earned a glare from Lauren for that, but she didn't argue.

"We'll be asking you to turn the spirit box off for the duration of this. Once you hear the chimes in the front of the store go, we ask that you blow out the candles immediately and pour the melted wax on the top of whatever vessel you let us use, sealing the top on it. I'm sure we can arrange reimbursement for the vessel you choose."

Lauren rose from the table and went over to one of her shelves. She chose a small brass urn with a top and brought it over to the table. "Will this do?"

"Yes, thank you, Ma'am," Snow said.

"Okay, what color candles do you need?" Derrick stood as he asked.

"White," replied Snow. "Six of them arranged around the vessel. Once you light them, would you be kind enough to turn off the spirit box?"

Derrick grabbed six white candles from Lauren's supply of candles in the shop. He then pulled his lighter from his pocket and lit them, placing them in a circle around the brass vessel as he did so. Aiden turned off the spirit box; the room suddenly seemed thunderously silent in the absence of static.

"This seems to be a very advantageous arrangement indeed," Croft said as the box went dead.

"We got lucky," Snow said with a shrug.

"Let's hope you stay that way," Croft said. "When we conclude this ritual, it will pull everyone out of the lair that Overton has concocted and imprison them in that," he said, gesturing to the new brass vessel. "You and Sam will need to get Cadence and get out of there before we finish the ritual. We'll give you ten minutes. Then we'll start the ritual."

"I understand," Snow said with a grim nod.

"Be careful. Be safe. Be successful," Croft said to them both. Sam and Snow both nodded. Then Croft bent down, whispered a few words, and touched the floor. It rippled in response, and a tear seemed to appear in the air in front of them above the ripples. Snow stepped through first, with Sam following after.

The corridor they found themselves in was dark, but they could tell from their footing that the floor of it was uneven. Dim illumination came from far ahead of them, a soft orange glow coming from two directions as if the hall they were in forked. Carefully, they both crept their way forward. Sam could feel the exhilaration and fear wash through him, and he suddenly understood the draw police work had had for his sister. It felt almost like he was alive again, with every ghostly nerve ending singing.

Snow stopped as they neared the fork in the tunnel. He couldn't see the end of either side, but both led somewhere with a light source. He looked at Sam and gestured for them to split up, for Sam to take the left tunnel while he took the right. Sam nodded, and each man began to creep off in his own direction.

When they heard Cadence's scream rip through the silence, both men immediately felt both relief and terror. Relief that there was confirmation she was still there, still existing, and not gone forever. The terror came from the knowledge that something awful was being done to her to draw that kind of sound from her.

Sam moved faster, in a hurry to save his sister, and got careless. He missed the tripwire in the tunnel near his feet. He felt the pull of the wire as he tripped it and moved, but it was too late to avoid being hit. From the wall, three darts exploded and hit him, but because he had moved, they hit his arm and shoulder instead of anything more important. At the same time, the tunnel collapsed behind him, cutting off the fork of corridor Sam was in from the main passageway they had come from. He had only one choice: to keep moving forward. His arm hurt, and he tried to pull out one of the darts, but it hurt too much to pull out himself. Snow would have to do it if, or when, they got out of here. Already the shoulder of his shirt was showing a slow spread of silvery blood.

Snow heard the collapse of the tunnel Sam had been in and only hoped that the young man had somehow managed to avoid being buried. He carefully stepped over the tripwire he had found in his tunnel. He would check out where this went, then look for Sam.

Snow wasn't the only one who heard the tunnel collapse. Overton grinned as he heard the sound and pulled the lever to close the trapdoor. Cadence's shoes were nonexistent at this point, her feet and lower legs seemed almost unrecognizable for what they were, and the floor of the cage beneath her feet seemed slick with silvery blood. Overton practically giggled with delight as he turned his attention to the doorway that was up a bit and on his right.

"Time to see who your would-be rescuers are, my dear Spitfire. That is, if they survived the cave-in and the darts."

Cadence had little left in her to reply; she just hissed in pain and feared for whoever had been caught in the traps Overton had set. She didn't even have the energy to call out a warning if her voice would even carry that far after being ravaged by repeated screaming. Movement caught her eyes, not from the archway that Overton was watching, but from the archway Overton himself had come out of earlier. The unmistakable salt and pepper hair of Snow shone in the light of the room as he came out of the archway.

Snow saw Cadence in the dangling cage and rage filled him. He could see the floor of the cage covered in her spirit blood and that the lower half of her body had been damaged. But from the distance he was at, he could not make out details. He left the shadows of the corridor and began a quick run down the steps, knowing that he would be seen, but also knowing that time was working against them.

Overton drew a knife from his belt, the knife Cadence had been carrying, and began nonchalantly walking over to where Snow was coming down. "Clever," he commented. "Trigger the trap in one tunnel, then come out of the other while my attention is on the wrong one."

Sam stayed in the shadows of the tunnel. He saw Overton's attention diverted to where he assumed Snow was. Once the man was no longer facing him, he tried to teleport down to the cage he could see his sister being held in. For whatever reason, he couldn't do it, though. He frowned and began to creep forward, trying to stay low while keeping a close eye out for any further trip-wires or traps.

"You're getting sloppy in your old age, Overton. First, you take a living, breathing cop, and now one of our own? Why did you take her?" Snow asked. "Why risk people coming after her? I would have thought a clean getaway would be smarter for you. We would have had no idea where to find you. You could have gone off and possessed another body, and no one would have been the wiser. This wasn't the smartest move to make, so why do it?"

"Why did I take her? Why not take her?" He laughed. "It seemed like it would be a good time. Besides, I was warned there would likely be at least one of your lot hanging around, waiting to stuff me into another prison again. It was suggested that I be ready to handle that and break up your little golden partnership." Overton stood at the bottom of the steps, watching Snow.

Snow glanced over to Cadence again, and this time he was close enough to see the burns. He could see the silvery energy of the ropes holding her to the chair and the blood beneath her charred legs and feet. He pulled a knife from its sheath in his belt. "You will pay," he said with a dangerous growl to Overton and launched himself over the last three steps to tackle him.

Sam took advantage of the distraction and hurried the rest of the way down the steps. Agent Whitfield had provided both Snow and himself knives; Sam pulled his knife as he crept to the cage that Cadence was in.

"Sam," she said, her voice hoarse, dry, and barely at a whisper in volume.

"Shh," he said softly. "It's my turn to protect you." He could see better than Snow the damage that had been wrought on his sister. Her lips were cracked and bleeding, some of her hair was blackened and singed, her hands were blistered and burned where they were tied to the chair, and her legs and feet were unrecogniz-able as such. Overton and Snow were still wrestling on the floor a few feet away. Snow was trying to plunge the knife into Overton and Overton was trying desperately to wrest control of the weapon away from Snow.

Sam crept around to the back of the cage and reached through the hot metal bars. He used the knife Whitfield had given him to cut the ropes that bound her hands. A small sound of relief escaped her and she brought her hands around to her front. She tried to flex her singed fingers, but the blisters made it impossible without excruciating pain. Her eyes moved from the fight with

Overton and Snow to Sam. She hated being the damsel in distress, hated needing saving, but she was glad they had come for her.

Overton managed to get the upper hand, if only for a moment, and flung the knife away, sending it skittering to the other side of the room, where it clattered against the stone wall. Without the knife in his hand, Snow relied on sheer strength and punched Overton square in the nose for all he was worth. Blood spurted from Overton's now broken nose and the man brought his hands up in self-defense to protect his face.

"You broke my nose!" he said in a muffled shout, tears in his eyes.

"You hurt my partner," Snow said in a calm, cold voice that belied the rage boiling in his eyes. Snow got to his feet and scrambled to retrieve his knife.

Sam had managed to cut Cade free of the chair, but her legs had been burned to the point that they were sticking to the legs of the chair. "This is gonna hurt, Cade. I'm sorry," he warned her.

Oh good, that will be a nice change of pace, she thought to herself. Her voice refused to work anymore, and even if it had, her throat hurt too much to make a smart-ass reply worth it. She scrunched up her face and braced herself. Sam tore her leg free of the chair and Cadence screamed in agony.

Overton was scrambling across the floor, still off balance from Snow's breaking of his nose. He was trying to make it to the stairs when Snow hauled him to his feet by the scruff of his neck. "No. You don't get to leave. We still have a score to settle, you and I." He plunged the knife into Overton's leg to hamper his movement.

Overton cried out in pain, his hands moving from his ruined nose to clasp his thigh.

Another scream signaled that Sam had torn Cadence's other leg free from the chair. A glance told Snow that Sam's wounds were taking a toll on him and that Cadence herself was close to passing out. He hauled Overton over to the cage, a singular look of fury on his face. Sam's death, the death of the others in the dorm, the siblings' current conditions, all of it was because of Overton.

Snow reached out and touched the lock on the cage. He wasn't about to give Overton the satisfaction of being in the position to haggle about giving over the key. A surge of energy went through Snow and into the lock, which fell open.

"Get her out," he said to Sam, his voice gruff and commanding. He hoped the boy was still up to the task despite the three darts sticking out of his bloody arm. Sam reached in and grabbed Cadence's arms, pulling her to him, then picked her up in a fireman's carry over the shoulder that wasn't wounded.

Snow took a moment to shove Overton into the cage and slammed the door shut. "You will never hurt another person, alive or dead," he growled to the now-caged man. He replaced the lock and then sent another surge of energy into the lock, fusing it shut. "Never. Again."

"You can't do this!" Overton protested. "I could be helpful to you! Let me go. I can give you whatever you want!"

Snow took Cadence from Sam, ignoring the pleas of the man behind him. They made their way toward the staircase Snow had descended, but Snow paused by the lever that Overton had been using to release the flames.

"Come on," Sam said. "I'd love to hear him scream, too, but we don't have much time." Snow nodded, and together the two made a break for the staircase back up to the unblocked side of the tunnel.

"Be careful of the trip wire," Snow yelled ahead to Sam, who had taken the lead in the sprint for the exit. Sam skipped over the trip wire, and Snow followed suit, as well as he could, carrying Cadence. They could see the exit portal ahead. They could see the table with the small brass urn and the ghost hunters. They could see Whitfield and Croft standing there, chanting.

"Hurry!" Sam yelled, and both men put everything they had into running for the doorway, which seemed to begin to shrink.

They emerged into the New Age shop and skidded to a halt just as Croft and Whitfield stopped the chant and the portal sealed behind them. The urn on the table seemed to shudder and Whitfield went to the front of the store, manipulating the crystals to chime. Derrick and Lauren blew out the candles and began pouring the melted wax over the top of the vessel. Aiden reached over and turned on the spirit box. Static filled the room as Sam and Snow tried to catch their breath.

"Did it work?" Aiden asked.

"They've got her," Whitfield said, his voice sounding every bit as relieved as he was. He blinked a bit as his voice came back to him through the spirit box.

"She's hurt. So is Sam," Snow said. "I have to take them to be treated. Thank you for all of your help. I appreciate it. We'll be in touch soon, but right now, these two are my priority."

"I hope they get better," Derrick said.

"Later guys," Aiden said.

"Glad we were able to help," Lauren added, which surprised Snow, given how angry she had been not so long ago. Aiden nodded to Lauren with a smile, glad to see his friend's change of attitude.

Snow nodded to Croft and Whitfield, who then followed him and Sam to Lexington. As usual, within moments of their arrival, Ramon was there. His usual greeting died on his lips when he saw Cadence being carried and then the darts in Sam's arm.

"Upstairs," he said, looking at Snow. "Same room I stitched her up in last time."

Whitfield showed Sam and Croft the way up the stairs, and Snow simply teleported with Cadence to the room. Ramon pulled the sheets down on the bed and then began pulling together the things he would need to treat her. The room was white, Snow noticed. He remembered how much his partner hated white rooms, but it wasn't like she could argue at this point.

"What happened?" Ramon asked as Snow laid Cadence down on the bed as gently as he could.

"That's what I would like to know," Croft said as the three others entered the room. Whitfield guided Sam to a chair and had the young man sit there.

Snow sank into the other chair in the room, feeling like he could sleep for a week straight. The energy he had poured into overriding the lock twice had wiped him out. "He had her in a cage, with some kind of fire trap underneath her. He'd been burning her."

"He had her tied up with some kind of rope that didn't burn," Sam added. "But the knife Whitfield gave me cut through it just fine. He had her hands tied behind her, and each leg was tied to a leg of the chair."

"And her legs fused to the chair, I see," Ramon said with a frown as he began cleaning her up.

"Had to pull them off." Sam winced. "She passed out not long after that."

"Given the pain it looks like she went through, I'm surprised she made it that long," Croft said, his brow creased in concern.

"She's nothing if not stubborn," Snow said with a sigh. "Overton and I fought, in part, so I could distract him from Sam freeing her. I broke his nose, stabbed his leg. Then we broke her out of the cage and I locked him in it so that he couldn't get free before we got out of there."

"Yeah, how were you able to do that?" Sam looked over to Snow as he asked that. "I don't know what was going on there, but I couldn't even teleport. How did you manage to zap the lock twice?"

Croft looked sharply over to Snow. "You did that?"

Snow shifted in his chair a bit under his former mentor's gaze. "You taught me how to circumvent certain energy-made situations. He had some form of bane up that disallowed anyone but him to use their energy. I did what I had to do."

A look of impressed respect crossed Croft's face as he nodded to Snow. He then turned his gaze to the younger Riley. "And what happened to you?"

"He had the place booby-trapped. I heard Cade scream and I guess I panicked. I ran toward the scream and didn't see the tripwire. I collapsed the tunnel I was in behind me, and darts shot out of the wall."

Croft nodded and moved toward Sam. "I can dissolve the darts for you, but you'll still have to see the doctor here to patch you up. Or we pull them out, your call."

"Dissolving sounds a bit less painful," Sam said. He looked to Croft to see the man chuckling.

"It is, trust me," Croft assured him. "Just stay still. It isn't an immediate thing."

As Croft began to dissolve the first of the three darts, Ramon tended to Cadence's legs and feet. The fire had exposed much of the muscle and sinew below her knees. Her feet and legs, or what was left of them, were going to be the worst part. Hopefully, there wouldn't be any lasting damage once she had healed from this, but healing would be a long and painful process.

Sam hissed slightly as the first dart dissolved. "I didn't say it would be painless, son. Just less painful than yanking them out," Croft said. "You two did well. You managed to save her, not get too badly hurt yourselves, and get out without allowing him to escape, as well. Snow, I must say you and the Rileys here continue to impress me." He glanced over to his old protégé and chuckled softly when he found the man fast asleep in his chair.

"Sir," Ramon said as he glanced at the imposing captain. "I'm not sure what you have planned, but she's going to need to be watched. Burns like these are tricky, even for us."

"How so, Doctor?" Croft asked as the second dart in Sam's arm successfully dissolved.

Ramon wasn't about to correct him about not being a doctor. He was the closest thing to one they had at this point, and he had almost graduated. He had been killed a mere semester before graduation. "It was spirit fire he used. As you can see, it did quite a bit of damage. She will heal as she rests, like any other damage we take as spirits. But it can leave lasting damage. And given how he burned her, with the chair right against her legs, there could be muscle damage. At least what we would perceive as muscle damage, anyway. Not to mention the risk of other injuries, despondency, things like that … There could be complications with the healing process."

"But you'll do everything to ensure there isn't, won't you?" Croft asked.

"Yes, sir. But the tools I have here are limited."

Croft dissolved the final dart from Sam's arm, which had started bleeding again with their removal. He then turned to regard Ramon for a moment. He nodded a bit. "You're right. These facilities do leave a bit to be desired. Can you take care of the two of them here for now? I'll need time to arrange something better."

"Yes, they'll be fine here tonight." Ramon nodded.

"I'd like a quick look around, if you don't mind?" Croft asked.

"Not at all. Just do one favor for me? Stay away from room 219? Ruby doesn't like men and I can't help them and take the time to calm her down."

"Of course, Doctor. Just focus on your patients. Whitfield, would you walk with me? I have things to discuss with you." Whitfield, who had stayed quiet and out of the way, nodded to Croft and left the room with him.

CHAPTER 26

The Hospital

Cadence awoke to a sharp stinging sensation in her feet and legs. At first, she thought she was back in the cage, but then she realized the stinging was far less than the burning she had felt. Not to mention there was no heat. The room around her was cool. She opened her eyes and was somewhat relieved to see she was in a room done in gold and pale blue. She looked to one side and saw Sam, his arm in a sling, asleep in the chair.

"Wake up, Buttercup," she called over to him, finding her voice was still rough, her throat sore. She could feel scabs on her lips. His eyes cracked open and he smiled.

"Well, look who finally decided to join us," he said, and she could hear movement in the room.

Snow and Ramon moved into view. "How do you feel?" Ramon asked.

"Like bacon, fried to a crisp. My legs, hands, and feet hurt," she said, wincing a little. "But I'll take the stinging over being in that cage again."

"No need to worry about that," Snow said, assuring her.

"Thanks for coming after me," she said with a tired smile to them. "What happened to you?" She looked at her brother.

"Took a few darts to the arm, no big deal." He shrugged and then winced as it pulled his shoulder wound.

"Careful," Ramon warned sternly. "What is it with the two of you liking to pull your stitches?" he asked, shaking his head and moving over to Sam to make sure he was alright.

"I'm good," Sam assured him.

"So why is it I'm always the one that ends up in the hospital bed?" Cadence asked with a sigh.

"It would seem you have a certain allure to the bad guys," Snow said with a chuckle, trying to make light of what had been a horrific situation. "Shadow creatures think you're tasty; psychopaths enjoy torturing you." He shrugged, still smiling at her, glad that she was there to tease.

"Just my luck." She chuckled. "So, how long have I been out this time?"

"Three days," Ramon replied.

"Three ...?" she said as her jaw dropped. "And no one thought, 'Hey, let's try to wake her up!'? You just let me sleep?"

"Doctor's orders," Snow said. "Remember, you have to rest to heal yourself, and given what you looked like three days ago, it was best you weren't awake."

"That bad, huh?"

"Not that great now," Sam said in a matter-of-fact tone. "But much better than when we got you out of there."

"Oh God, Croft is going to be so pissed at me," she said with a groan.

"And why should I be?" Croft asked from the doorway. He smiled at the pause that his entrance brought to the conversation. He did enjoy making an entrance. He strode into the room and joined the congregation around her bed. "You were held captive, tortured, and burned. Why on earth would I begrudge you the time you need to heal?"

"Because I was dumb enough to get captured in the first place," she said, the anger at herself evident in her voice.

"No. The job is dangerous. Just because we don't face mortal dangers as often as the breathers doesn't mean there are none. So no, I am not angry with you."

Cadence nodded, then frowned. "So, where are we? This doesn't look like Lexington."

Ramon chuckled and shook his head. "It's not. There have been a few changes while you've slept. I didn't have the facilities there that I needed to take care of your wounds. I told them that you were going to have to be moved and that someone had to look after you very carefully."

"Instead of moving you into the care of someone who may or may not have been able to handle your burns, we simply took him with us when we moved you," Croft explained.

"Wait, what? What about Lexington?"

"Edith Brewer, a former nurse there, will be holding the stewardship of Lexington now," Snow replied. "Ramon has come over here."

"Where is here?"

"We're starting a hospital for the officers and agents," Croft answered. "With the increase in non-human activity and evil human spirits, more and more are getting hurt in the field. We need someone like Dr. Suarez and others with his skills to tend to those hurt instead of leaving them to, in most cases, tend their own wounds."

"Seriously?" Cadence asked, her eyebrows lifting in surprise and curiosity. "Doesn't a hospital in the afterlife sound like the punch line to some kind of joke?"

"Joke or not, you aren't the only person getting hurt. Though your regularity with the experience is somewhat alarming," Croft said, smiling to indicate he was joking. "Also, your brother is no longer a monitor."

"What? Why?" She looked over at Sam, who gave her a guilty smile.

"I kind of threw a fit and made them take me with them on your rescue mission."

"Yeah, I remember you cutting the ropes. I was so damned glad to see you that I didn't stop to wonder why you were there at the time."

"Well, that's why. Bethany went to the dorm while I was with Snow. Julie and Nelia moved on. That only left Bridgette, and she's residual."

"Sorry to hear that, Sam," his sister said. He shrugged, but only with one shoulder this time.

"It sucks, but it was bound to happen. So, with no one there to watch over anymore, I don't have to be there."

"Going to join Mom and Dad?"

"I thought about it," he said with a sigh. "But I decided not to. They've offered me a position," he said, pointing to Snow and Croft.

"Sam, you're not a cop. You wanted to be a teacher."

"True. But I have to admit, I kind of liked being along on that rescue mission."

"I thought you would be happy at the prospect of having your brother join your team," Croft said in surprise.

"I am," Cade said with a smile. "I am. I just worry about him. Old habits die hard. What happened to Overton?"

"Oh God, Cade, you should have seen it," Sam said, leaning forward, an excited smile on his face. "Snow here beat the shit out of him."

That nugget of information stunned her for a moment as she swung her gaze across the room to look at her partner in disbelief. He offered her a somewhat embarrassed smile. "I served as a distraction for Sam to free you."

"Dude!" Sam objected, shaking his head. "That wasn't a distraction. That was pure vengeance."

"I think young Sam here is overstating things just a tad," Snow demurred.

"You did admit to breaking his nose," Whitfield said with a shrug.

"Not to mention stabbing him in the leg," Croft added.

"And then you shoved him in the cage he had kept her in and used some kind of magic mojo to fuse the damn lock shut," Sam finished. "I saw your eyes, man. You were pissed."

Snow shuffled his feet a little and looked down to the floor. "Yes, well … you could say I don't take kindly to people hurting those I care about."

"Here, here," Ramon chimed in. "I only wish I could have gotten a crack at this guy, too."

Cade smiled at her partner, who still looked embarrassed. It touched her that he did care so much. After a moment, she looked over to Ramon. "So, when can I get out of here?"

"When you can walk again," Snow said.

"Which is going to take time and rest," Ramon said, giving her a sympathetic smile. He knew her and knew she would be itching to get out of there.

"We made sure the room wasn't white, so you wouldn't freak out," Sam said, hoping to cheer her.

"Come along, gents," Croft said. "Let's leave Officer Riley to the care of her doctor and let her get some rest."

Snow reached over and gently hugged her. "I'm glad you're alright."

Sam got up from his chair and walked over to her, then leaned down and kissed her forehead. "I'll be back later. Take care, sis." The two men followed Croft and left the room, and Sam shut the door behind him.

"So, doc, what's the prognosis?" she asked with a smile.

"That eager to leave huh?" He grinned.

"You know me. I'm a pain in the ass patient, especially when I feel fine. Well, except for my legs. And hands. And feet."

"Let's see if you can handle sitting up." He tossed back the sheets and she saw that aside from the bandages she had felt on her hands, from her thighs down, her legs were completely wrapped in bandages. Even her feet were covered. It was like someone had put her in thigh-high mummy boots.

"Guess I know what I'll dress up as next Halloween," she joked.

"Very funny." He chuckled. "We'll see how much you laugh in the next minute. Very carefully swing the first leg out of bed."

She winced as the movement pulled on muscles and skin in both legs, but she got the first leg down. She drew in her breath sharply as her foot landed on the floor. "Oh, holy shit, that hurts!"

"Want to stop?" he asked.

"No," she replied, gritting her teeth. "I can do this." She moved the second leg, swinging it down to the floor, and couldn't help the yelp of pain as that foot hit the floor.

"Okay, okay," he soothed. "Pull your legs up a little so that your feet aren't on the floor." She put her hands behind her and leaned back a little, using her thighs to pull her feet up. Her hands stung in reply to the pressure, but not nearly as bad as her feet had felt. "You've actually healed very well so far. But getting back on your feet is going to be hard work and painful. Maybe in another day or so, you'll be able to take sitting up as your feet regenerate."

"They were the worst, huh?" She sighed, shuddering as she recalled how the flames had melted away her shoes. She tried easing her legs back down and winced as her feet gently touched the floor.

"Yeah, they were." He frowned, watching her. "Not that anything below the knee was very pretty."

"And here I thought you thought I was always pretty," she joked, trying to take her mind off of the pain. She tried putting more weight on her feet, and once more cried out, lifting them back up as she cursed.

"Okay," he said softly, "enough of that. Get your legs back up into bed." She followed the doctor's order and within a few minutes, and with his help, Ramon was settling her sheets over her legs again.

"This sucks." She sighed, feeling exhaustion wash through her.

"Just rest; it will get better."

A knock sounded on the door and Snow poked his head back into the room. "How is it going?"

"Well, she sat up for a couple of minutes," Ramon answered. "But she can't put her feet on the floor much yet."

"How long before you think she can at least sit in a wheelchair of some sort?"

Cade's brows furrowed. "Why? What's up?" She knew he wouldn't be pressing the issue unless there was something going on.

"Our paranormal group has had a letter."

"Lauren's not getting into trouble over the Caulfield thing, is she? He decided to die. He told me that. She didn't kill him." There was something else he had told her that she needed to tell Snow, but she couldn't think of it at the moment.

Snow shook his head. "No, she was cleared of any wrongdoing. This is from another ghost hunter group." He frowned. "It's one of those groups that has a television show of their own. Apparently, they have taken an interest in some investigations our group has done and will be coming to town."

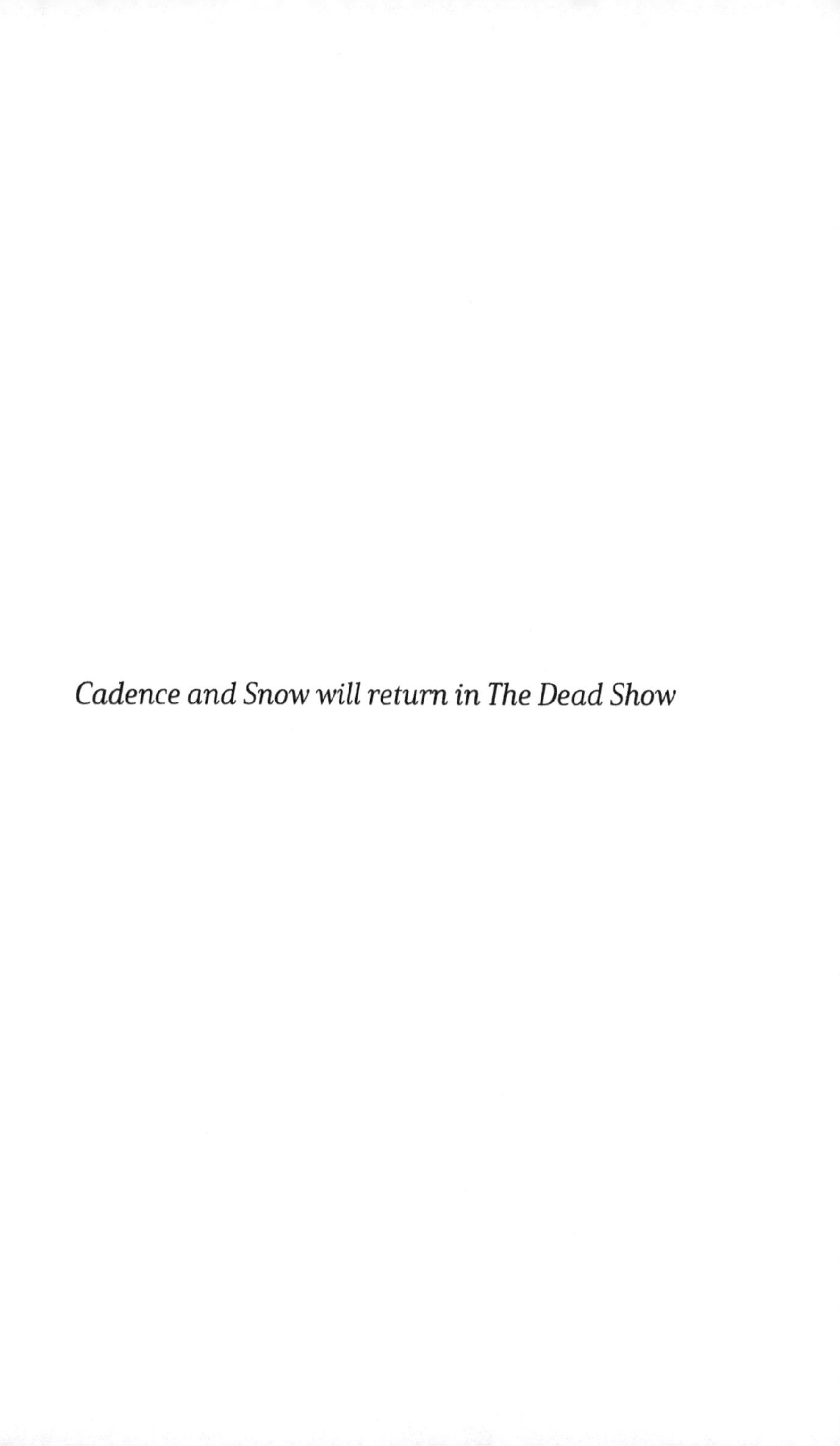

Cadence and Snow will return in The Dead Show

"We're here with Derrick Getty, the youngest member of Southern Paranormal Investigations and their team researcher. Derrick, we're standing here outside of Barrington Prison. What can you tell us about it?"

Derrick took a breath to steady his nerves and began. "Barrington Prison was built in 1940 and remained in operation for less than half a century, closing its doors for good in 1985. This is where the area sent the worst of its criminals. The death sentence was enforced here, and rather than upgrading to the electric chair or lethal injection, Barrington Prison kept it old-fashioned. There was a dedicated gallows building in the same yard where the prisoners would have their exercise time. So, every day when they went outside, they were faced with death.

"In the early days, the first few wardens of Barrington used to have the prisoners line up outside, rain or shine, to watch a soon-to-be executed inmate's last walk from the prison to the gallows building. That practice stopped when a riot occurred that killed not only prisoners, and ironically the man that was to be hung, but also the medical examiner and some attendees of the execution. That was in 1954.

"This was a prison; it doesn't have a quiet history. There were murders, rapes, attacks, but other than the riot I just mentioned, there were two other major incidents. The first was in 1968. A prisoner overpowered a guard in the rec room, and some prisoners barricaded themselves in there, demanding more humane conditions. Apparently, some of the guards were notorious for their treatment of the inmates. It took about nine hours, but the warden and other officers diffused the situation. Or so they thought. When they entered the rec room, the errant guards and some of the less-than-popular inmates were found stripped, hanging from the overhead pipes by their bound wrists, and they had been mostly skinned. There were seven deaths in total at that time. Two were guards, and five were other inmates."

Teeny couldn't hide the look of shock and disgust on her face at that. "Oh my God," she murmured.

"As I said, these inmates were the worst this area had to offer." Derrick gave Teeny a bit of an apologetic shrug before continuing on. "The second riot happened less than a decade later, in 1975. This one occurred in the cafeteria and was stamped out by the guards pretty quickly, but not before there were deaths. No one seems to know really how or why, but a fight started. It only took about 45 minutes for the warden and his guards to regain control, but that was plenty of time for blood to be shed. Three guards and eight inmates died that day.

"As newer prisons with better security measures opened, Barrington became less used. When the state did away with the death penalty, Barrington's doors were closed for good."

Author Bio

Growing up in a haunted house and having a father who loved horror set the stage for Amanda's creative life. This Urban Fantasy author has been writing since her teen years, blending horror, fantasy, and the paranormal. Amanda balances a day job, her writing, her family, and helps her husband run a board game group and YouTube channel, Tabletop Misfits. Local to Southwest Florida and a total geek, you can often find her conventions, either as a vendor or an attendee.

Book Club Questions

1. How has Cadence developed over the series so far?
2. What was the biggest surprise to you in this book?
3. How do you feel about the way the Cadence/Andy relationship is playing out?
4. How do you feel about the way the Cadence/Ramon relationship is playing out?
5. Is Lauren in the right to still be angry at Cadence?
6. How do you feel about Croft? Is he sketchy? Hiding something? Or just trying to shield his officers from the "higher ups"?
7. Which character would you like to see more of? Less of?
8. After the events in this book, what do you think might happen with Sam?
9. After the events in this, how do you feel about the formation of this task force?

10. Should Mike have been given the chance to return to his body, or should he have moved on?

MORE BOOKS FROM
4 HORSEMEN PUBLICATIONS

CRIME, DETECTIVE, AND NOIR

A.K. RAMIREZ
Secrets & Photographs

MARK ATLEY
Too Late to Say Goodbye
Trouble Weighs a Ton

JOE DAVISON
Journey to Hell

PARANORMAL & URBAN FANTASY

AMANDA FASCIANO
Waking Up Dead
Dead Vessel

An Eye for Emeralds
Swimming in Sapphires
Pining for Pearls

BEAU LAKE
The Beast Beside Me
The Beast Within Me
Taming the Beast: Novella
The Beast After Me
Charming the Beast
The Beast Like Me

CHELSEA BURTON DUNN
By Moonlight

J.M. PAQUETTE
Call Me Forth
Invite Me In
Keep Me Close

JESSICA SALINA
Not My Time

KAIT DISNEY-LEUGERS
Antique Magic

LYRA R. SAENZ
Prelude
Falsetto in the Woods: Novella
Ragtime Swing
Sonata
Song of the Sea
The Devil's Trill
Bercuese
To Heal a Songbird
Ghost March
Nocturne

MEGAN MACKIE
The Saint of Liars
The Devil's Day
The Finder of the Lucky Devil

PAIGE LAVOIE
I'm in Love with Mothman

ROBERT J. LEWIS
Shadow Guardian and the
Three Bears

VALERIE WILLIS
Cedric: The Demonic Knight
Romasanta: Father of Werewolves
The Oracle: Keeper of the
Gaea's Gate
Artemis: Eye of Gaea
King Incubus: A New Reign

FANTASY

D. LAMBERT
To Walk into the Sands
Rydan
Celebrant
Northlander
Esparan
King
Traitor
His Last Name

DANIELLE ORSINO
Locked Out of Heaven
Thine Eyes of Mercy
From the Ashes
Kingdom Come
Fire, Ice, Acid, & Heart
A Fae is Done

J.M. PAQUETTE
Klauden's Ring
Solyn's Body
The Inbetween

Hannah's Heart

LOU KEMP
The Violins Played Before Junstan
Music Shall Untune the Sky

R.J. YOUNG
Challenges of Tawa

VALERIE WILLIS
Cedric: The Demonic Knight
Romasanta: Father of Werewolves
The Oracle: Keeper of the
Gaea's Gate
Artemis: Eye of Gaea
King Incubus: A New Reign

KYLE SORRELL
Munderworld

DISCOVER MORE AT
4HORSEMENPUBLICATIONS.COM